MW01127194

Men of Winter

Books by Ted Morrissey

Figures in Blue, a novelette
The Beowulf *Poet and His Real Monsters*, a monograph

Men of Winter

A Novel

Ted Morrissey

A Revised & Expanded Edition

Preface New to This Edition
A Conversation with the Author, by Beth Gilstrap
Afterword, by Adam Nicholson
Discussion Questions

Twelve Winters Press

Sherman, Illinois

Published by

Twelve Winters Press, LLC

P. O. Box 414
Sherman, IL 62684-0414

TwelveWinters.com • xii.winters@gmail.com

Men of Winter was first published by Punkin House Press in 2010.

Men of Winter, a Revised & Expanded Edition, was first published by Twelve Winters Press in 2013.

An abridged version of "A Conversation with the Author" by Beth Gilstrap was published under a different title in *Fourth River* and is used by permission of the author.

Cover & Interior Page Design: Ted Morrissey
Cover Photo, *Amandine, Usedom, Germany*: copyright © Gina Glover
Author Photo: copyright © Shannon O'Brien

ISBN
978-0-9895151-0-8

Printed in the United States of America

For my parents,
among whose many gifts was the love of story.

Contents

vii

Acknowledgments

The first chapter of *Men of Winter* was published in *The Sleepy Weasel* (fall 2004), edited by Peter Ellertsen, under the title "Men of Winter," and chapters fifteen and sixteen appeared in *Slush Pile Magazine* (No. 1), edited by M. R. Branwen, also under the title "Men of Winter." The interview, written by Beth Gilstrap, that appears herein is a longer version of an interview that originally appeared in *Fourth River*, edited by Robert Yune. The author would like to thank the following: Gina Glover (ginaglover.com) for the generous use of her photograph on the cover; Pamm Collebrusco for her diligent and expert editing and proofreading of the manuscript; Adam Nicholson for writing the afterword; and Lindsey Siders for her reading the novel closely enough to spot a plot error that all other eyes missed. And he would also like to acknowledge Homer and his innumerable gifted translators, especially Robert Fitzgerald, who brought the *Odyssey* to life for him for the first time. The epigraphs that appear at the head of each chapter are the author's interpolations, owing much to the translations by Fagles, Fitzgerald, Lombardo, and Rieu. Single quotation marks indicate that the epigraph is dialogue in the original.

A Note on This Edition

This edition of *Men of Winter* is expanded in that the preface, interview, afterword and discussion questions were not part of the original 2010 edition. As far as its being revised, I have included epigraphs from either the *Iliad* or *Odyssey* at the beginning of each chapter, and I have made a few changes in word choice or phrasing here and there. I have also attempted to correct any errors that managed to slip through the cracks in the 2010 edition (without, hopefully, creating new ones). Otherwise the text of the novel is essentially unchanged.

— T. M.

Preface

Publishing in the Wild West of the 21st Century

I suppose every book has a long, strange history, at least as far as its author is concerned. I certainly feel that way about *Men of Winter*, which began as a short story and just kept expanding as I wrote it. From my experience, there are two types of fiction writers: planners and, well, not planners. I'm definitely in the latter camp, and perhaps it's appropriate that the label I've just ascribed to it is spontaneous and ill-defined because that's how the creative process works in our camp.

I admire the planners—writers who construct a story or a novel as if it were an edifice that required a detailed blueprint before ground can be broken. They have character sketches, and chapter-by-chapter outlines; and they systematically write one scene after another, always knowing where they are in the story, how close to the middle, and how close to the end. My former mentor and thesis director, Kent Haruf (*Plainsong, Eventide, Benediction*), writes like that. He always claimed that his friend and Iowa Writers Workshop mate John Irving (*The World According to Garp, The Cider House Rules, A Prayer for Owen Meany*) wrote that way as well; in fact, Irving begins by writing the end of the novel, then plots his way in reverse. I experience vertigo just thinking about his method.

For a long time I worked under the assumption that that was how *good* writers did it, so I had to be a planner, too. The process didn't work for me, however. I felt . . . hemmed in and constrained by my own plans—"cabin'd, cribb'd, confin'd," said Macbeth, "bound in [t]o saucy doubts and fears." Meanwhile, I discovered that not all writers were planners. Indeed, some of my other favorite authors were much more organic in their approach. Ray Bradbury (*Fahrenheit 451, The Illustrated Man*) comes to mind, as does my own literary idol, William H. Gass (*The Tunnel, Middle C*). For me, pre-planning put my conscious mind in control of the narrative, and the best writing comes from the unconscious mind. Interesting discussions of this unplanned process can be found in Bradbury's introduction to the graphic novel adaptation of *Fahrenheit 451*, by Tim Hamilton (Hill and Wang, 2009); and in Gass's 1976 interview for *The Paris Review*, by Thomas LeClair (actually in a lot of Gass's interviews and essays).

I can't explain my own process with much precision, but when I write I, in essence, keep putting pieces on the board (characters, plot details, bits of setting, images), and at some point I get the sense that I'm roughly half way to being done and it's time to start maneuvering those pieces in a way that will draw the narrative to a close. I may get that half-done sense on the third manuscript page, so I know I'm writing a short story (in fact, a rather short short story), or I may get that sense around the hundredth manuscript page, as I did with *Men of Winter*.

These two distinct approaches to writing fiction, to storytelling— the planned versus the unplanned—no doubt go back to our earliest ancestors grunting cause-and-effect scenarios as an essential survival skill.

However, what happens once the story is told, how it becomes something an audience can experience . . . that has been changing with accelerating rapidity for the last twenty years or so. The model that was in place in my youth—learn to write, publish in respected magazines, write a book, land an agent, publish with a reputable house—has mutated into something quite different. It is too complex of a situation to discuss adequately here, but the highlights (or lowlights) include a shift in the commercial publishing industry toward profit almost exclusively, and a drastic reduction in the number of those commercial publishers. Thus, there are fewer and fewer commercial houses publishing a narrower and narrower band of authors. This situation has led to what I think of as "the James Patterson Syndrome," whereby an author becomes a book-writing machine (perhaps even overtly enlisting the aid of a team of subordinate writing partners) whose only goal is to produce as much text as possible in the least amount of time and carpetbomb the marketplace with titles (hopefully catchy, gimmicky ones that readers will easily remember and associate with the author brand).

So big publishers only want big books by big-name authors; and the quality of the writing doesn't even enter into consideration.

Every release has to be a million-dollar seller, or it isn't worth their while. Obviously there are exceptions. There are some excellent writers who manage to place their work with large, commercial publishers—but their example is increasingly exceptional.

During this same time span, technology has evolved which makes writing, printing, publishing and distributing on a small scale (a microscopic scale even) not only possible, but relatively easy. On the plus side, talented writers overlooked by commercial houses (and, yes, I count myself in this group) can get their work to a potential audience. Literary journals and small presses have sprouted like springtime mushrooms across the publishing landscape. The downside is that the technology has turned publishing into a kind of Wild West, where lawlessness and quackery run rampant. Anyone with a few dollars can establish a webpage, don the title "publisher" or "editor" (or "author"), and begin churning out material, digitally and traditionally. There are no standards, virtually no rules, and if there are any watchdogs, they are cloudy-eyed and toothless.

Men of Winter and I fell prey to such publishing quackery. After years of so-close-but-have-to-pass rejections, I accepted a publishing contract from a new press, Punkin House (the name itself made me uneasy, but what did I have to lose at that point?). Punkin House's publisher meant well, in the beginning, I believe, but a lack of know-how, and, ultimately, integrity led to a frustrating and disappointing publishing experience. Not that it's about the money, but I have no idea how many copies of *Men of Winter* were sold. I was paid less than twelve dollars in royalties, and nothing in the past two years. Punkin House's publisher won't communicate with me, let alone respond to any business-related questions. I thought the house went out of business in 2012, but people have been buying the 2010 version of the novel in digital formats all along, so Amazon and Barnes & Noble have been making money from it, and presumably my old publisher; but not a penny of that has made its way into my PayPal account. I could retain an out-of-state attorney or accountant to get to the bottom of things, but quite frankly I can't afford to pay someone five grand to unearth the fact that my old publisher owes me twenty bucks.

So, if you can't beat 'em, join 'em . . . at least part way. I established

Twelve Winters Press in 2012 to get *Men of Winter* back in print and to gain control of it in the marketplace. I hope to use the press to keep my work circulating, but eventually I'd like to assist others in finding an audience for their deserving work as well. In the Wild West, you had to take matters into your own hands from time to time. I'm glad it's only a metaphor because I have no doubt I'm far handier with a keyboard and mouse than I would be with a six-gun and Winchester.

T. M.

Sherman, Illinois

June 27, 2013

Men of Winter

By night our ship ran onward toward the Ocean's
bourne, the realm and region of the Men of Winter,
hidden in mist and cloud.
     —Homer's *Odyssey* (translated by Robert Fitzgerald)

I

'A man should never say all that he knows—
some details should remain obscure.'

Odyssey 11

SHE BOARDED THE TRAIN at one of the overnight stops, at Yaroslav or Amir. I vaguely recall the subtle commotion of her settling in, a few seats ahead of me and across the aisle. When sunlight crept into the car I noticed her long black hair, intricately braided and pinned in place. The braids formed a geometric shape, something like a star, across the back of her nearly child-size head. She had a wrap around her shoulders that was a deep purple color, like the Urals in winter. The skin of her neck was as white and unblemished as porcelain, as a china teacup—no, as the snow on the peaks of the Urals.

Indeed, her skin was so flawless and her hair so black and lustrous, I assumed she was little older than a child traveling alone to meet a guardian aunt for a holiday in the country. A few years earlier I might have concealed the ring on my finger and found some pretense for making her acquaintance. I might have tried to coax her to the dining car for a glass of sherry. I could have spotted some traveler in a threadbare suit, an old man with a tobacco-stained beard, a guiltless fellow on whom to affix some outrageous lie. "That man over there—*do not look*—he bears a striking resemblance to ... yes ... the Butcher of Belgrade (or the Rapist of R—, the Murderer of M—). I am not certain of course. Not certain enough to alert the conductor. But perhaps it would be best if you accompany me to the dining car—if you are traveling alone. Our friend may disembark at the next station." And if I were lucky, the innocent old man would choose that moment to look at the poor girl; and if I were really lucky, the old man would not disembark: he would stay right there for the duration of the trip, a few feet away, hacking violently every so often into a frayed handkerchief, oily with phlegm.

But there was too much white in my mustaches for such machinations. I twisted the plain silver band on my finger a quarter turn; and, out of habit, I checked my coat pockets for my notebook and leather pencil case. Then I set about rereading my newspaper, for perhaps the twelfth time. I had a byline in that edition, a story about a vagrant in the city. The pitiful creature claimed to be the Prince of Ithaka. I thought at first I was pursuing a humorous story—but there was a sadness that shone through each outrageous remark he made, like the light of a candle's flame seen through a comic paper.

I interviewed the strange fellow in the police's interrogation chamber. I got to him before the detectives, who were busy with their lunches. (Over the years I had made friends among the police—a bottle of vodka now and then for the young ones, cigarettes for the old ones—for the newlyweds, a pair of theater tickets.) At first I thought the vagrant was older than I, then I soon realized the thinning hair was due to malnutrition and the rings under his eyes were more city dust than age. The room was an empty gray space, save for two straight-back wooden chairs which faced each other in its exact center. A single lightbulb hung on a cord above the chairs; its intensity wavered with the electrical needs of the city. There was a pair of gas sconces on the wall where there were black halos on the gray paint, but gas was nearly as hard to come by as electricity. The floor showed the dark and permanent stains of past interrogations. The building had been the police headquarters of a dozen different regimes for more than a century. Petty thieves, murderers, political agitators—all manner of detainees had been questioned here. But probably none was odder than the Prince of Ithaka.

As I began to interview the man, I noticed the framed painting on the wall: a lavender sea rolling onto a deserted beach dotted with colorful flowers. An inappropriately cheerful picture for the gloomy chamber.

At first he was unresponsive, his eyes roaming erratically, his neck twisting in a violent tic now and again. His clothes were shabby, his shoes beyond worn; a hole in the top of one revealed they were also too big for his feet. Many things were scarce because of the war effort but shoes especially so. Nearly all of the material and know-how were used for boots. Apparently at the beginning of the war, the dead soldiers were buried in their uniforms, including their boots. The wastefulness soon became obvious, however, and the newly dead were stripped of their possessions before being interred. There were even rumors that the army had sanctioned grave robbing, that it had encouraged troops to exhume the bodies of the first-fallen for their boots and belts and whatever else was useful. Government officials denied the rumors of course.

I asked the man his name again and this time he uttered a disturbing little laugh, a laugh more closely related to a wince of pain than an ejaculation of mirth. "My name?" His grin was a gash chopped through the crust of a frozen sea. "I am Nobody—is it possible you do not know?—I am Nobody." He laughed in pain again. He spoke with an accent I could not place. Why are you in the city? "I am traveling, forever the traveler. Perhaps that is my true name: Traveler." From where have you traveled? "From everywhere, from the ends of the earth—no, from beyond the ends—do my shoes not show it?" He uttered his broken-glass laugh as he made his feet dance upon the floor. I could not help but notice the light in the stranger's eyes and the play in certain features of his unshaven face as he spoke. The man had been handsome in his youth, that was certain. (Later, the police artist made a quick sketch of the man for me—it only cost me three cigarettes—but my editor decided he did not have space for it.)

I tried again: Do you have friends or family in the city? This question seemed to stun him. His eyes stopped roaming the interrogation chamber; his head and his hands became as steady as a diamond cutter's. "No. There is no one. No one for Nobody." His wild eyes and his tic returned.

The report I had from my friends in the police was that he was caught stealing from a secondhand store: a wine skin, a knotted rope, an oar and of all things—a silk opera cape. When the shopkeeper confronted him, the stranger hit him so hard that his jaw was broken. The commotion caught the attention of patrolmen in the neighborhood—probably drinking or seeing a prostitute, unlikely they were merely patrolling. He gave the police quite a chase. It eventually required the two officers and a dozen spontaneous vigilantes to subdue the stranger, who apparently sent a patrolman and another man to the hospital when the mob at last cornered him.

I asked the Prince of Ithaka about the odd assortment he had tried to steal. "I am forever traveling," he repeated. The police said they suspected he had come from Iiloskova, which was fewer than fifty miles from the northern front. Very little normal citizenry remained in Iiloskova. There were taverns and brothels and gambling houses, and, of course, the infamous Iiloskova Sanatorium for the Insane. So if the stranger came from there he was probably a deserter, an escapee from the sanatorium, or a pawn of some black-market profiteer. Each seemed equally likely to me.

My editor, Mezenskov, had been trying to coerce me to go to the front for some time. We received news in the form of official army dispatches but they lacked color—and, no doubt, accuracy. I had been putting Mezenskov off, but retracing the journey of the Prince of Ithaka attracted me. The publisher of our rival paper, *The Nightly Observer*, had been trying to seduce me to write for him for a while. *The Observer* specialized in lurid tales. Journalistically, it was inferior to Mezenskov's paper but there was no questioning its circulation. *The Observer*'s publisher offered me five times the money, assuming of course the story was acceptably licentious. Obviously, I did not mention this as my true motivation when I spoke to Mezenskov about going north. He retrieved the lock-box from his desk and gave me traveling money. He reminded me to pack my warmest clothes and said that he wanted me to return in a fortnight. I felt a stab of guilt at using Mezenskov's money to pursue a story for his chief rival. But I thanked him and bid him adieu.

I took the watch from my vest pocket and checked the time; it would be several hours before reaching Iiloskova, literally the end of the rail line. I decided to go to the dining car for a bit of breakfast. I wanted to be conservative with the newspaper's allowance—no telling how expensive things would be in Iiloskova. I stood and stretched. Several vertebrae popped. The train seats were thinly upholstered and quite uncomfortable for such a long journey. As I was gathering my heavy coat and my valise, someone brushed past: it was the woman who was traveling alone. I briefly saw her face in profile, and she was not a mere girl—though there was a youthful radiance about her fine features. She glanced over as she said, "Pardon me," and her eyes were a flash of deep purple, like electric current passing through amethyst. I nodded and managed a quick smile; I was too late, however.

I took up my things and followed the braided woman through the aisle. The movement of the train made us both appear intoxicated. We passed between the cars, she and I, and the air was bracing. The next car was a sleeper. Most of the curtains were drawn tight—the few others revealed empty berths. The woman was nearly as tall as I—I glanced down to see if she wore a heel, but her gray muslin skirt touched the floor—and there was an erectness about her bearing I was not used to seeing. It seemed the weight and the weariness of war had stooped everyone: an entire population simultaneously carrying a heavy load. Yet there was nothing unifying about this burden. Each man, woman and child bore the weight in isolation.

This made me suspect the woman was a foreigner, and when I thought of it, there was a hint of accent in the two words she spoke to me.

The commodes were at the rear of the sleeper car. The woman stopped and knocked on the door of one of these little compartments, then entered. I decided such was a good idea and used the adjacent commode room. I finished quickly. When I stepped out, the woman was not to be seen. I continued to the dining car.

A few passengers were having their breakfasts but several tables were still available. I chose one on the east side near a window, where the light would be good. The cook, in his white uniform jacket, came over and took my order: a slice of ham, a fried egg, and black coffee. I had had the ham the previous evening and it was very good. I opened the valise and removed a sheaf of papers tied together with plain string. The cook brought my coffee in a simple porcelain cup. To my surprise, it smelled rich and strong; I was used to everything being rationed and watered down, especially coffee.

I drank the good hot coffee as I flipped through the papers. It was a group of poems I had been working on. Before the war began I published a few sonnets in the literary papers. At one time I hoped to publish a collection but very few books were being produced, due to the scarcity of paper and ink—and interest. A friend was planning to leave for Paris in the summer. He offered to take my poems there in hopes of finding a publisher but I was not sure I would be ready to part with them. They had grown from me so gradually they felt a piece of me, the way that a lover can.

The cook brought my ham and fried egg. I continued to glance at my poetry as I ate.

The door of the dining-car opened and the braided woman entered with a gust of frigid air. She steadied herself on the back of the first chair she came to. She looked unwell: her fine skin was flushed and there was perspiration on her brow in spite of the cold. She appeared to be faint. I was the closest to her, so I put my fork down and went to her. "Here, please sit." I led her to my small table; she was too weak to protest. Her brilliant eyes said "thank you." I helped steady her in the chair, then took my own. "May I order you something?" It took her a moment to respond. Perhaps she was gathering the strength, or perhaps searching for the words. "Just tea please—tea would be lovely." I relayed her request to the cook.

"May I order you something to eat?" I asked.

"No thank you—but please eat your breakfast while it is still warm." She definitely carried an accent but I could not place it.

The cook brought her tea in a moment. She sipped at it and the drink seemed to improve her. I wondered then if it was simply hunger that troubled her. Her face, though of a graceful structure, was unnaturally thin; her neck was the swan-like neck of which the poets of old wrote. Her blouse and long skirt were of good quality, but they were worn to the point of shabbiness and did not fit her properly, as if they were secondhand or as if she had lost a good deal of weight. I noted that she carried no pocketbook.

"Please," I said, "may I order you some breakfast? It may help to restore you. My reward is that it will induce you to sit here with me a bit longer."

"Yes, Mr.—"

"Pastrovich."

"Yes, Mr. Pastrovich, an egg and a slice of toasted bread would be very nice. Thank you." Some of the ruddiness had left her cheek.

I signaled the cook and communicated her order, and requested more coffee also. For a time we sat in silence while I finished my breakfast and she drank her tea. The woman seemed lost in thought as she observed the passing countryside beyond the window. Now snow covered the ground and the barren tree limbs were laden in crystal. Compared to the city, with its shades of dirty gray, the country in winter almost seemed a fairyland. Briefly one could imagine the soldiers fighting the war with magic wand, incantation and pixie dust, instead of rifle, mortar-shell and bayonet.

The cook brought her plate. She immediately broke the egg's yolk and soaked it up with a corner of toast. I sensed that she was profoundly hungry. The smell of my food and the sight of my eating it must have been maddening for her.

I ordered her more tea. She was soon finished with the egg and toast. The cook took our plates when he brought her fresh tea. Her face was no longer flushed and the electricity had returned to her eyes.

"Thank you, Mr. Pastrovich. I feel myself again."

"I am glad. Traveling can affect one's health, especially traveling in winter." I wanted to ask why she was on the train alone, destined for such an inhospitable part of the country, but that would be prying. She would explain all in due course if she so intended.

The sheaf of papers on the table drew her attention. "Are you a writer or a publisher?"

"Journalism puts the bread on my table but I try my hand at poetry now and then."

"A poet—how wonderful." Her delight sounded sincere. "May I have a look?"

I nodded. She turned the title page of my manuscript so that she could read it; it took her a moment, no doubt translating. She said, "*The Singing Poet*—?"

"Very nearly. *Songs of the Poet*. It is a working title."

"By Hektr Pastrovich. Hektr: it is an uncommon name in this part of the world."

"My father was a devotee of the Greek poet Homer."

She smiled. "Your father was a scholar then?"

"No, my father was many things but scholar was not among them. Mainly he was a fish monger."

"Then how did he come to know Homer?"

"My grandmother cooked and cleaned and sewed for the Orthodox priest in the village; in exchange the priest tutored my father. In addition to the Bible, the stories of Homer were his lessonbooks."

"Did your father teach you to read them too?"

"No. He told me the stories when I was very young. I am afraid I recall little of them." I had not thought of Homer for many years. "I remember the death of my namesake, how he was tricked by Athena outside the walls of Troy."

The braided woman smiled; there was electricity in that too. "Ah yes, Pallas Athena, the goddess of wisdom, sprung from her royal father's head." Something like bitterness was in her voice.

"You know classical mythology then?"

"I have a . . . familiarity with its characters, yes." She sipped her tea and looked at the snowcountry.

I had many questions but I still sensed that she would be reluctant to answer. After all, she had not even offered her name. I tried one nonetheless: "What is your destination, madam?"

She returned her gaze from the window. "The terminus of the line."

"To Iiloskova then—that is the end of the rail. The train must turn around there." I could not imagine why a woman would be traveling alone to such a godforsaken place. "That is my destination as well."

She nodded but did not comment on the coincidence. We had finished our coffee and tea, and suddenly there was nothing more to say. I paid the cook; the woman thanked me for her breakfast. We returned to our car and found that our respective places were still vacant. She smiled politely to me before returning to hers. I settled into my seat and prepared for the final hours of our trip.

II

'Lend me a hand, friends, for I am alone and afraid.'

Iliad 13

THE PENSION SEEMED QUITE PERFECT for my needs. My room had a comfortable chair, a sturdy table for writing and eating, a coal-burner, and a large bed whose springs were not too noisy. It was on the second floor, so it was the beneficiary of the little heat rising from the building's lower half. Its only window, double-paned, looked across a narrow alley to a featureless gray wall. The pension's landlord guaranteed me a scuttle of coal every other day; of course, I could obtain more for an additional cost. He was a short fellow, but muscular, with unkempt mustaches that covered his mouth even when he spoke. I assured him I would make do with the basic allotment. An electric light fixture hung from a black cord in more or less the center of the room; however, I was told not to depend on electricity. There was an oil lamp on the table, along with an assorted handful of stubby candles. More were available from the landlord—for an additional cost.

I had picked up a small metal pail of turnip soup from the landlord's skinny wife, and I immediately placed it on top of the coal-burner, as some warmth would no doubt improve the soup.

The pension was a twenty-minute walk from the railway station, toward Iiloskova's central business district—what remained of it. The offices that once handled money and valuable commodities of trade now dealt in basic necessities: used clothing, alcohol, and pharmaceuticals. Or they were vacant altogether. At the rail station I had opened my suitcase and took out my fur hat and my heavy gloves. I wound my scarf about my neck and hefted the suitcase to my side. With it and my valise, my hands were quite full.

In spite of the cold, the air seemed stale. Frost formed on my mustaches, which felt as stiff as pig bristles. Snowflakes descended erratically, but I could not tell if they came from the leaden sky or were merely blown off the severely slanted rooftops. Great piles of snow, some twenty and thirty feet high, stood at every street corner, where they had been doggedly shoveled, scraped and swept by the citizens in an attempt to stay winter's steady avalanche. On my way to the pension I stopped at a store selling alcohol. Its front windows were nearly black with soot. I needed a break from my burden so I stepped inside and immediately placed my heavy suitcase on the floor. There was a man behind a glass display counter. He was probably close to my age but appeared older. He was mostly bald and had long gray side whiskers, giving his face a thin, protracted look. He wore a black horse-hair vest over a heavy fisherman's sweater.

"Hello, friend," I said. "What do you have for the cold?" Wooden crates were littered about the room, some open, many not. Straw and glass bottles protruded from the open crates; straw also lay in clumps on the filthy floor. The shelves and display cases were somewhat ornate. The molding which ran along the high ceiling was hand-carved wood. This place had probably once been an apothecary. Well-to-do businessmen, physicians and litigators were no doubt among its heyday patrons.

"Nothing for the cold like mother's milk, *friend*." He set a small bottle of vodka on the greasy glass counter. He wore black wool gloves with half-fingers. The tips of his nails were as black as the wool.

"Of course. I will take it." The price he asked was too high but I did not feel like haggling. I slid the bottle in the pocket of my big coat and took up my suitcase. I was quite certain that if I had asked for something more potent, I would have been supplied accordingly from the back of the store.

In my room at the pension I sipped the grainy vodka and held my hands near the coal-burner. I was beginning to feel warmer.

My mustaches had thawed and I used my jacket sleeve to wipe at the moisture. Having no tableware, I drank the turnip soup. It was bland but probably nutritious.

The long train ride had taken its toll; I was suddenly very sleepy. I shed my jacket and my necktie and my shoes, then crawled under the blankets on the bed. The mattress was lumpy and smelled slightly of something unpleasant, wet poultry feathers perhaps, but overall it was heavenly to lie down. I balanced the bottle of vodka on my breastbone and took an occasional taste. The only light was the diffused illumination from the alley way. The little room grew gradually darker as the long boreal night approached. Half intoxicated, I imagined the night as a great black beast, plodding toward this remote city from the barren north. It came on—pigeon-toed and relentless as winter—without malice, but dangerous nonetheless. The great beast could gobble up a man before he knew it, I thought. One moment ignorant bliss; the next . . . nothing.

With this black thought I took a last drink and set the bottle on the floor. Instantly I was asleep. My brain soon caught hold of a familiar dream of my wife: Tasha is the young girl I courted, before sorrow had imprinted itself around her eyes. She wears a knitted cap and pushes a noisy baby carriage along a cobblestone street. She appears quite content. It is a lovely day; it must be springtime. Then a wheel of the carriage strikes a dislodged stone, nearly upsetting the carriage. Concerned, Tasha checks her baby, only to find she has been pushing an assortment of rotten fruit. Tasha becomes despondent; she has known all the while there was no baby in the carriage, that she has deceived herself into contentment. Tasha's face of despondency is the wife with whom I was familiar—the woman who cooked my meals, who laundered my clothes, who dusted my books, who lay with me at night—all out of wifely obligation. She cooked bland meals, she removed only the least tenacious of soil from my clothes, she ran her duster along just the spines of my books allowing great quantities of dust to collect on the edges. And she lay with me like a corpse, silent and rigid. Only the dampness between her legs implied anything like desire.

In sum, I had nothing with which to be dissatisfied—and yet everything too. Often, at the conclusion of the dream I arrive at the scene and devour the rotten fruit, as blissful and as ignorant as swine at trough.

Perhaps this was in part why I was fascinated with the Prince of Ithaka. Between the lines of his lunatic ramblings, I read that he had, if nothing else, truly lived life. He had eaten meals exquisitely prepared, he had worn clothes finely tailored, and he had slept with women expertly trained. Maybe I was merely projecting my own wishes onto an anonymous canvas.

When I awoke it was quite dark and cold in the room. There was barely a discernible orange glow within the coal-burner. A band of spectral light entered through the curtainless window. I had the sense that it was very late, that I had slept for some time—but it may have been only an hour or two. I was comfortable under the blankets, except for a strong urge to urinate. There was a pot under the bed but I did not want to smell it for the remainder of the night.

I rose from the warm covers and used a box of matches to light the oil lamp on the table. It was filled with whale or even seal oil and smelled very badly. However, it did illuminate all but the corners of the room. I slipped on my shoes and fished the heavy key from my pants pocket. Taking the lamp, I stepped into the hall and locked my door. Mezenskov's money was in my wallet jammed under the mattress. There was a commode on the first floor; I hoped it was not occupied. The pension was quiet as a crypt—perhaps most of its rooms were vacant. I descended the stairs as stealthily as possible. While I am not a huge man, I tend to be heavy-footed. Several of the steps creaked but there was nothing to be done about it. I found that the first-floor commode was available. I took the lamp inside and was finished quickly. Returning to the hall, the crack of breaking glass startled me, over-loud in the silent pension. I realized there had been voices all along but almost below hearing. I assumed it was the landlord and his wife, possibly arguing about something.

I placed the lamp upon the floor and crept along the darkening hall toward the landlord's rooms. Light shone through the keyhole. Just outside their door now, I was not certain their voices were tinged with anger. They could have been just as plausibly engaged in lovemaking. I bent to one knee and peered through the keyhole, an odd sort of genuflection. I could see a cluttered table and a shattered cup on the wooden floor, but there was no one in view. I heard their two voices but could distinguish no words. I plodded quietly back to the lamp then to my room.

Hearing the couple, possibly violent, possibly amorous, had put ideas in my blood. I thought of the place where I had purchased the vodka. Surely there was a shopkeeper who peddled more than "mother's milk"—but the tit and all, I mused. My room was cold and I felt a lonesomeness I had not known for some time.

I had told myself I would not be unfaithful on this journey away from my wife; therefore, I also told myself I was not going out to solicit a whore as I prepared to leave my little room. I merely wanted some air. I was in a quandary about what to do with my money. On the one hand, I did not want it all on my person, but I did not care to leave it in the room either. I put my two largest bills in each sock and an equal amount of money in my valise with my manuscript, stuffing the valise behind the bed, then I kept the remainder of the money in my wallet. I put on my vest and suit coat but not my tie, then my big coat, scarf, beaver hat and gloves. I carried the oil lamp downstairs, extinguished the flame, and placed it by the pension's side-door, which I left unlatched.

The night was exceedingly frigid. I looked up expecting to see a clear sky but the stars were not visible. In a moment I saw a dull semicircle among the clouds that was the moon. I anticipated the Iiloskova streets to be teeming with people of the night but I saw very few people at all. And those who were out were huddling within themselves against the severe cold. I presumed they were men who roamed the dark streets; however, it was difficult to say for certain.

I walked in general toward the rail station. The dark streets seemed entirely unfamiliar and I could not recall precisely how to find the vodka dealer. I was suddenly afraid I would not be able to find my way back to the pension. I retraced my steps in my mind and was reassured. The darkness allowed me to think of the buildings as they must have been in the city's heyday. I imagined brightly painted store fronts, cornices and window frames highlighted in gold leaf, and trimmed hedges along the boulevards, and even colorful flowerbeds in the summer months. I thought of the well-dressed businessmen and the socialites traveling the streets in fine carriages and motor-cars.

But a downturn in the economy changed all that more than a decade before, and the war hastened the city's demise. In the dark, it smelled of decay and desolation.

My fingers were growing cold even inside my big gloves and stuffed inside the pockets of my coat. My nose was numb and my mustaches had turned to pig bristles again. I must return soon, regardless of whether I found what I was searching for. What *was* I searching for on these strange and lonely streets? I could not think of a reasonable reply.

Four dark figures crossed to my side of the street and were walking toward me. Their silence alarmed me; I would have felt more at ease if they had been crooning some bawdy drinking song. I imagined they meant to rob me. I suddenly scolded myself for stashing money in my socks: with the war shortages, my shoes and socks would probably be the first items they would take from me. I had a vision of myself hobbling in the dark on frostbitten feet trying in vain to locate my pension. It occurred to me I had not seen a police station or, for that matter, one policeman since arriving in Iiloskova. Perhaps it had become a place of lawlessness. I considered turning and fleeing—but they would no doubt overtake me: I was no longer a young man. Too, some bit of pride, some part of me that did not want me to be a coward, kept me moving forward, albeit unsteadily.

Only a few paces before we were to meet on the boardwalk the four figures stopped in front of a building and entered through its double doors. Light from the building's windows spilled onto the boardwalk and street. It was incandescent light and the building shone like a beacon upon a dark sea. The proprietor must have had significant civic clout to keep so much electricity flowing to his establishment. I came to the building—it was tall, at least three stories rising into the gloom—and I peered through the windows. At first the light dazzled my eyes. There was no question as to the nature of the business: the lobby of the building, once an accounting office perhaps, was decorated like a parlor, and a dozen painted whores sat about on silk sofas and footstools smoking and drinking from china teacups, but probably not tea, and chatting with the men who had just arrived from the night. The whores wore formless dresses of gray and red and blue; they wore stockings but no shoes.

I stood on the boardwalk and watched until my breath on the icy windowpane completely obscured the view. I turned and began retracing the route to the pension. Now the streets were deserted except for the bitter wind and an occasional pricking snowflake. I wished that I had brought the bottle of grainy vodka; I yearned for a warming swallow.

I could no longer feel my feet. The impact of my steps seemed to travel directly to my knees. I tried to hurry but I did not want to stumble on the invisible boardwalk. I realized I was a little afraid—but the fear quickened my heartbeat and warmed me: a cozy blanket of fear: I appreciated the irony and made plans to use the image in a poem. Suddenly and irrationally I had the sense I was being followed. I had not heard the echo of footsteps, nor noticed movement out of the corner of my eye. Yet I wondered if one of the men from the whorehouse had followed me. No, they were otherwise occupied. Some other night wanderer then?

I came to a corner where I had to turn right, and when I did so I glanced behind. I saw nothing in the dark. It was not perfect darkness. Here and there lamplight shone from a window, or the ruddy glow of burning coal. The sky itself was very slightly illuminated—the tiniest bits of moonlight and starlight fell through the filter of snowclouds. I had gone several yards when I realized something was not right. Ahead a group of people huddled around a barrel keeping warm by a fire. Their bodies at first hid the flames. I had not passed such a gathering on my excursion. I was lost; I had made a wrong turn.

I stood stock still and squinted at the nondescript buildings on either side of me. My eyes watered in the cold. Nothing looked familiar, or rather everything did. Why had I left my room? What brand of stupidity had precipitated it? Think, Pastrovich! What do you do? Maxims about being lost in the forest or in the mountains came to mind—worthless globs of words. My heart pounded. I felt warm, even my feet.

I could try to find my way back to the brothel and begin again. But I had no confidence at all in my sense of direction. I imagined becoming even more lost—hopelessly lost. Then I must speak to the nightpeople around the barrel; I must ask for their assistance. My natural fear of strangers was suddenly acute. However, there was no help for it. I approached the nightpeople slowly, straining all my senses—even, I hoped, a sixth sense—to detect if they were malignant or benign. But they were as unreadable, as unpredictable as a pack of feral dogs. In their layers of clothing, with a strange contrast of harsh firelight and total darkness, I could not even tell their sexes. Five androgynous figures surrounded the barrel.

At the instant that I might have spoken, my trepidation surged and I walked past them, mute and trembling. I was only a few steps beyond when one of the streetpeople spoke in a feminine voice: "May I accompany you, sir?"

I halted but did not respond. She repeated, "May I accompany you, sir?" I turned; she was a black form against the crimson light.

I spoke, my words shivering in the cold air. "I am en route to my pension." She waited; I supposed all the streetpeople did. "I am en route to my pension but I am disoriented."

She stepped forward, closer but not clearer. "I know this part of the city, sir. May I accompany you?"

May I accompany you?—it must be an Iiloskova prostitute's solicitation. I put that aspect of her question out of mind. I clearly needed a guide. I could not wander the black streets all night. Dawn would be slow to come in this northern city.

I considered her age. She sounded youthful and she seemed small in spite of her winter layers. "Yes . . . please."

We left the circle of light together.

Presently she took my arm as if we were sweethearts out for an evening stroll. Her touch was light; in fact, I could barely sense her at all. Seeing her was difficult. I half suspected that even if we passed a lighted window she would cast no shadow upon the boardwalk. I sniffed in hopes of detecting some trace of cologne. The hairs of my nose were as stiff as pine needles and I smelled nothing, not even a trace of smoke from the fire. I listened for her quick steps but heard only my own heavy plodding. I spoke just to provoke her voice: "The pension is on Division Street, I believe."

"Yes, it is in the next street, to the left." There was a hint of accent in her voice—different from the other northcountry folk I had met.

She was an able guide and we reached the pension shortly. "Yes, this is it," I said standing at the walk which led to the side entrance. Her hand was still on my arm. "Thank you for your service. Let me give you something for your trouble." I reached into my coat pocket for some coins.

"You are kind, sir, but could I not warm myself a bit at your fire? It is a deathly cold night."

I tried to see her countenance, to see if she was playful or sincere, but the street was too dark. I glanced around, fearful that some of her companions had followed us. I saw no one of course. I was too chilled to consider the issue any further. "Yes, come in for a bit. To warm yourself."

We went to the side entrance of my home-away-from-home and entered. I latched the door behind us and lighted the lamp I had left there. I kept the wick low, so I still did not have a plain view of her face. The pension was perfectly quiet as we ascended the stair. My cold fingers fumbled with the key but at last I unlocked my door. The coals had all but died and the room's temperature was not a vast improvement over the city streets. My companion went immediately to the coal-burner to work up the heat. I set the lamp on the table and increased its illumination, anxious to see her face and determine her age. Her back was to me as she knelt at the burner. She was experienced with fire and soon a flame danced among the fresh coals she had applied.

She took off her mittens and was wearing half-finger gloves beneath. She held her hands near the heat. "That is better," she said, speaking toward the warmth so that I could barely hear her.

I removed my hat and gloves and coat. The fire was making a difference already. We stayed there in that way for some time. I did not know what to say or do. It was a great relief to be back in my room and secure—that was enough for now.

Yet the silence grew heavy. I was about to speak, something about her parents or her friends on the street, when she said, "Is that turnip soup I smell?" The pail was still atop the coal-burner. "May I have a taste, sir?"

"Yes, please, finish it. I am sorry but I have no tableware."

She took up the pail in her small hands and began gulping down the cold soup. She must have been very hungry. Even when the soup was gone she held the pail tipped to her mouth letting the last few drops of milky broth run out. She finally replaced the pail to the burner. "Thank you, sir; I had not eaten today." Her face was in profile. She looked pleasant . . . and young. "I do not mean to be forward, sir, but do you have anything to wash it down?"

I hesitated before offering her the bottle of vodka, which was still on the floor by the bed. I bent over and picked it up and she took it from my hand. She sat on the edge of the unmade bed and removed the cork. Her steadily increasing familiarity unsettled me. She took a long drink and I expected her to choke, but she did not: she was accustomed to hard liquor.

"Please," I said, "you have gotten something to eat and drink to warm you. You must go. You must return to your friends."

She looked puzzled. "But I have not thanked you properly, sir. Do you not want my thanks?" She untied and removed her cap, then shook free her thick dark hair. She appeared older then, perhaps not the child I had guessed.

"It was I who was in your debt, miss, for guiding me back to my room. Thank you for that."

She stared up at me. I looked at her but I tried not to think of the shape of her face, of her eyes, her mouth. I reminded myself she was a stranger from a strange street, that she might be a thief or a murderess even.

"Though you do not want my thanks, sir, could I not stay here until morning? Your room is comfortable and the streets are so cold in winter." She watched me closely for a sign. "I promise to leave when the sun is fully up and you will not be burdened with me anymore."

She seemed earnest. And the cold was severe. I recalled the profound lonesomeness I had known earlier—it was gone now. This strange girl had exorcised it from my room, from my heart. Like a priest casting out evil.

"I will sleep here on the floor in my coat," she offered. "I will be fine."

I thought of her sneaking off with my things while I slept like an old bear in his den. "You may take the side of the bed nearest the wall. But be certain to keep your promise in the morning."

"Thank you, sir, indeed."

"It is late and I am exceedingly tired."

She removed her boots and heavy coat and crawled to the far side of the large bed. I took off my shoes and lay beside her, turning my back to her and pulling the blankets over us both. I dozed off quickly but not before I heard her sleep rattle.

It was one of those sleeps that seems over in an instant. I had no dreams—I do not believe I even moved—but I was suddenly awake. Light streamed in from the window. And just as suddenly I knew she was gone. It was not for my money or my winter coat and hat that I was immediately concerned. I reached across the bed where she had lain and pulled up my valise. I unlatched its top flap and dug past my poems and money until I found the sketch of the Prince of Ithaka. I breathed with relief when I found it in its place. I looked for a moment at the Prince's eyes (the artist had captured them exactly). Traveler, he called himself. Was he often unnerved in his travels? A foreigner upon foreign soil or seas. There were tales he could tell but he kept them locked within, like a priest's bread inside his tabernacle. Christ's body closely guarded, and doled out sparingly and mysteriously.

I put the sketch away and secured my valise. I stepped over to the window in my stocking feet. I had the sense that my visitor left via the window. It was a foolish idea as it was a full two-story drop to the brick-paved alley. I checked the window nonetheless and it was firmly shut and latched. It annoyed me that she had left me asleep in an unsecured room. In the instant that it took for me to glance at the door, I imagined that it was latched, making a mystery of the girl's egress—but it was in fact undone.

She either had great faith in humankind that I would not be robbed or murdered in my sleep, or she simply did not care. The latter seemed most probable.

The landlord's wife had promised me tea with warm milk and biscuit for breakfast. There was also a washroom off the kitchen at my disposal. I decided that I should clean myself and eat, then go about the business that had guided me to this godforgotten place.

III

All the rivers were diverted into a single great flood.

Iliad 12

A FTER BREAKFAST, I set about finding the news bureau office. I had an address, given to me by Mezenskov, but I needed directions from my landlord. He said it was about three miles to the bureau office, and that I might be able to procure a cart or even a carriage going the right direction. He doubted that a motor-car could be found as the army had already commandeered virtually all of them in the city. The day was cold but sunny, and after fresh biscuit with butter and honey, and good strong tea, I felt up to the walk—should it prove necessary. I had my valise with me, and it could easily grow heavy. The streets of Iiloskova were almost bustling and my fears and forebodings of the previous night seemed distant and foolish. I was a child afraid of bogeymen under his bed. In the light of day, being well fed and well enough rested, I felt the city offered a certain charm, like an elderly woman who retains the hint of her girlish beauty, though bent and crippled now. Many of the former municipal buildings revealed their architecture's ornate Turkish roots. In between were more brutish structures, built solidly and lower to the earth, ready to withstand a northcountry winter. They were often constructed of red brick and heavy timbers, the windows small and square.

Deep ruts, frozen hard, were cut into the city streets. Pedestrians, both two- and four-legged, had to mind their steps or risk a broken ankle. Snow as fine as face powder blew in swirls through the ice-covered streets. I kept my eye out for a horse-drawn conveyance of some sort but none came rattling along. Every so often a child or small woman would pass me on the boardwalk and I thought of my young roommate of the night before. I wondered where the streetpeople went when the streets were filled with daytime folk. I imagined them to be nocturnal creatures, like vampires, who had to retire to dark places while the sun was out. Perhaps they slept in alleyways and ate from garbage bins while Iiloskova went about what remained of its business.

I heard squeaks and rattles behind me. A rickety cart drawn by an aged swayback horse was navigating the treacherous street. I hailed the cart's driver, a man with a graying beard and worn coat. The cart continued to move at its same pace while I spoke to the man and requested a ride to the news bureau. I offered to pay a pair of koppers and he consented with a nod to let me hop onto the back of his slowly moving cart. I concluded I would not reach the bureau any faster but the ride would save my legs and feet some hardship. As I found a place on the cart among wooden crates and a rolled up carpet and sour smelling milk cans, I thought of the Prince of Ithaka and his wornout shoes and shabby clothing. I wondered how many miles he had walked and if in fact he had traveled these same streets. I had no proof of it but it seemed to me that he had. I looked at the people on the boardwalks and could imagine him there, moving hunched through the crowds, as silent and separate as an assassin among bishops.

I arranged myself on the old carpet, which smelled of pine pitch and ammonia. I asked my driver where he had been headed when he came along but he either did not hear me or decided to ignore my query. I removed paper and pouch from my coat and made myself a cigarette. I struck a match on a milk can lid. It was cold riding in the back of the cart and the smoke in my lungs warmed me. There was no reason to be in a hurry, so I leaned back and enjoyed my smoking and the bright day. I was carefree only for a moment, however. My thoughts turned to Tasha, at home alone except for her washing and mending and cooking, which only half occupied her. She went through her days in search of other activities. It was the labors of motherhood she desired, to prepare meals for and tidy up after children that were not to be. I once suggested that we take in children—there were orphans in plenitude thanks to the war. Tasha did not respond, which was often her way. She went about her pretend housework, sullen, like a cow licking her stillborn calf.

After a time, the horse-drawn cart entered a section of the city with no ornate buildings whatsoever; they were all of the squat working-class type. Without warning, my driver halted the cart and pointed to a building with a gray façade and window shutters of peeling black paint. A wooden sign with tarnished metal letters confirmed that this was the news bureau, so I climbed down from the cart and gave my man the two koppers I had promised. He put them in the pocket of his coat and got the old horse moving again with a shake of the reins. The sunny skies were giving way to clouds, snowclouds no doubt.

Fewer people were on the streets here. I walked up to the door of the news bureau and thought about knocking: it looked closed-off and uninviting. But, after all, it was not a private residence, so I turned the knob and went inside. I expected to feel a rush of warm air but it was nearly as cold as outside. There was a long hallway lit only by a window near the ceiling at the far end. It took a moment for my eyes to adjust. Meanwhile, I heard the clack of a typewriter from somewhere in the gloom. There was an overlarge desk shoved into the corner of the foyer. I suspected a receptionist once occupied the desk but had probably been let go for want of work and salary. There was a disheveled stack of newspapers atop the desk, and a felt writing pad, and a nearly empty bottle of black ink, probably half frozen.

I called hello and received no response. I started moving toward the sound of the typewriter. I noticed the dust on the floor of the hallway and cobwebs in each of the corners. Clearly, the cleaning woman had been dismissed along with the receptionist. The typing sound was coming from an office at the far end of the hall. The door was ajar and my first view into the room was of just the typewriter itself and its carriage jumping along with the energetic bursts of the typist, who was smoking a pungent cigar. A puff of smoke hung over the paper in the typewriter's carriage like a stormcloud.

I knocked on the door and stepped inside the office. "Hello," I announced.

The man looked up startled and a second later his fingers finished their flurry of letters. He wore half-finger gloves. At first he appeared nearly my age but I quickly realized it was his furrowed brow and unshaven cheeks; in reality he was probably a good deal younger than I. He also wore a shirt of dingy white, the collar almost yellow, and an undone black tie hung lank from his neck. His sleeves were rolled up revealing a heavy gray shirt underneath. He wore a black vest with silver piping on the shoulders; it was part of a naval uniform. The cigar protruded from his lips like a misplaced organ.

"Hello," I said again. "I am Hektr Pastrovich. My editor, Mezenskov, was to have wired you about my coming." I went to the man's desk and extended my ungloved hand. I had a letter of introduction from Mezenskov in case telegraphy failed us.

"Pastrovich," he repeated through the smoldering cigar as he shook my fingers. "Pastrovich." He pawed through paper strewn across the desk and produced a little yellow sheet. "A boy brought it only within the hour." He reread the short message to himself. "Says you are here to *investigate* the front."

"Yes . . . that is true. . . ."

"What? My dispatches are not sufficient?" He laughed and emitted a thick cloud. "It is all right. As you can see, I am understaffed." He had a southeastern dialect.

"Are you alone here in the bureau?"

"No—I have two writers, if they can be called such, but I told them to only come to work when they are sober, which leaves a very narrow window of opportunity." He jerked open the bottom drawer of the desk. "Can I pour you a drink?"

It seemed early to me but I did not want to offend. He pulled an unlabeled bottle of vodka and a pair of mismatched glasses from the drawer. He half filled the glasses and I took the shorter of the two. The vodka was tart; I imagined that in the whole of Iiloskova there was not a drop of liquor more than a few hours old.

"Please, pull up a chair," he said. "I am Bushkov, by the by— editor, star reporter . . . navy lieutenant, errand boy, publican—you name it." He removed the cigar long enough to drink down most of the vodka in his glass.

I took hold of the nearest chair and turned it toward Bushkov. The chair had an uneven leg.

He continued, "What exactly do you want to accomplish, Mr. Pastrovich, now that you have come all this way?"

"To be frank, I do not have specific objectives. I am hoping to gather background for a piece or two on the city, how the war has affected it. And I should like to get to the front, to report the war with my own eyes—that is what my editor has in mind, I know."

"I see." Bushkov puffed on his foul cigar. "I can help you arrange transportation, perhaps point you in the right direction. Trucks come from the front irregularly, once every week or two—sometimes less frequently in winter. I can provide you work space, as you can see. Where are you staying?"

"At a pension, near the rail station. It is reasonably comfortable and affordable."

"It is some distance from here then. In the room across the hall are some cots with blankets. If you find yourself nearer this part of the city some evening. There is always a key above the front door frame."

"Thank you." I supposed there were pensions closer to the news bureau but I felt the need to keep my distance, from Bushkov, who at some level represented the government. "There is another matter," I said as I reached into my valise and retrieved the sketch of the Prince of Ithaka. "Does this man look familiar to you? Has he been in the news?"

Bushkov angled the picture to catch the light from the window. "Who is he?"

"I am not sure. I suppose I was hoping you could tell me."

"He is from Iiloskova?" Bushkov continued to study the drawing.

"I believe he spent some time here, yes." I sensed some suspicion in Bushkov.

"No, he does not look familiar. I could ask my writers when they come in."

"That is all right." I reached out and reclaimed the drawing. "Do you have a paper morgue? Perusing some old reports may be a good way to begin."

"Such as it is." He got up from the desk chair and shifted the position of the cigar in his mouth. Carrying my valise and glass of bad vodka, I followed Bushkov to the hallway and two doors down to a larger room with a pair of windows and three tall bookcases, from floor to ceiling. Each bookcase contained shelf after shelf of leather-bound papers. Bushkov pointed to the bookcases from right to left: "City, the war, and everything else. The oldest starts in the bottom right, the most recent top left. And over there—" He indicated a table against a wall. "—are about six months' worth of dispatches that have not been organized." Stacks of disheveled papers covered the table top. I knew then how long ago the receptionist had been dismissed, or had evacuated herself. "You may peruse to your heart's content. Let me know if I can be of further service." He left behind a cloud of smoke. I noticed that his black pants had silver piping up the leg to match the vest. Cleaned and pressed, it could have been a smart uniform. I supposed it was some government official's idea of a joke to post a navy-man in the news bureau in Iiloskova, a thousand miles from the nearest coastline. The River Hadz that ultimately connected Iiloskova's lake to the ocean was so clogged with chunks of ice one could make the journey by foot just as easily, or uneasily, as by boat.

There was a rolltop desk in the morgue-room with the top up and a bit of clear space to work. So I removed paper and pencil, and went about looking through the old dispatches and taking notes. I did not want to go back further than six months, so I began with the table of papers. I found that they were not completely disorganized; there was a kind of method to the madness, and I was able to sort out "city" stories from "war" stories. I was not certain what I was looking for. I figured that I would read for general information and if anything seemed related to the Prince of Ithaka, no matter how obliquely, I would make note of it.

Outside the morgue windows, the day had turned from bright to overcast white. And it was becoming more difficult to read the dispatches, some poorly typewritten, others scribbled in cursive. There was an oil lamp on the floor near the desk, so I lit the stubby wick and hung the lamp on a nail protruding from the wall that was there for just such a purpose. I also fixed myself a cigarette and used

an ash bucket that I found in the corner of the morgue-room. There
was something cozy and comforting about sitting alone in the cold
room amid the dispatches, smoking and sipping the bad vodka,
hunting for some clue to a mystery I could not yet articulate.

I accumulated a few notes. Among the city reports were ones
about petty thievery and troublemaking vagrants. I recalled the
incident that landed the Prince in jail at home, his stealing from the
secondhand shop, and it seemed that any of these reports might have
to do with the stranger. I found nothing about escapees from the
asylum, or army deserters. In fact, it occurred to me there were no
reports of serious crimes whatsoever. Iiloskova had to have its share
of murders and beatings—more than its share—yet after two hours
I had read no dispatches regarding homicides, brutal robberies, or
rape; nor bootlegging or prostitution for that matter. Could it be
the government-controlled press reported nothing so unseemly?
We had long suspected government censorship, but we imagined—I
imagined—it only pertained to issues of national import, like the
progress of the war. What would be the point of polishing Iiloskova's
image? Perhaps officials were hoping for the return of trade after
the war. To me, such thoughts were beyond hope: they were of the
realm of fantasy, of fairies and elves, witches and dragons.

The city's death rattle was on the cold breeze.

It was after midday when Lieutenant Bushkov stepped into the
morgue and invited me to dine with him at his landlady's. He was
without his disfiguring cigar for the first time and he had lost ten
years from his face. I was hungry and beginning to get a headache,
from the poisonous vodka and the close reading. We donned our
heavy coats and went outside, where nearly invisible pellets of snow
were cutting the air. We talked very little as it was difficult into the
wind. He asked how my researches were coming; there might have
been a touch of sarcasm in his voice but it was difficult to tell with the
wind. I said they were coming along.

It was only a few blocks to his landlady's house, yet my face was
numb by the time we arrived. I thought of how one would not last
long exposed to the elements in the northcountry. I wondered what
sorts of hardships the troops were enduring to keep the enemy at
bay.

The landlady's house was a two-story brick edifice with a white-painted rail fence and a spacious porch. It was the first homey home I had seen in Iiloskova. Inside, it was actually warm. A fire roared in the livingroom hearth. I removed my winter things in the foyer and soaked in the heat, like a toad taking in the rays of the sun on a cold morning. Madam Ilychka was stately in her elderliness; gray-haired, yes, but tall and willowy. She wore a touch of rouge on her cheekbones. Her hands were long and white beneath her lace cuffs. A blue-eyed Siamese cat moved around her feet, which were hidden under a long, striped skirt.

Madam Ilychka told Bushkov he was the only boarder to return for supper, so a guest was no trouble, "welcome, in fact," she said.

We went to a table in the dining room, where another fire was alight, and soon the landlady brought us steaming bowls of red bean and ham soup, with wheat bread and mugs of black coffee. I had not felt this warm and comfortable since boarding the train for Iiloskova. Once we were served, Madam Ilychka sat at the head of the table drinking coffee with cream from a china saucer, the Siamese draped across her lap. She encouraged us to eat heartily and to spread butter to the point of excess on our thick slices of bread. Bushkov was used to such treatment and readily complied, whereas I was more timid.

"Is this how all southerners eat, like sparrows?" she chided me. I supposed that to the northcountry people, all visitors were southerners, though I certainly did not consider myself such.

I wondered about my decision to remain in my current pension—perhaps Madam Ilychka had room—but the strong coffee was making me clear-headed if nothing else, and keeping my distance from Lieutenant Bushkov still seemed wise. Not to mention, the cost was probably well beyond the allowance Mezenskov had provided. While we ate, Madam Ilychka asked me about my family back home; I told her I was married. She asked about children; no, I said. My tone, I am certain, made her drop the line of inquiry. Soon the landlady went to the kitchen with our bowls and spoons, and returned with bread pudding on saucers with cream. The desserts were steaming as if recently from the oven. I was convinced I could not afford her rent.

After the dessert, Bushkov offered me a cigar in Madam Ilychka's parlor, but I declined. "I should probably gather my notes from the bureau and begin making my way back to the center of the city," I said. "I may have to walk the entire route and your days are short here." I stepped into the kitchen for a moment and thanked Madam Ilychka for her excellent meal; I offered to pay her but she said it was already taken care of by her tenant.

Bushkov and I returned to the cold day. The boardwalk was a bit slippery with the new-fallen, powdery snow. We were passing a low brick structure when the lieutenant said, "Come in for a drink before you are off, Pastrovich." We paused at its entrance.

"I probably should go."

"Pish. It will warm you for the journey. You said you wanted local color. This establishment is positively vibrant."

Still wary, but still not wanting to offend—Bushkov could prove useful here—I accepted and we walked into the tavern. It was surprisingly busy for the middle of the day but it was mainly old men. The war had taken most of the men who were in their prime. There was a long oaken bar along one wall but no stools. When I looked closer, I realized there were dark squares on the floor where stools had once been anchored. At almost the same moment I noticed an empty frame on the wall behind the bar that looked as though it might have held a mirror in place. Perhaps the tavern had sat empty for a time and had been looted. In fact, once I considered it, it seemed likely.

Bushkov and I went to a table near the center of the tavern, and an old man in a dirty apron came to take our order. Bushkov ordered a vodka. I asked the old man if he had beer and he did. Bushkov removed a cigar from his coat, clipped off the end with a little pair of scissors he kept in his vest pocket, and lighted it. "So," he said through a cloud of smoke, "tell me about your home, Hektr. What is it like?"

I thought for a moment. "I never considered it special; yet having spent some time here, it seems to have improved in my esteem."

"Yes, Iiloskova is a real rat hole. I have been here nearly eighteen months. Imagine that—when a year is like a life sentence." The old man brought our drinks. There was no exchange of currency; perhaps Bushkov ran a line of credit. "What else?"

"There is a river, a branch of the Vulpa, not far from my house. I often go walking there in the mornings. It is very pleasant." I knew these responses were not what Lieutenant Bushkov had in mind but I felt like being abstruse. The thought of painting him a vivid picture of my home seemed like a violation of privacy. Had he not represented the government in my mind, I might have responded differently. I drank my beer, which was a bit flat, but an improvement over the vodka I had had since arriving. "And you, Lieutenant, where is your home?"

"I too have a river," he said, "and I have been walking there myself."

Touché, I thought. We drank in silence for a time. Suddenly two men in a corner of the tavern broke out in a noisy disagreement. Just as suddenly, they were on their feet grabbing each other by their lapels. Both men were as dark-skinned as gypsies. A chair was knocked over; the drinks on their table spilled. I was frozen by the spectacle. I watched as the old tavernkeeper walked up behind one of the men and hit him in the back of the head with a small wooden club. The old man hit him hard, hard enough to stun him into submission while he reached for the back of his head and felt the blood-sticky wound. He mumbled some words in an unfamiliar language—probably something like "you old bastard." But the tavernkeeper lifted the club as if to strike again and both men began hurrying toward the door. As they left, the old man hurled a phrase at them in their own tongue, perhaps "and do not return."

"Say what you will about the rat hole, but there is always something to break the monotony," said Bushkov through his cigar.

As he returned to the bar, the old man wiped the club on his white apron and left a streak of blood that looked like a backward "L."

We finished our drinks and I stopped at the news bureau long enough to collect my valise, which contained the notes from the morning's researches. I thanked Lieutenant Bushkov for his help and generosity, then I began the trek back to my pension. The snow had stopped but the night was already creeping toward the city, and with it the bitter cold. I walked briskly to keep up my internal heat. Bushkov promised to send me a message when a truck had arrived from the front. In truth I had little desire to go there, farther north, deeper into the relentless winter and whatever grim realities of war resided there. I imagined some great beast, chimera-like, who hoarded corpses as other monsters of myth hoarded treasure. I pictured the beast's great talons wrapped around bloodied soldiers, its great rump resting on a pile of bones. The northcountry had fanned my creativity but not necessarily in a productive way.

IV

Sing the singular story once again.

Odyssey 1

MY LANDLORD SERVED TURNIP STEW and biscuits left over from breakfast, not the fare of Madam Ilychka but nutritious and welcome after the long walk. At dinner I met some of the others staying in the pension. There was an older gentleman, Kritch, who was visiting relatives in the city. No one pursued his story: What kind of family makes a relative stay at a pension? Or, what kind of man is made to stay at a pension by his family? There was a salesman of glass, Polozkov, who had a large hooked nose and an absurd scheme for becoming rich: It seemed that he expected the war would eventually come to Iiloskova, thus shattering virtually every window in the city. After, he would be on hand to make his fortune. Our landlady was refilling teacups as Polozkov elaborated on his plan; he quickly assured her that such a calamity would not befall her residence, "so close to the heart of the city." It appeared to me that Iiloskova did not have a heart. A ribcage perhaps, and a large and small intestine, and a liver . . . but not a heart. In any case, the war was still some distance away, and I wondered how long the glass salesman intended to wait. There was a woman staying at the pension by herself, a woman of middle age, though she wore bangs like a schoolgirl. She was polite and listened respectfully to her fellow lodgers, but she did not volunteer anything about her situation, which of course made me—made everyone, I am sure—imagine all kinds of wild stories about her. She was a witch, a spy, a prostitute, the wife or mistress of a fallen politician—perhaps all of them.

After the landlord and his wife cleared the dishes from the table, Polozkov and I set up a chessboard that we had been told of. The other lodgers went to their rooms. The chess pieces were carved from hardwood (linden perhaps), half left natural in coloring, the others stained dark. The hooked-nose salesman and I were well-matched; we played two games, each winning one. I was the victor in the second game. I had noticed that he appeared vulnerable to diagonal attacks, so I used my bishops in combination with my queen to place him in checkmate. I made a mental note of this weakness in case we played again. After we put away the chessboard and Polozkov excused himself to his room, I looked at my pocketwatch and it was only a few minutes beyond seven o'clock—a long northcountry night still lay before me. I was in the mood to write. The images of Iiloskova, the train ride, the braided woman with whom I ate breakfast, my young guide of the previous night, Bushkov and his ubiquitous cigar—all of these things were cluttering my mind. I felt that I must put them down on paper in order to clear my head. Once on paper, they could be properly arranged and organized, like tools in a well-maintained shed, then stored until needed.

My host and hostess were still cleaning in the kitchen, so I went and asked for a pot of tea. The landlady was scrubbing a large stockpot at the butcher-block table, her sleeves gathered at her elbows; her husband was putting cups away in the cupboard. My request did not please them, but my landlord said that he would bring it to my room presently. I thanked him and went upstairs.

I tried the electric light hanging on the cord from the ceiling but of course it was not working, so I lighted the fetid oil lamp and stoked the coals in the burner. I opened my valise and arranged my writing things on the table, my paper, and nibs, and my bottles of ink. The room was chilly so I spread my great coat over my legs like a shawl. I filled the nib of my pen and looked at the blank paper, as blank as a frozen pond, yet full of possibility too. My eyes moved up to the black, square window directly across from me; the window worked as a mirror against the night beyond its thin panes. I saw myself there, behind the flame of the lamp, looking like an unholy surgeon, my pen a rusted scalpel, my ink bottle a specimen of bad blood.

I touched the nib to paper and began. I thought of the woman on the train and how I had mistaken her for a mere girl . . .

A child she seemed, her black hair braided
Like a schoolgirl's. Her slender nape of
White flesh, her slender hands clutching her cloak.

The words flowed, line by line, until I had a fair poem about her. Four stanzas, with some images I liked even upon a second reading. I recalled her "elfin waist," her eyes "like stones of amethyst / in the bed of a mountain stream," and an unsettling aura about her reminiscent of "air before a storm." All in all, though, she was "a creature of awe and sympathy," I wrote. I wondered where she was now, on this cold dark night. She seemed ill-prepared for life here. I sensed that no one was waiting to greet her. She was, even more than I, traveling alone.

There was a knock on the door and a muffled voice beyond said, "Your tea, Mr. Pastrovich." I had nearly forgotten. "Come in, please," I said, expecting my landlord to open the door, but it was his skinny wife who entered, balancing the white teapot and cup against her aproned bosom. I reached out to assist with the burden but she was already placing the pot and cup on the table.

"Thank you," I said. She continued to be of service as she poured the hot tea into the cup. She held onto the teapot with a kitchen rag. Her eyes, gray I recalled from seeing her in better light, glanced to my papers. She set the pot, rag and all, on the table when she was finished.

I expected her to leave quickly; instead, she said, "My husband said you was a newspaperman." There was skepticism in her voice: I was obviously writing poetry.

"It is true, madam. Your husband told you correctly. But I also enjoy writing verse." I had an urge to cover my newborn poem with another sheet of paper. I was not ready to show it to the world yet (as if the world were curious). A moment of intimacy between father and child was being violated.

"I used to write little poems, when I was a girl," volunteered my landlady. I noticed the curls hanging down from her cap. I wondered how long her hair would be if released—a mane of curls may soften the angular quality of her face, I thought.

"Little poems," I repeated.

"Yes, silly little poems, I suppose." She smiled a bit to think of them; it was an attractive smile, in spite of a twisted tooth. "I grew up on a farm, my papa was a farmer, and I wrote little poems about chickens and ducks and such."

I no longer felt the urge to cover my poem. Both my visitor and I were in a moment of intimacy now. "Have you retained your poems, madam? In a scrapbook perhaps?"

Her smile vanished. "Nah. I wrote near all of 'em in the dirt. At most they lasted a day or two before something would trample them away."

I could tell the thought of her lost poetry saddened her; I understood completely. "Thank you—for bringing the tea. It was most kind of you." I wanted to comfort this poor woman but it was not my place to comfort her. Besides, she was so thin, it looked like a firm hug would crush her. I thought of my first night's eavesdropping and the sounds emitting from her and her husband's private chamber. She was no doubt hardier than she appeared.

The landlady took her leave of me, nodding politely as she shut my door, embarrassed perhaps that she had spoken of her childish poetry. I drank the tea. It had a slightly piney taste but was good. I filled my nib and wrote . . . about the buildings of Iiloskova, of their mix of grand and commonplace, each standing solitary, though side by side, like mausoleums and headstones along the streets. I wrote a long description of the central railway station, of its marble columns and Turkish spires, of its filthy steps, and of the oak benches inside its cavernous hall where streetpeople slept, wrapping themselves in rags against the cold.

I wrote and wrote and wrote, drinking the good tea all the while—I kept the pot warm on top of the coal-burner. I grew stiff in my chair. Papers were spread across the table, the tight loops and lines of ink drying in the chill air. I stood and stretched; my vertebrae popped like small-caliber pistol shots. I went to the black, mirror-like window. I could not see out but I heard pellets of snow against the panes. It was a brutal night and only just beginning. In the news bureau's morgue there were reports of people dying from exposure in the streets. I examined my reflection in the window: I had not shaved since my arrival and my face showed the beginnings of a black and gray beard. I decided I would let it go here, that the additional insulation was prudent.

When I left home, there were harbingers of spring, but not here. Winter's grip was still as tight as a drowning man's hand upon a buoyant oar.

I went downstairs to prepare for bed. The other lodgers were quiet in their rooms. I listened at the door of the landlord and even they were silent this night. I was about to return to my room when I noticed a faint light under the door to the kitchen. I went through the dining room, which still smelled of turnip stew, and listened intensely. For some time I heard no sound at all and thought perhaps a candle had been left burning, then there was the creak of a chair. I wondered who would be up at this late hour, sitting in the dimly lit kitchen, probably alone. I thought of the various lodgers and tried to imagine why each would be holding such a vigil. Clearly I should return to my room and not intrude upon the person in the kitchen, but curiosity was getting the better of me.

As I reached for the doorknob, a convincing lie formed in my mind: I saw the light and was concerned about a candle left unattended. I pushed open the door and discovered the landlady sitting at the butcher-block. She was startled and embarrassed and immediately began to push back her chair. Her hair was hanging loose and fell over her shoulders, which were covered by a dark shawl.

"Madam . . . I am sorry . . . I saw the candlelight. . . ." I stopped my story because I noticed what she had been doing in the kitchen. She had spread flour on the butcher-block and was using her finger to trace words, to trace poetry no doubt. I walked up to the table; the candle flame flickered in the cold air. I knew that if anyone else had interrupted her, she would have quickly erased her words. For me, she stayed seated, the light playing tricks with her features. I stood beside her and read what her skeletal finger had made in the flour dust: "Mother Duck quacks to the breeze of the far shore / Where her ducklings have gone missing in the reeds—"

"That is lovely," I said, meaning it, "quite lovely." I gently squeezed her shoulder to communicate my sincerity. She put her hand in the flour. "You must not," I said quietly. But she wiped out the words anyway.

"It is all right," said the landlady. "I will remember this time." She put her finger to her forehead. I could not see in the poor light but I imagined there was an imprint of flour above her eyebrow. I had an urge to kiss it away.

A sound in the dining room surprised us both; I took my hand from her shoulder. I had left the door ajar and lamplight came toward the kitchen. It was the landlord in his nightshirt and cap. "Hello, sir," I said, probably sounding too subordinate, too guilty. "I saw a light and thought a candle must have been left unattended." I stepped toward the doorway. "Well, good evening to you both." I left the landlady to explain herself to her husband.

I went through the dark house quickly and up the stairs two at a time, anxious to get away from the kitchen. Nearly reaching the second floor, I tripped on the top step and made a racket as I caught myself with my hands and regained my footing. Before I could abscond to my room, two doors opened in the hall: Polozkov, the glass salesman; and the middle-aged woman, her bangs sticking out of her cap. Polozkov said, "Everything all right out here?"

"Yes. . . ." I was short of breath. "Everything is fine. I tripped on the stair is all."

Polozkov and the woman, both dressed for bed, continued to look at me as if expecting more.

"I apologize for the noise. In the future, I will take a lamp." Probably not what they wanted.

"It is perfectly all right—just be careful. Good evening," said Polozkov, closing his door.

I nodded to the woman, witch or whore or spy. "Madam," I said and went inside my room. I was embarrassed, about many things. I latched my door and collected the papers on the table into a neat stack. I looked forward to having a warm drink and reading back through my writings on the morrow. I added some small lumps of coal to the burner, extinguished my lamp, and crawled beneath the blankets. Wind rattled the window. Snow peppered it. It seemed that the city was under assault. I pulled the covers over my head like a hood, feeling secure in my bunker.

Soon I was asleep. For how long I do not know.

I sensed some commotion in the house. Not noise exactly, but commotion. Perhaps I felt it through the floorboards and the legs of my bed and the springs and mattress—as a spider senses movement. I tried to ignore the sensation and return to sleep but it was too potent. I slipped out of my warm cocoon and pulled on my pants. I stood at the door in stocking feet. I still could hear nothing per se, yet sensed the agitation in the house. I wondered at the hour: it must have been the proverbial middle of the night. I quietly unlatched and opened my door.

The hall was dark, cold and drafty. Keeping a hand upon the wall, I walked toward the stairs. Standing at the top, I strained to hear. Yes, there were voices, distressed voices, angry voices. It could only be the landlord and his wife. I crept down a step or two, which made the voices louder but no more distinct. I tried to imagine where they were: the kitchen still? in their rooms? I thought of rows Tasha and I had had, often over the silliest of disagreements, at times over things of more weight. I was always ready to forgive and forget after a few minutes, after the venom had drained from my fangs— but not Tasha. Her hurt and anger would smolder for hours, for days. In fact, it seemed that a small ember of each argument never did become completely extinguished, so that after all these years she had a full belly of hot embers that were ready to be set ablaze with the smallest bit of fuel.

My woolgathering was interrupted by the slam of a door. I realized there were angry footsteps in the hall bearing down on the stairway. I tried to retreat to my room but I did not make it. I was still in the hall when a dark figure rushed past, probably not even noticing me in its state of agitation. I could tell by the figure's height and scent and lack of girth that it was my landlady moving by in the dark. The smell of flour lingered for a moment. She went to a door at the far end of the hall, next to mine, and entered. She did not slam the door as such but closed it with some force. The click of the latch was like the cocking of a pistol in the night.

She would not be sharing her husband's bed.

The hall was suddenly as silent as it was cold. I expected the landlord to come upstairs in search of his wife but no one ascended the steps. I returned to my room and took a moment to enliven the coals in the burner. Kneeling on the floor, I could see my breath in the faint orange light. I sat in bed with the blankets wrapped around me. I stared at the wall beyond the coal-burner; I wondered what she was doing on the other side of it. Crying? Seething? Plotting? I considered tapping on the wall, just to let her know I was thinking of her. I thought of the times I tried to connect with Tasha after one of our fights and how she could transport herself a million miles from our home. She would be there but not be there too, adrift in another realm, adrift and alone. To stew and to pick at the wounds I had opened. My weapons were always words, of course. Never fists or anything physical. Tasha, however, in her rage, would slap at me. Once she shoved a door against me, cutting my forehead; another time I was burned by a fistful of hot noodles.

But always in a short time I would forget and forgive, tired of the fighting. Then it would require patience as I waited for Tasha to completely return to our home. It happened little by little, like the creeping of a vine. She would be returned for some time before I would even realize it, as I had grown used to her absence: the way one can become used to a toothache or sore back. I thought that Tasha and I were fortunate that we did not have a large house; if we did, she would spend all of her time wandering in empty rooms. The closeness of our home forced us into the same space. Proximity was a kind of priest who counseled us to stay together in spite of our differences.

I lay in the pension's bed wide awake on this strange, cold night. I wondered if all my nights here would be strange, if strangeness was the way of things in Iiloskova. I listened for a sound from my new neighbor, a sob or a creaking spring, but she was completely silent in her room. I knew that I could not go to her, to comfort her—I had already overstepped the bounds of a good guest. Yet I wanted my landlady to know that, if nothing else, she was not the only one awake at this lonely hour. I thought again of tapping on the wall. I guessed that if she were lying in bed, her head would be just beyond my coal-burner. Still wearing my blankets, I went to the wall, reached around the burner pipe, and knocked gently on the flaking plaster, three times.

I held my breath. My heart began to pound in my ribcage. Nothing, except for the wind shaking my window and my pocketwatch ticking on the table. I returned to the bed and lay under the pile of covers. I turned on my left side and as the bed springs subsided I heard a single, quiet rap on the wall. Somehow it both gladdened and saddened me. I was glad that she had responded to me, that we had found a way to connect. But the thought of two lonely souls hibernating in our cocoons of ice made my heart heavy. Then I imagined all the other lonely souls in the world: my little guest from the previous night, the woman on the train, the Prince of Ithaka, Tasha, my landlord, probably even Bushkov and Mezenskov. A whole country of lonely souls, perhaps at war with a country of kindred spirits. I was on the verge of tears in my cocoon when I had an idea.

I unwrapped myself from the bed clothes and found my valise on the table. Operating only by the feeble light from the faintly glowing coals, I removed some blank sheets of paper, half a dozen perhaps, then I took a pencil from my leather case. I stole into the hall and slid the paper and pencil under the landlady's temporary door. I quietly returned to my bed, and sooner than expected sleep overtook me.

'Seek for word of your lost father,
even if nothing more than a traveler's tale.'
Odyssey 1

I N THE MORNING the landlord and his wife were at work serving breakfast for their lodgers with no hint of a change between them. He directed everyone to be seated with his usual reserved and requisite politeness, while his taciturn wife brought the meager fare from the kitchen. I had slept until past daybreak and did not hear my neighbor stir from her room. As with all couples, they must work things out themselves.

Breakfast was the northcountry's version of a potato pancake— mostly flour and a bit of shredded potato, served with a teaspoon of butter—and tea. Afterward, I set out for the Hotel Slopek, which I knew was near the rail station. The hotel was the site of a disturbance some months back, according to one of the reports at the news bureau. There were innumerable reports of disturbances, but the alleged perpetrator of the one at the Hotel Slopek sent three men to hospital.

It was a day much like the one before: sunny and cold with the promise of diminishing sun and increasing cold. I did not bother looking for a ride of some sort; it was not a long walk. En route I passed the brothel I happened across my first night. Of course it looked different in the light of day, much more like an accounting office or some such, which no doubt was its original purpose. It was quite close to my pension, and I thought about my foolish fear at being lost. Yet it was a city that inspired fear, or at least a lack of confidence in the world. The whole of the city, citizenry and all, seemed perched on the edge of some precipice, ready to topple into a black unknown. I imagined the snow and ice would quickly cover the spot where Iiloskova stood, leaving no trace of the once prosperous bastion of civilization.

It occurred to me that the army should allow its enemy to advance, allow it to march straight through the Great White Desert all the way to Iiloskova, unopposed. For surely when it arrived in the city and took stock of the place, its commanders would immediately give the signal to retreat. As they returned through the snow desert heaped with the dead, they would surely ask themselves what they had been fighting for all those years. The soldiers would return to their home country, put down rifle and bayonet, and take up the implements of farming, to try to scratch out a life amidst the frozen rock and earth.

It was a whimsical notion. Who could understand why armies engaged each other? I thought of the long-ago war in Troy, fought over a woman—no doubt my conversation on the train sparked the recollection of such knowledge. If two men can knock each other's brains out over a beautiful woman, why not two armies of men? I tried to imagine two armies of women clashing over a man but it was an impossible premise. If they did, it is certain the losers would get him.

The hotel was tall by Iiloskova standards and I saw its sharply pitched slate roof from some distance. Nearly all the buildings of the city had severely pitched roofs; it was not wise to allow snow and ice to accumulate. A winter storm could stave in a flat roof. Two men in black coats were shoveling and sweeping snow from the hotel's wide steps as I approached. They wore scarves around their mouths and noses, but their breath still came in puffs of smoke. The façade of the Hotel Slopek was cream-colored stucco, and there was a high pointed arch over its entrance. I went through the heavy doors and stamped the snow from my shoes.

The lobby of the hotel had a high ceiling, almost as high as the rail station's. Windows near the green-painted ceiling allowed in a copious amount of light, casting a verdant glow throughout the lobby area. It was similar to the light in a forest when a midday sun is shining through the leafy canopy. I breathed deeply, hoping the scent would be that of a forest, but of course it was the same stale, indoor smell I had encountered in all the buildings of Iiloskova. I also detected a whiff of pipe tobacco and at the far end of the lobby, in a crushed velvet chair, was a bald man in an old-style black suit having a smoke.

I removed my hat and gloves, shoving them inside my coat, and approached the wooden counter where the guest registry was spread open like the chest of a cadaver undergoing autopsy. I stood at the counter looking around for a hotel-man. No one was in sight except for the peaceful old fellow with his pipe. There was a small brass bell next to the registry, so I picked it up with my thick fingers and shook it. It emitted a delicate little jingle that was immediately lost in the high-ceilinged lobby. I shook it harder but my zeal had no effect on its volume. I imagined that I could hurl the bell against the wall and it would sound like a wad of wool hitting the plaster.

There was a door behind the counter and I was about to call toward it in hopes of conjuring a hotel employee, when the old man with the pipe rose from his velvet-covered chair and began to stroll in my direction. He kept the pipe between his teeth and a trail of smoke followed his leisurely path. There was so little purpose in his gait it did not occur to me he was answering my summons until he removed the pipe from his mouth and said, "Yes, may I assist you?" His voice was gravely, as if he had been sitting and smoking without interruption for some time. He was bald except for a half ring of white hair around the back of his head. Dark age-spots stood out on his pate.

"Yes, hello, my name is Pastrovich. I am here for some information. Are you in the hotel's employ?"

The fellow drew from his pipe, as if considering a difficult question, then said, "I am the proprietor, Golokov." He offered his hand, which was icy and arthritic. "Would you sit, Mr. P—"

"Pastrovich—yes, thank you." We slowly made our way to the velvet-covered chairs. I unbuttoned and removed my coat, then folded it over the back of one of the chairs, which was low to the floor on thick, dark-wood legs. I sat and located the sketch of the Prince in my valise without removing it. Meanwhile, the old fellow was smoking peacefully in his chair. I suspected he would not care if I never got to the point of asking him questions; he would probably soon forget I had mentioned it. I began: "Mr. Golokov, it appears the hotel is not overrun with guests."

With the pipe in his teeth, he said, "No, sir, I would not describe it as 'overrun,' not for many a year now. There was a time when one could not obtain a room without having some little in with the family. Fine gentlemen, gentlemen of business, and their wives filled the hotel."

"The family?"

"Yes, the Slopek family." He removed the pipe for a moment and exhaled a great cloud of smoke, then returned it to its place. "A fine family indeed—pillars of the city. There was a day when Vlad Slopek had the ear of every noteworthy official." I had the impression these were thoughts that often ran through old Golokov's head, sitting here in his velvet chair in the abandoned lobby, but I had given him the opportunity to speak them aloud. I had noticed on a wall of the lobby the portrait of a regal-looking gentleman in a blue coat of military cut. The figure had an aristocratic brow and an intricately trimmed beard. It must have been an oil painting of Vlad Slopek.

"Do any Slopeks remain? Do they still own the hotel?"

He glanced down at the floor, as if the answer could be found there. "A single Slopek," he said, "Vlad, like his grandfather, but not his grandfather." He held the bowl of his pipe and chewed the mouthpiece for a moment.

"Does this Vlad Slopek live at the hotel?" I asked.

"He has some rooms—there are plenty of rooms these days."

I thought perhaps Vlad Slopek may be worth interviewing, if I was in the market for lurid details. I switched to the business for which I had come: "Mr. Golokov, do you recall an incident of some four months ago? A man who was arrested at the hotel?" I had nothing in hand still, no notebook, no pencil; I wanted to keep the mood conversational.

"A man arrested," he repeated, smoke seeping from his lips. "The police are not a presence any longer; they too have gone elsewhere."

"Yes, but four months ago, or longer—perhaps my information is not accurate—the police were here, and they arrested a man because of a disturbance. Do you recall it?"

The old fellow was lost in thought, as it were. He sat smoking, his eyebrow drawn down almost covering his eyes. I had nearly given up on him when he said, "There was an episode. It involved a woman, if it is the incident of which you inquire." He stopped suddenly, recalling something. "I think I should not discuss it."

"A woman? A guest at the hotel?"

Golokov worked on his pipe more quickly, the little puffs of smoke a barometer of his agitation. He did not look at me.

I took a stab at the truth: "Was this woman a prostitute?"

His pipe stem was suddenly a tit and Golokov a famished babe. The chill air around us became thick with tobacco smoke. It seemed I would get nothing more from the old man. I looked around the empty lobby thinking there must be someone else I could interview. I recalled the workmen on the steps but was skeptical of the help they could provide. Figuring I had nothing to lose, I removed the sketch of the Prince of Ithaka from my valise. I held it out for Golokov to see. "Was this man involved?"

At first it did not appear that Golokov even saw the drawing. I wondered if I had chosen a lunatic to question, if he had fabricated his recollection of the incident, if there was no Vlad Slopek at all. I was about to return the sketch to my valise when some emotion began to form on Golokov's wrinkled face—slowly, like frost forming on a window pane. It started with an increased furrowing of his brow, then spread to his eyes, to his mouth. Yet it was not precisely recognition that I saw on the old man's countenance. "You know this man?" I said, half question, half statement.

He took the pipe from his mouth and reached out with his other arthritic hand toward the drawing. I assumed Golokov was going to take hold of it but he merely touched the Prince's rough likeness with his trembling fingers. He said in his raspy voice, "You know this man?"—half question, half statement.

I considered my complicated connection to the Prince. "Yes," I said, and it did not feel like a lie. "How do you know him?"

"He was here." He moved his fingers away from the drawing and pointed toward a shadowy corner of the lobby. I looked, almost with a sense of anticipation, as if I might see him there—not lurking in shadow, but rather standing erect in a beam of sunlight truly like a prince. He was not of course. Golokov resumed without prompting, "No one knew him, so it was said after." He lowered his arthritic paw to his lap but continued to stare at the phantom Prince in the corner. I discreetly returned the sketch to my valise. "It was summertime. People were in the hotel, eating, drinking. *Friends* of Vlad Slopek. Plates littered the lobby, plates with discarded food. Chicken bones with meat still upon them, crusts of bread, melon rinds. And bottles of wine and of vodka, so many bottles."

Golokov remembered his smoldering pipe and placed it in his teeth. He took a long draw and I was worried that the tale was finished. "What about the man?" I said, pointing to his phantom in the corner.

A long moment passed before Golokov said, "They noticed him there, picking through their food, through their garbage. Vlad Slopek's friends became angry, or they simply wanted to be angry. He desired only to take the scraps and leave but they had him in the corner. Drunk, they were quite drunk. I thought, 'I must call the police,' but policemen were there, among the friends of Vlad Slopek." Golokov rubbed the wrinkles in his brow as if trying to remove them, or perhaps he was attempting to purge the memory. He puffed on his pipe but was nearly out of tobacco. "The stranger's eyes, darting to and fro, like the eyes of a caged animal. I did not know what to do, then there was the crashing. . . ."

"Crashing?" I scolded myself for interrupting.

"Yes, upstairs. . . ." I looked at the wide staircase, once grand no doubt, at the far end of the lobby. "Vlad Slopek and one of his . . . one of his . . . ladies. She was half down the stairs, clinging to a sheet to cover herself. She held something in her hand. A broken bottle. Vlad Slopek was at the top of the stairs laughing. He held his sides he laughed so hard. He had no modesty. She pointed the bottle at him. She warned him." Golokov mimicked her motion with his withered claw. "The man. . . ." He looked to the phantom's corner. "He could have escaped at that moment. The friends of Vlad Slopek had found new amusement. But he did not. He pushed through them, he went to the lady on the stair. She was not frightened of him, she accepted his protection immediately. . . ."

Golokov's voice had trailed off. I wanted more but I was patient. Golokov's eyes wandered the empty lobby, perhaps much as the stranger's had that summer night. I realized my toes were numb with cold. I wiggled them to try to regain some circulation. I could imagine the end of the story, of course, assuming the news bureau dispatch was at least partially accurate: a fight ensued, the stranger did some damage, but was ultimately overwhelmed by their numbers. Yet I wanted something more from Golokov, some detail that was not in the official report.

I noticed there was spittle on the old man's stubbly chin. Perhaps all this was only half-remembered, bits and pieces of childhood recollections, sewn together with rumors. I was on the verge of giving up when he said: "Like a queen . . . like a queen."

"What? I am sorry—did you say something about a queen?" I ached to take my notebook from my pocket and jot down some of these details but I did not want to spook old Golokov.

"Yes, like a queen. The stranger took the sheet from the lady and spread it about her shoulders like a queen's robe. She stood on the stairway looking like a queen. The broken bottle glittered like a jewel. Green, like an emerald." Golokov realized his tobacco was completely gone. His face was suddenly at peace again, as if the incident had been exorcised from his failing memory. He fished in his suit pockets for his pouch and matches. My journalist's instincts told me there was nothing more to be had from him. I thanked the old man and took up my coat. I thought I might wander about the hotel for a few minutes and gather some details of setting.

I went to the stair and found that the carpet on the steps was threadbare, and the gold paint on the rail was peeling in long curls. I reached the second floor, where the hall seemed wide compared to my pension's upstairs. In one corner of the hall was a stack of eight or ten wooden chairs, all worn and chipped. The carpet in the hall was probably supposed to be red, but dirt and neglect had given it a dun color. A foul odor permeated the chill air, like bile and sex. I took down a chair from the top of the stack; I wanted to sit and record some of my thoughts and impressions. I removed my notebook from my coat and my leather pencil case. I was already getting used to the foul smell.

Even if Golokov's recollections were only half true, they could be the basis for a sensational tale for *The Nightly Observer*. I scribbled the details in a notation system I had invented, then I went about describing the Hotel Slopek. I wrote about the men in black coats shoveling snow from the entrance and the pointed arch, about the green-tinged lobby and the smell of the old man's pipe tobacco, of the velvet furniture and the threadbare carpet. I tried to imagine the "lady," as Golokov called her, and a clear picture would not form in my head. I wished that the old fellow had given some specifics, like the color of her hair or the shape of her body. His use of the word *queen* made me imagine her tall and golden-haired—a goddess. But probably she was not. I had seen very few people with light hair in the northcountry; like their architecture, the northerners seemed to be of Turkish descent. It bothered me that I had no true details of the lady on the stair. It was silly to be troubled: no one would know or care, as long as I provided a description that was plausible. The story did not have to be true—but it had to seem true. It was a writing maxim I had adopted from somewhere. Its origin would not come to me.

I heard someone plodding up the long stairway. His or her steps were heavy on the nearly bare wood. I put my notebook and pencil away, and I quickly and quietly replaced the chair to the stack. Though I was doing nothing wrong, I did not want to be caught there. I imagined it might be old Golokov or Vlad Slopek the younger or, impossibly, the queenly lady from Golokov's story. I was standing there, I suppose stupidly, when one of the men who had been cleaning off the hotel's steps appeared at the end of the hall. He had undone the scarf from around his mouth and his face was crimson from the cold and exertion. He had long black mustaches and a heavy black eyebrow.

I was off to the side, near the chairs, so at first he did not see me; then his peripheral vision took note of me. He stopped and stared. I felt I owed him some explanation, though I did not know why. I said, "I am a newspaperman," as if that made everything clear. He did not respond at first. I thought he might be catching his breath, although his wide chest was not heaving. He spoke with a thick dialect, his words seemed caught in his throat: "You are here about the woman."

I wondered if there was a question mark at the end of his statement, but he had emphasized all the syllables wrongly so it was difficult to tell his exact meaning.

"The woman." I waited for more from him then added, "The woman on the stair."

Now it was his turn to be puzzled. He gave up on language and motioned for me to follow him as he resumed his plodding gait. We went to a room at the opposite end of the hall. He knocked gently on the door, surprisingly gently for his size, but there was no response. He slowly turned the knob and called hello with his clumsy tongue. We stepped inside a spacious room with flowered wallpaper and a tall wardrobe whose doors were left open revealing nothing inside. The bed was made but there was an impression in the middle of it as if someone had been napping recently. He removed a mitten and felt the woolen bed cover. So did I. It was cold to the touch; the bed had not been slept on for some time.

The man went to the wardrobe and soaked in its emptiness for a moment, then took two paces to the room's only window. A lacy blind was half drawn over the window's double panes. Using his hand still in the mitten, the man lifted the blind aside and peered down to the street, perhaps looking for the absent woman.

"Who was she?" I said from behind him. He did not respond, possibly not comprehending my meaning, but I had the impression he was not in the mood to speak, in his or any other language. I knew it was not the lady from old Golokov's story who had occupied this room. But who then? And why did he think I might have anything to do with her? I tried one last time: "Perhaps she will return."

He said something to himself, a mumble of his native tongue, without turning around. That is how I left him there, staring out of the second-story window, perhaps continuing his quiet soliloquy after I had gone.

I returned to the lobby, which was completely vacant now. Even old Golokov had taken his pipe elsewhere. I exited the hotel's doors and went down the steps to the boardwalk. I began walking back toward my pension. I looked up to the second-floor windows but with the daylight's glare I could not pick out the one behind which the black-coated man watched the street. Years before, I wrote a juvenile poem about a ghost sentry who stood watch atop a castle all night. I recalled the poem just then and a line from it: "The spirit spied the battleground once soaked in blood." I wondered what had become of the poem, awful as it was. Probably Tasha had thrown it out, in one of her tirades. No doubt that is why I carried so much of my work with me. In my valise it was safe from Tasha's pendulous mood.

Clouds were gathering but the sun still had the upperhand. I thought my trip to the Hotel Slopek had been a success. I was confident now that the so-called Prince of Ithaka had been in Iiloskova and not so long ago. Yet his behavior here made him no less enigmatic to me. Where else had he been? He also called himself "Traveler" and "Nobody." Perhaps a soldier deserting battle would think of himself as such.

The day was still young. If the Prince had been at the Hotel Slopek, he no doubt had visited other places in the district. A simple canvassing may yield some information. It was good, old-fashioned newspapering. And even though I was in pursuit of something lurid for *The Observer*, it was invigorating to take the role of the hunter again. The story was a game fox, flushed from the wood and on open field. Luck was no longer involved: it would only take effort and concentration, and the prey would be mine.

These were my thoughts as I moved along the city's street, my valise feeling light in my hand and my breath smoking before me. It was becoming a good day indeed.

VI

A death-like night was cast over the field of battle.

Iliad 16

AMONG THE FIRST BUSINESSES I NOTICED was a coffee and tea shop. The smells were very potent and reached me before opening the heavy shop door. A brass bell tied with a red ribbon tinkled shrilly when I entered. The shop appeared mainly to sell its products in bulk as shelves along each wall displayed canisters and paper packages tied with string. The shelves were mostly vacant, however. Either the shop had recently been overrun with enthusiastic customers, or the shopkeeper's suppliers had been niggardly of late—I figured the latter. There were a couple of marble-topped tables in one corner of the shop along with some wooden benches, which indicated one might have a hot drink here. In the center of the shop was a black stove emitting a modicum of heat and a hint of woodsmoke.

In spite of the bell on the door, no one came immediately, though I thought I heard some faint noises from the room behind the shop's glass-case counter. The scents were overpowering at first and I felt a bit light-headed, but I was quickly getting used to them. Browsing along the shelves, I read the names of the various teas and coffees—mostly teas—which were hand-printed on little cards. Some of the cards had turned yellow with age; I hoped the product itself was not so antiquated.

Finally, after I had nearly perused the entire shop, an old woman came from the backroom. She was dressed all in black, as if in mourning, even with a black scarf over her white hair. She breathed through her mouth like walking was an exertion and I noticed she was nearly toothless. "May I help you?" she asked with a strangely deep voice, her words a bit mushy with so few teeth for articulation.

"Yes." I came towards her. "I am hoping for something hot to drink. Coffee perhaps." I had had mainly tea or vodka since arriving in Iiloskova.

The old woman glanced over her shoulder as if she could see through the wall into the room behind. "Coffee would take some time to prepare. I have a nice ginger-root tea available now. It would definitely warm you."

"I am in no particular hurry; I am happy to wait for the coffee."

She glanced over her shoulder again, perhaps expecting someone to emerge from the backroom. "I am afraid I must charge you excessively for coffee—it is a rare commodity these days."

I had no desire to be robbed as if by highwaymen, but I felt myself in something of a competition with the old shop-woman: my will versus her stubbornness. And winning out was suddenly important to me. I said, "I will pay you its worth, understanding that your coffee supply is one of the casualties of war."

"Make yourself comfortable then. I will bring it as soon as it is ready." She was not happy and made no pretense of rushing to fill my order. I really came to ask her about the Prince's sketch but had forgotten once the game between us began. No matter. I would have time when she brought my overpriced coffee.

I removed my heavy coat and gloves, and I sat at one of the marble-topped tables. The story Golokov told me was still fresh in my mind, so I took pencil and paper from my valise and, using my notes, set about recording the incident in full narrative. I titled it "Queen on the Stair" and began:

It was to be an evening like any other, unforgettable. Local boss Vlad Slopek and his cronies took up residence in the lobby of the hotel Vlad's grandfather had established half a century earlier. Then, it was a showplace of elegance and sophistication. Every well-to-do person in the North Country stayed at the Hotel Slopek at one time or another. Men of business, men of politics—all men of power. But over time the hotel declined along with the city, until its dilapidated interior reflected the moral decline of its current owner, Vlad Slopek. Vlad was tall and thin, an aristocratic stork among the mud-flapping birds who were his friends. A robust weed among rocks. His side whiskers and mustaches connected to form a sharp, black "V" on each pale cheek. "V" for Vlad; "V" for violent; "V" for vermin.

Vlad's party began early, while the summer sun was still peeking above the horizon, so it was well underway by nighttime. The cronies ordered grotesque amounts of food, wine and vodka. Quantities which only black marketeers could provide in a city run down by war. The "businessmen of the night"—as they are sometimes called—also supplied Vlad's gang with "ladies of the night"—as they are often called. Young girls and women of middle age who had in common a desperation for money and a dependence on drink and drugs.

But one among the "ladies" was unusual. She was not native to the city. She had come in search of her lost love, a young infantryman sent to the front. They had corresponded for over a year, then suddenly his letters ceased. The army was no help, nor the government. Her young man had simply disappeared. She had taken the train as far north as the rails would allow. Then, penniless, she threw herself on the mercy of the city. It was not kind.

Soon she found herself in this den of debauchery, far from home and from the man she loved. Vlad Slopek noticed the girl of course. All the men did. She was tall, statuesque, with the bearing of a goddess. Her hair golden. Her skin as pure as the snow that covers the skating pond every morning in winter. Vlad, the bent stalk who grew from good seed, could be charming. He was indeed as he invited the girl to escape the crude crowd gathering in the lobby of the hotel. The host of the party did seem a cut above his guests and she was fearful of the rowdy, drunken men. She had been raised by her mother and an aunt, so therefore knew very little of men and how they behaved when full with alcohol. She accepted his invitation and he escorted her up the stairs, which only hinted at the hotel's long ago splendor. The carpet on the stairs was threadbare, and along the handrails long strips of gold paint curled like serpent tongues.

Vlad unlocked the door to his private apartment on the second floor. He encouraged her to enter with a gentlemanly little bow. She

hesitated for a moment, thinking about her choices: this secluded
room with a strange man, or the riotous party downstairs, or the dark,
unfamiliar streets. She stepped inside Vlad's chamber.

Meanwhile, the party continued in the lobby. . . .

The old woman in black brought my coffee in a large glass. She
used her shawl to protect her hands from the heat. Still, she shook
them as soon as she had placed the glass on the table. "Thank you,"
I said. She named her price. It was high but not as expensive as
I had imagined. I fished a silver coin out of my pocket and two
koppers. It was a bit more than she had requested but I hoped the
extra would encourage her to take my inquiry about the Prince of
Ithaka seriously. "Just a moment, Madam," I said while I opened my
valise and removed the sketch. "Have you seen this man within the
last few months? I believe he was observed near here."

At first it appeared she had trouble focusing on the sketch and I
wondered if she suffered from cataracts. I looked closely at her eyes
trying to detect a cloudiness within them. Instead, I saw teardrops
form at the corners and leak onto her white cheeks. She used her
shawl to wipe at the tears. I waited for her to speak. "Are you an
inquisitor, with the police?" she asked, glancing at the table top,
trying to determine if pencil and paper were the tools of a police
inquisitor. They could have been.

"No, I have no connection with the police whatsoever."

"I, I do not recognize this man. I thought at first I did, but my
eyes are old." She had regained her composure.

"Please—I only wish information about him. I am a journalist; I
am writing a story." It occurred to me a police inquisitor might tell
just such a lie.

"I know nothing. Truly I do not. Now drink your coffee while it
is hot." Her deep voice was broken with emotion. She moved toward
the backroom with alacrity I would not have guessed possible.

I was not sure what to do. Clearly she recognized the face in the
drawing and had some emotional connection with it. The aroma of
the coffee drew my attention. It had a slightly nutty smell, and when
I sipped it, a slightly nutty flavor—but it was very good. I placed
the Prince's sketch on the papers I had been writing, then focused
my attention on the surprising coffee. I considered returning to my

story about Vlad Slopek but the spell was broken for the time being. Hopefully, back in my room later, I could conjure it again with little effort.

I wondered if everyone in this district of Iiloskova had had an encounter with the Prince, or was it just dumb coincidence? I sipped the coffee, which was cooling quickly in the cold shop. I kept both hands on the glass to warm my fingers and to impede the drink's dissipating heat. I heard voices in the backroom though the words were indistinct. It sounded like two men having a heated discussion but probably one speaker was the old woman in black.

The sound of the voices stopped abruptly and in a moment the door to the backroom opened. I expected the old shop-woman to appear but it was a man about my age, though thinner and with more white in his hair. I noticed dark circles under his icy blue eyes. He approached me directly; he seemed to favor his right leg but in the short distance it was hard to be sure. "Good day, sir," he said. His eyes were quickly drawn to the sketch on the table. "May I?" He picked it up and studied the Prince's picture. I watched his expression for some sign but his face was of stone.

He returned the sketch to the table and said, "You must excuse my mother-in-law. My son is at the front and has not been heard from for some time. This picture bears a slight resemblance to him but it is not."

It seemed that he was about to return to the shop's inner sanctum until I stayed him with a question: "If I may ask, why did your mother-in-law fear that I was an inquisitor for the police?"

He did not respond at first, perhaps wondering if it was prudent, perhaps wondering if I was indeed an inquisitor. Finally he said, "There were malicious rumors in the neighborhood that my son had deserted his unit. They were quite false of course. But the burden of the unfounded accusation has only added to our worry for his safety. If you have a son, you understand surely." The rings under his eyes seemed to darken as I watched his haggard face.

"Yes, of course." It was only partly a lie. Though I did not have a son, I did understand.

"Please, enjoy the rest of your drink," he said and began his return to the backroom. He did, in fact, walk with a slight limp.

"Sir," I said, almost surprising myself, "what is your son's name? I am going to the front in a few days—perhaps I could make some inquiries."

He turned, leaning his hands on the glass counter. "He is Anatoly . . . Anatoly Shatrov. His friends call him Toly." I anticipated that he would thank me for my unexpected offer but he merely continued on his way and disappeared behind the door. I opened my notebook to a blank sheet and scribbled the young man's name. I wondered how many families were in a state of pre-mourning, wasting away in ignorance, not knowing if their sons, brothers and fathers were alive or dead. Perhaps that would make an interesting story, for Mezenskov's paper of course, not *The Observer*.

I finished my coffee, now merely tepid, then gathered my things and headed out to the street. The day was still young, though I felt I had been working for a long time already. Snowflakes floated down irregularly from the white sky. I was not sure what to do with myself. Just ahead, a bench, which someone had dutifully cleared of snow, was on the boardwalk next to a building of tan brick. I was feeling warm from the coffee and decided I could spend a few minutes sitting and watching the people in the streets of Iiloskova.

I placed my valise next to me on the bench and went about making myself a cigarette. Soon I was smoking and observing the passersby, few though they be. It was quite pleasant. In my mind I continued my story of Vlad Slopek and the queen on the stair, so that when I had a chance to write it would be as much recollection as invention. Snow appeared to be increasing in the air but I did not mind. In a moment I thought of a particular turn of phrase that I liked, so I began going through my coat pockets for my notebook and pencils, fearful that I would forget the exact wording if I did not jot it down.

My gloved fingers had just touched my pencil case when someone delivered a sharp blow to the back of my head. The sudden pain pitched me off the bench and onto my knees. I held my head with both hands trying to orient myself with what had just happened, then I noticed a mittened fist snatch my valise from the bench and the thief began running down the boardwalk. I got to my feet and began following the dark-coated figure as best I could. I believe that

I called to him to stop but my words may have only been internal, like a silent prayer.

The thief was very fast and I very slow. I thought of my precious manuscripts and my notes and my pens and ink bottles, and also of the money. And tears clouded my vision. Perhaps it was the sharp blow to my head, or the cold air that caused them. Several blocks ahead I saw the thief turn in somewhere and vanish. I was getting my legs back and made it to the approximate spot fairly quickly. There was a narrow alley and I supposed that the bastard had retreated there. The alley appeared to end at a brick wall, thirty or forty paces ahead. But there were a few doors and several windows in the alley, not to mention all sorts of rubbish partly covered in snow: crates and great piles of newspaper, rotting scraps of food and God knows what else. It all smelled terrible, and it was winter—I could not imagine its summertime fetidness.

I began moving cautiously through the alley. I desperately wanted to retrieve my things but I had no desire to be murdered in the process. I realized there was something in my mouth; I spat it onto the brick pavers. It was tobacco and paper that I must have bitten off my cigarette when I was struck on the head. I wondered what had been used for the operation, a rock, a club, the butt of a gun?

The buildings were tall on both sides of the alley, thus casting its entire length in shadow. Each door that I passed appeared secure and I saw no signs of entry at any of the windows. As I said, the alley ended in a brick wall that must have been thirty feet in height. I was about half way along the alley when a window opened somewhere above me. I looked up to see a pair of arms pitch the contents of a piss-pot into the air. I moved in time to avoid being struck directly but the splatter soiled my shoes and the cuffs of my pants. "Damn, damn, damn!" I uttered into the air. No wonder the alley reeked so. Now I reeked too.

I continued toward the dead-end of the alley, with less caution than before. Anger and frustration can cure you of your fears. I checked the final door. It was made of heavy boards and iron hardware, and was quite secure. Suddenly there was a rustling in a pile of debris, and a lad in a blue coat bounded out—with my valise in his hand! He was several paces from me and I had no hope of catching the fleet-footed little rascal. "Hey!" I called stupidly and began my heavy plodding.

The fellow's shoes found the mess from the piss-pot and he completely lost his footing. In fact, for an instant his feet were literally over his head before he landed on his back in the foul puddle of excrement. Even I was not too slow to catch him now. I was quickly there picking him up by the shoulder of his coat. With my other hand I retrieved my valise, which had landed on a pile of rotten pears a stride away from the mess. I shook him hard in spite of my one-handed grip for he weighed nothing. "What now, thief? What now eh?"

His sock-hat fell from his head, and greasy hair spilled to the thief's waist: the culprit was a girl. She was as wispy as a nine- or ten-year-old, but she could have been a malnourished adolescent. Her cheeks were dark with soot. The discovery startled me and soured some of my taste for vengeance. I realized my head was throbbing from the blow and exertion.

"What did you strike me with?" That is what came from my mouth but even as I said it I wondered what difference it made.

She had eyes as green as a summer meadow. I expected them to well with tears but life on the street had hardened her no doubt. Yet there was a trace of fear in them, like a rabbit's eyes when caught in a snare. She slowly reached into the pocket of her coat in response to my query. She removed a wad of pink stocking. When it was completely out of her pocket, the toe of the stocking sagged to the ground as it was filled with stones. Clever little scamp, I thought. Her nose was beginning to run profusely due to the cold, so she used the end of the pink stocking to wipe it. Then she put the makeshift weapon back in her pocket. I considered relieving her of it, but she no doubt needed it on the street.

I let go of her coat and removed two koppers from my side pocket. I handed them to her. "Try asking for assistance before whacking someone on the head," I said, quite certain my advice was falling on deaf ears. She closed her mitten around the coins while at the same time retrieving her wool hat from the puddle of filth, then ran off without a word of thanks. I removed my beaver hat and felt the back of my head. There was a large knot but my gloved fingers showed no trace of blood. She either delivered a glancing blow or simply struck with the impotency of a hungry child; her weapon had the potential to kill a man. I put my hat back on and, holding my valise tightly, I began making my way to my pension. Perhaps a drink and some rest would dull the pounding in my brain. Snow was falling more thickly now, and my room felt like it was at a great distance. I thought of my real home for a moment, and it seemed to be in another country altogether. No, more than geography separated me from Tasha and our little cottage. We occupied different spheres—as if somewhere between home and Iiloskova the train left the world I knew and entered an entirely different one.

The literary papers would sometimes publish tales about impossible events. Such fantastic stories were not to my taste so I usually did not read them in earnest. Yet there was one I recalled about a man who went to bed and awoke the next morning as a dung-beetle or some such thing. It was titled "Transformation" I believe. I glanced down at my legs—I knew it was foolish—to make certain they were still quite human and I wiggled the fingers of my free hand. Everything was in order, except for my throbbing head and my valise, which felt as if it had tripled in weight. In spite of my difficulties, I had a profound sense of relief—the relief of someone who has narrowly avoided some great calamity. In a word, I was happy.

VII

'It was I who rescued him from the sea god's cruel clasp.'

Odyssey 5

I WAS SOUND ASLEEP FACE DOWN in the covers when I realized that the tapping I was hearing was not simply my racing heartbeat against my pillow. Someone was at my door. There was still some daylight leaking into my room. I guessed that it was around three or four o'clock. "Just a moment," I called to my visitor but my throat was thick. My head ached and I rested for a moment at the table, feeling that I might fall down. My visitor lost patience and slipped a piece of paper under the door. I heard footsteps retreat in the hall.

In a moment I picked up the paper and discovered it was a crudely printed handbill. I took it over to the window to read it without lighting the foul smelling lamp. It was advertising a meeting of the Society of Forensics and Poetics, featuring a reading of classical verse by Doctor Wittinski. The meeting was that very evening at six-thirty, at a place called the Luminarium. I had not heard of it, nor the Society for that matter. It was difficult to believe some shred of culture remained in this corrupted city. On the one hand, attending the meeting was quite attractive but on the other I did not feel well. In addition to my sore head, my stomach was queasy, perhaps from the consistent pain or from the foul vodka I drank when I finally reached my room. I carefully touched the bump on my head. Maybe the swelling was somewhat less, but it was very tender.

I wondered who might have brought the handbill to my attention. It had to be my landlady for she was the only one in the pension who knew of my interest in poetry. She would probably like to attend the meeting; her husband, of course, did not seem the type. They were as mismatched in that way as Tasha and I. I often attended readings at the local debate club. I had even read some of my own work from time to time. Tasha had never heard me. I found her lack of interest in my writing something of a relief. It left me free to explore our relationship truthfully without fear of offending or upsetting her. She would not understand the artist's need to probe under the surface, to press on the sore tooth to see just how great the pain could be.

I knew that my landlady would be in the kitchen by now preparing the evening's meal. It was to be flatbread with some sort of bean soup. I pulled myself together, knowing that I still looked very rough. I had not shaved since arriving in Iiloskova but I did not have a beard yet—I merely looked like a madman. I was certain my skin was ashen and my eyes sunken from the headache and the sour stomach.

I put my vest on over my white shirt but not my jacket. I left the vest undone and did not button the collar of my shirt. I had pulled my collar together but it seemed to constrict my throat and intensify my urge to vomit. I went downstairs and as I approached the kitchen I heard the sound of work. I opened the door and there was my landlady preparing the flatbread at the butcher-block. A large stockpot was beginning to steam on the stove behind her. Her husband was not in sight.

"Hello, madam," I said, trying my best to smile. "I am not feeling well—I slipped on some ice and struck my head—could you prepare a pot of tea and provide me with a slice of bread or two? It is all my stomach can take I am afraid." I leaned against the frame of the door, feeling a bit faint.

She came forward wiping the flour from her hands on her apron. She took me by the arm and directed me to a chair in the corner of the kitchen near the stove. "Rest here," she said. "Just a moment and I will fix your tea." She completed the pan of flatbread she had been preparing when I entered the kitchen, then she slid the pan into the oven and immediately filled the kettle from a bucket of water she had no doubt pumped earlier. I did not realize how chilled I had been until I sat next to the stove for a few minutes and it began to warm my bones. The pains in my head and stomach eased a bit. I found that closing my eyes helped too, so I dozed in the chair while my landlady went about filling my request. I was glad my landlord stayed away; I would be embarrassed to be found in such a sickly state and would feel obligated to act well.

Soon the tea and bread were prepared. My landlady had produced a small serving table from somewhere and placed it by my chair. Just the smell of the tea helped to make me more alert. It smelled good but unusual. I must have had an inquisitive look on my pale face for my landlady offered an explanation: "Honey and tiger-root."

"Tiger-root?"

"It is a local herb. It probably has other names elsewhere. It will cure your aching head. You look like Death hisself."

"Yes, I am sure." I sipped the hot tea; the taste was not medicinal at least. The bread was stale but dunking it in the tea made it quite palatable. I began to feel better almost immediately, so much so that my appetite was encouraged. However, I did not want to push my luck by consuming too much. I hesitated to drink the last drops of tea. "Thank you, madam, you have put me quite in order again." My landlady was busy with preparing the meal and had paid little attention to me. "I will be going out this evening, I believe, so there is no need to hold my place at supper."

"I am glad you are so much improved," she said, hurrying to stir her pot.

"One more favor, madam—can you direct me to the Luminarium? It is there I must go this evening."

She stopped stirring but did not look at me. "The Luminarium? You should ask my husband; he will be in shortly I am sure."

Her reaction was enigmatic. She may have been the deliverer of the handbill, or not. I finished the rehabilitating tea. I was reluctant to leave my corner of the kitchen; it was a pleasant enough place. I was about to ask my landlady to let me know when her husband had returned when I heard him at the backdoor. He entered with a canvas tote of firewood. He had a dark hat pulled down low, and his cheeks were scarlet on either side of his too-long mustaches. Perhaps he had been somewhere chopping wood, though I had not heard the sound of the axe. I sensed that he did not like finding me in his kitchen again. Alone with his wife again.

I rose from my chair. My balance was not completely returned and I nearly knocked over the little serving table. "Hello, sir. I have been waiting for your return." Did the landlady glance at me in my lie? "I must go to the Luminarium tonight. Can you direct me?"

He was taking off his mittens and hat; his thinning hair was damp with perspiration. "The Luminarium," he repeated. "Yes, it is not far, only a few blocks." He gave me clear directions, assuming he was being honest. Perhaps he was sending me into the lair of robbers and cut-throats. What would my murder matter to him? One less guest to care for, one less man prowling around his house at night. Yet I must trust his directions.

I excused myself to my room and dressed for the evening. The tea had worked marvelously, almost miraculously. The knot on my head was still tender of course, but the pounding had ceased. I opted for a red necktie instead of the brown wool one I had been wearing since I left home. Tasha did not like my "work tie," as she called it, but it was my favorite in winter. I thought of changing my shirt. It was clean enough, however. While I dressed, I thought about what to read at the meeting in case there was the opportunity. One of the poems from my manuscript no doubt. Yet my new poem about the braided woman on the train came to mind; perhaps I would share that with the audience.

Suddenly the lightbulb hanging down from the ceiling on a serpentine black cord came to life and its harsh light filled my little room. I held my hand up to shield my eyes as they were unused to such brightness. The bulb faltered for a moment then went dead entirely. I cautiously reached out and poked the bulb with my finger, which started it gently swinging but produced no light of course.

I exited the pension through the front door and set off for the Luminarium, which my landlord described as a domed-structure of moderate size (I am paraphrasing). The evening was cold of course. I felt cheered at the prospect of meeting with others who appreciated culture. I imagined that all such people had left Iiloskova long ago, that there must have been a mass exodus of poets, writers, painters and musicians, that they had fled south in search of a saner place to practice their arts. Perhaps they had—and the homeless and depraved had taken their positions in society. Or, at best, second-class poets and other hacks had moved up in the ranks.

My mood was becoming gloomier, though not by much.

It struck me again how dark the nights were in this northern city. The shortages of electricity, coal and oil accounted for much of the darkness, but beyond that it seemed that the city itself absorbed light, that the buildings took in all that the heavens offered and did not allow it to shine on the streets, on the boardwalks, on the populace. I wished that I had some sort of lantern, even an old-fashioned bull's-eye that did little more than illuminate the tops of one's shoes. It, at least, would be a comfort.

In spite of the dark, I found the Luminarium just as my landlord had described. Its silvery dome reflected a trace of early moonglow. Perhaps that is where it derived its name. There were several dark shapes on the street making their way to the uniquely shaped building. Perhaps the Society would have a good turnout, perhaps the good citizens of Iiloskova were starved for culture.

I entered the structure through tall double doors and stamped the snow from my shoes on worn purple carpeting with an ornate scroll of yellow running through it. There was a woman just inside the door wearing a shabby gown of golden silk. Her face was over made-up with rouge and red lipstick that only emphasized her age and hardships, rather than masking them. Her hair was dyed black, blacker than a gypsy's. "Hello," she said, "and welcome." She handed me a program on a single sheet of paper. Like the handbill, it was cheaply produced. "Please seat yourself. The program will begin in a quarter hour." She smiled as she motioned me toward the auditorium doors. There was a smudge of crimson lipstick on her yellow teeth.

I nodded and said thank you. As I approached the auditorium, I heard her repeat her greeting to another visitor. A mishmash of lamps and candelabras lighted the lobby, which was no doubt a showplace in an earlier day. Its printed wallpaper was probably once vibrant; the brass doorknobs and fixtures probably shone brightly. The auditorium itself was a traditional design with the rows of seats curving around the stage, which was about two thirds surrounded. The back of the stage was a long curtain of purple velveteen. There was a podium on the stage along with several straight-back chairs. Like the lobby, an eclectic assortment of candles and oil lamps provided light in the high-ceilinged room.

The turnout seemed only fair in such a large auditorium and there were plenty of open seats. I chose one more or less in the middle on the aisle. If the meeting proved to be a bore, I wanted to be able to sneak out without causing a fuss. I removed my coat and hat and gloves, placing them on the adjacent seat, then I sat with my valise in my lap. The air was chill. I read through the short program. There would be a few welcoming remarks from the president of the Society, who would then introduce the featured speaker, Doctor Wittinski. Afterward, questions and answers, and an opportunity for what the program called "open readings from the audience." On the back of the program was an announcement for the Luminarium's next event, an operetta titled "Ulas Ulasovich." Apparently someone had set the old folkhero's stories to music; I hoped it was not intended to be serious theater.

I turned my thoughts to the question of what to read. I unlatched my valise and brought out my manuscript tied in string and several other sheets of paper. I thought of a sonnet about the Urals, based on an experience when camping in the mountains as a boy. An earlier version of the sonnet had been published, so it was a safe reading. I did not particularly want to untie my manuscript to remove the Urals poem. I sifted through the loose papers until I found the handwritten poem about the braided woman on the train. "Beautiful Traveler" I had tentatively titled it. Glancing through it, I was suddenly insecure about some of the phrasing. The images seemed trite, the rhythm plodding.

The grating sound of wooden chair legs being dragged across a wooden stage broke my concentration. An elderly fellow with a yellow-white goatee and a very old-fashioned reddish brown suit was rearranging the chairs on the stage. Actually he was not affecting them whatsoever as he would move one a bit to his right, then left, then back, then forward—thus arriving at its original spot. But he did this with each of the four chairs on the stage, and even gave the podium an ineffectual little nudge. He was remarkably thin and the odd-colored suit hung on him like a relaxed sail waiting for a gust of wind. Then the fellow carefully sat in the chair to the immediate left of the podium as if his bones might snap if he seated himself too roughly.

I glanced around me and was surprised at the number of Iiloskovites who had come out on such a frigid night. The men generally wore dark suits and the ladies evening dresses, some in black while others were in gayer colors. All appeared shabby and well-worn to me. It was as if the entire audience was poking fun at theatergoers and their fancified dress. I wondered if I would be a match with my fellow audience members to an outside observer. My suit was not new but I believed its cut was still in style. I was suddenly self-conscious of my red tie and thought of taking it off.

Fortunately the program began and there was no more time to dwell on my appearance. The thin fellow in the baggy brown suit was joined on stage by a short, round-bellied man in black wool coat and trousers and a blue silk scarf; the newcomer's wispy white hair was combed straight back revealing a ruddy over-wide forehead. But his eyes were a startlingly bright green—even viewed from the middle of the auditorium—and his grayish mustaches were neatly trimmed. He sat and held a leather document case to his chest, resting it on his belly like a shelf. The thin man in brown stood up to the podium and cleared phlegm from his throat:

"Good evening, ladies and gentlemen. Welcome to the quarterly meeting of the Society of Forensics and Poetics. I am vice-president of the Society, Grigory Yanov. As you may know, our esteemed president, Mr. Shaferavich, has taken quite ill and has been bedridden for some weeks. We pray that he will recover soon and be able to join us for our summer meeting . . ."

It occurred to me then that this must be the Society's spring meeting; I thought of the frozen world around me and it did not seem possible that it was springtime. When I left home, spring was in the air: the earliest flowers were beginning to bud; geese were returning from their migration to the sea; the earth showed signs of thaw. But Iiloskova appeared deep in winter's grasp still, a miser holding onto his last frozen coins. In a few weeks the gardens would be ready for planting back home. I always enjoyed sowing the wax beans, carrots, turnips, and summer squash, the lettuces, onions, and parsnips. I used to think gardening would be something Tasha and I could share, sowing and weeding and reaping together, but she always left the vegetables to my doing—even the cleaning of them when they were harvested. Once ready, Tasha would steam or boil them, or cook them with a soup bone—kitchen activities from which I was excluded. Tasha seemed intent on making us live the most difficult kind of solitary existence: together.

Mr. Yanov, reading his prepared statement, continued from the podium. ". . . it is my great honor to welcome our distinguished scholar, Doctor Lek Wittinski, recently Lecturer-in-Antiquities at Rotterdam University, but between posts at the moment, and just arrived, I understand, in the last few months from the Mediterranean . . ." Doctor Wittinski nodded in confirmation from his rickety chair on the stage. ". . . where he was researching his current book, tentatively titled *Classical Verse Form of the Aegean Isles*." Mr. Yanov cleared his throat again and squinted myopically at the paper in his trembling hands. "We are honored that he will read newly translated verse, and discuss 'Language in Metamorphosis.' Please, assist me in welcoming our speaker for this evening, Doctor Lek Wittinski." The audience joined in politely applauding Doctor Wittinski's ascension to the podium, while Mr. Yanov took a chair to the doctor's left.

I hoped that Wittinski's translated poems would be decent and that his discussion would be brief. I mainly was interested in reading my own poetry to an audience; it was a self-centered streak that sometimes complicated my marriage—but it was a deep-set part of my personality, like another man's drunkenness, or another's womanizing—a curl of dark color in the marble not easily expunged.

The scholar unbound his document case, arranged a pair of eyeglasses with oval lenses on the end of his stubby nose, and gathered his thoughts for a moment by surveying the papers in front of him, which were out of view behind the lip of the podium. Candlelight danced on his glistening pate in two patches like squares of bandages slipping on new wounds. The stage, the whole of the auditorium, was drafty; and the candle flames snapped to and fro, always on the cusp of being extinguished. I thought for a moment of the whorehouse and its radiance of electric light, and of what it said about a society in which only whorehouse proprietors had the clout to draw power to their businesses.

Doctor Wittinski addressed his audience with a distinct accent, one perhaps generated by the knowledge of too many tongues. "I echo Mr. Yaslov's welcome and thanks to you all. I am honored to be here, in Iiloskova, so near the war but still a member of civilization." His opening was no doubt intended as some sort of compliment to the Iiloskovites, but it sounded more like a farewell. The final remarks of a captain to his crew while he watches the waterline rising in his ship. "It is my deepest pleasure to recite for you some lines I have recently translated from an indigenous Aegean language— ancient Greek, if you will allow me to employ a crude generality. While there is no definitive proof in the matter, it is my thesis that these are lost verse of the great poet Homer. I have colleagues who disagree with my assessment, but to my eye and my ear, the cadence and syntax, the diction and imagery are unmistakable. Moreover—"

A loud spasmodic sigh from the audience interrupted Doctor Wittinski. It sounded like something between a whimper and a laugh, and maybe feminine too. I glanced behind me, toward the sound, but gained no knowledge of its source. The doctor continued,

"Moreover, I believe the verse, though fewer than ten poems, or two-hundred lines, represent a bridge between the famous poet's epic works, and will thus end centuries of debate as to the origins and order of said works." I felt my shortage of formal schooling quite poignantly at that moment as I had no idea about the debate to which the scholar referred. My father, in his recitations of the ancient stories, spoke of no mystery about their origins. If he had, it would have piqued my curiosity and I no doubt would have been more attentive to the details. I assumed the other audience members, sitting there not stirring in their shabby clothes, were fully aware of the mystery of Homer. I had second thoughts then about reading my poetry; I felt unworthy.

Doctor Wittinski was letting his earthshaking hypothesis settle in the auditorium a moment before continuing. He opened his small, finely mustached mouth to speak and was again interrupted by the whimper or laugh, this time louder. It was followed instantly by the sound of many people turning to locate the position of the rude audience member. I was not certain if anyone did; I did not, though I looked around.

A trace of annoyance mixed with his distinct accent as Doctor Wittinski said that he would read the first verse translation.

Sunrise creeping over the peak of pink;
Stunning Apollo flashes his bold arrows
From the Heavens, Father Zeus' golden throne.
Morning's charioteer clutches the reins,
And his subjects know of his lordly presence.
Athene, too, basks in Apollo's glow—

"Fine, white bitch!" The woman's voice, full of alcohol, was slurred from the back of the auditorium. Doctor Wittinski slammed shut his leather case; three candles near the podium went out in a column of smoke; his eyeglasses went askew at the end of his nose. He blurted out something in his mother tongue—whatever that might have been—then remembered himself: "What is the meaning here? Who is this woman?"

"Fine, fucking, white bitch!"

Several members of the audience were moving in on the rabble-rouser. I heard murmuring in the back of the auditorium. I decided it was unseemly to be too interested in the spectacle of the drunken woman, but as a journalist I had a professional responsibility to at least see what was happening. So I stepped into the aisle and made my way toward the gathering crowd, which I soon discovered was made up of mainly women and old men; thus I had little trouble forcing my way to its center. Onlookers were in the aisle and in the space between rows in front of and behind the focus of their attention. I saw a very thin woman stretched across three or four seats; her face and throat and hands were so ashen she actually appeared to glow in the dim light at the rear of the auditorium. A purple shawl was draped haphazardly across her body, and she wore a blouse and skirt of summer weight. The reek of sour vodka surrounded her like a cloud. The old woman who greeted everyone at the door, the old woman with red lipstick on her yellow teeth, was taking the pulse of the listless younger woman. "Like ice," said the greeter, "her hands are quite like ice." The listless woman's head rolled so that she could look up at us all through half-closed eyes. And I suddenly knew her: the swan-like neck, the amethyst eyes. It was the woman from the train. I thought of my poem in my valise about her; the one I thought of reading to this audience, "Beautiful Traveler." She was not beautiful now; unless, of course, one could consider a corpse beautiful. The old woman said, "Who is this woman? Is she alone here?"

Like the other onlookers, my eyes glanced from one to another. I hesitated a long moment before volunteering, "I am her acquaintance of sorts. We arrived on the train together." The Iiloskovites no doubt noted my southern dialect and were immediately suspicious of me, a stranger in their increasingly strange city.

The old woman with yellow teeth continued to lead the inquiry: "Do you know where she is staying? Is she staying with you? She is near dead from exposure." Her statement seemed to imply I was somehow to blame. I, a bear-like man—not a ferocious denizen of the wood bear, but rather a performing circus bear—a bear-like man in my red tie. Perhaps I looked a little guilty, felt a little guilty. I recalled reading that Oriental actors who wear masks learn to concentrate their thoughts on an emotion to such a degree that the emotion is transferred to the face of the otherwise sterile mask and thus communicated to the audience. "No," I said, though no longer certain what I was negating. "I can secure her lodging and food. Does she require medical attention, do you think?"

The old woman, who had not removed her fingers from the stranger's seemingly paper-thin wrist, pondered the question carefully. "Perhaps, if food and warmth have not brought her round in short order, then a doctor will be necessary." An onlooker, an old man with but one front tooth, said, "Beft of luck finding one."

I said, "I must convey her several blocks to my boarding house, and she is obviously not dressed for the travel." I was wondering how on earth I was going to get her to Division Street when someone touched my arm and said, "I shall help you transport her." It was Polozkov, the glass salesman with the hooked nose. I wondered then if it was he who had put the handbill under my door and not my landlady after all.

The old woman said, "Bring her and follow me." Polozkov

assisted me in lifting up the woman—she weighed nothing—and I removed her from the auditorium. The doors closed behind us when we reached the lobby, and I assumed Doctor Wittinski continued his presentation. I felt a twinge of relief that this bizarre happening had prevented me from possibly making a fool of myself reading my undercooked poetry.

"Wait a moment," said the old woman as she disappeared behind a previously closed door. Polozkov and I sat the listless stranger in a chair with torn upholstery in the lobby while we waited. I thought of making small talk with Polozkov but did not know what it would be. Most of the lanterns and candelabras that had lighted the lobby previously had been removed to the stage and auditorium, so the lobby was very poorly lighted. The old woman returned in a moment with a bundle in her arms. Polozkov helped her to deposit the bundle on the floor near my feet; I steadied the stranger in her chair, her head rolling back and forth as if it might just fall off.

"I have raided the prop room," said the old woman, and I noticed the lipstick on her teeth. She knelt on the thinly carpeted floor and sorted out the bundle. The largest item was an old bearskin coat that was missing large patches of fur here and there and smelled of mildew and mange; there was an equally ratty woman's hat, of some long-haired gray fur, perhaps goat. And there was a lengthy swath of golden-yellow cloth; the old woman proceeded to tie a knot at each corner. I got the idea that this cloth would be used as a stretcher or hammock in which to carry our charge to the pension. "It is the best I can do," said the old woman who had welcomed us all to the Luminarium not an hour before.

Polozkov and I wrapped the woman in the massive bearskin coat then lowered her onto the hammock. "Just a moment," I said; I returned to the auditorium long enough to retrieve my things at my seat—Doctor Wittinski was reading another poem, this one about the god of the sea. In the lobby again, I put on my own coat, hat and gloves. I placed my valise in the hammock next to the woman, then slid the goatskin hat over her head. Her hair was still neatly braided in the star pattern I had first noticed on the train. Her head was so small, like a child's, the hat could have been pulled down to her chin, but I stopped at her thinly arced eyebrows, making sure her ears were protected from the cold.

Polozkov took the feet-end of the hammock, his back to me, while I lifted the head-end at the same time. The old woman held the door for us as we carried the stranger into the raw night. The woman opened her eyes for just a moment and looked at me, upside-down of course, in the fading light from the Luminarium, and her lips seemed to form my name—*Mr. Pastrovich*—before she slipped from consciousness again.

VIII

Messengers brought gifts of treasure to the hall.

Odyssey 8

W HEN POLOZKOV AND I RETURNED to our pension, the landlord and his wife were not up. We placed the unconscious stranger on the couch in the parlor and added coal to the burner in what used to be a fireplace. While I prodded the coals into quicker combustion, Polozkov disappeared for a moment; he returned with a bottle of sherry and a tumbler intending to administer the drink to the woman for medicinal purposes. I convinced him that she had had quite enough alcohol, so he drank the sherry himself. I felt her hand, which had been inside the cocoon of bearskin, and it did not feel quite as icy. I removed my coat and placed it on top of her in addition to the animal fur.

I said, "She needs to eat something, and have something hot to drink." Polozkov was sitting in an embroidered chair pouring himself another sherry. "Watch her a moment while I fetch something from the kitchen." He nodded while putting the tumbler to his lips.

I went to the kitchen and began snooping about. I had been more awake than I realized when my landlady made my tea earlier, so I knew right where to find the leaves and packet of tiger-root. The kettle was already on the stove, and there was some fire glowing in the cast-iron belly. I placed a quartered log inside and stirred the embers a bit with a soot-black poker. I shut the door on the stove then began looking for some biscuit and butter. The kitchen door opened. I hoped it was my landlady but instead her husband entered. He was in his long-sleeved undershirt and wool trousers, the suspenders hanging slack at his knees.

"What are you doing?" he said. "Who is this woman in my house?"

Surely Polozkov had explained a little. "She fainted at the Luminarium. Mr. Polozkov and I brought her here—she could not be tossed onto the street."

"I am not operating a house of charity for streetpeople; this is a business . . . and my home."

"I understand, but I met the woman on the train . . . I felt some responsibility toward her."

"What is her name? Where does she come from?"

I was found dumb. "I . . ."

"You have no idea, do you?" He pulled up his suspenders but got them twisted. He appeared not to care.

"You have an extra room. I shall pay for her lodging." What was I saying? Mezenskov's money was not infinite. I tried to do the mathematics in my mind but I was too flustered. Somehow I would make do.

"At full rate."

Was it a question or statement? "Yes—full rate." I reached into my vest and removed some money, enough for a couple of days at the pension. "Now," I said, "may I get the woman some food and drink before she dies and I have to ask for my money back?"

My landlord folded the currency and tucked it into his back pocket. "Go see to her; I will bring something in a moment."

His wife entered the kitchen. She looked at me but not questioningly. Perhaps Polozkov had spoken to her. "It will do no good to feed her now," she said. "She has vodka poisoning; she will need a purgative before anything else." Ah, reliable countryfolk—they know what to do in any circumstance.

I left the kitchen and the matter in their hands. I returned to the parlor, which was becoming quite warm. Polozkov had fallen asleep in the embroidered chair; the sherry bottle and tumbler were about to slip from his hands. I took them and told him to go to bed, that I would handle things from here. He appeared too tired to care one way or another as he left the parlor and headed for the stair. I put my hand on the woman's cheek and it was cool. Her eyes fluttered open for a moment but I saw only their whites.

Now I sat in the embroidered chair, which was a bit narrow for me. I watched the woman and wondered where she had come from and why she was here in Iiloskova. I recalled her taciturnity on the train. Except for a hint of pink at her cheek and the subtlest of movement under her covers as she breathed, she looked to be a corpse on the sofa. I imagined that had she not found her way to the Luminarium and therefore here, she would have been dead by morning. The smell of unripe vodka and the muskiness of the bearskin coat were a potent combination in the parlor. The room was beginning to warm me, and I felt a little drowsy.

Perhaps I did doze for a moment, because soon the landlord and lady were there, he carrying a tray with a teapot, cup and toasted bread, and she with a wooden pail, a towel, and a glass half-full with a bilious liquid. The landlady placed the towel and pail on the floor, then said, "We must get this in her," referring to the purgative drink. I took my great coat from atop the woman and loosened the bearskin and removed the overlarge hat from her head. Then I propped her up on my arm as I knelt beside the sofa. The landlady opened the woman's slack mouth and poured in a bit of the liquid; it smelled foul, even compared to the awful vodka and musky animal skin. The landlady stroked the woman's throat to make her swallow. The woman immediately began to come to—no doubt the horrid taste of the purgative was forcing her toward consciousness. The landlady coaxed a bit more into her. She began to retch, so I aimed her toward the pail, which the landlady had grabbed and brought closer to her patient. After a minute or two of violent heaving, the woman had expelled a quart or more of rancid vodka. And no food. We all waited for a while to make certain the woman's stomach was empty, then the landlady used the towel to clean her lips and chin and tip of her nose. "There you are, dear," she said, almost under her breath, her pent-up maternal instinct used on a drunken stranger.

The woman dozed on my arm, but now she seemed more asleep than passed out. After a while, the landlord poured a bit of tea; and the landlady and I helped the woman to eat a few small bites of toast and drink some tea with tiger-root. She was half awake but did not appear to have the energy to question where she was. We let the food settle a few minutes before the landlord and I used the hammock, which was still under the woman on the sofa, to carry her upstairs to the available room next to mine. The landlady went in after we had gotten her to the bed and probably arranged her under the covers, taking off her shoes and smelly coat—I had already gone to my own room.

It was almost midnight and I was utterly exhausted. My headache from earlier had returned, though not as acutely. I lay in bed and reflected on the events of the evening, but only for a moment. I was soon fast sleep.

I thought I heard birdsong outside my window then knew it was only remnants of a dream. A dream of home and of springtime. I realized, though, I was thinking about my boyhood home, not my marital home with Tasha. I remembered the woman in the next room and pulled myself out of bed. I felt hung over from drink, yet I had not been intoxicated the night before. Sitting on the side of the creaky bed, I let my head hang down and I noticed I was still wearing the red tie. Its vivid color made my eyes hurt. I took off the tie and hung it over the back of the chair, then I put on a clean shirt and went downstairs to see if there was something for breakfast. I craved coffee and a smoke, but a bit of tiger-root tea and a fried egg or two would do. I assumed the woman was still sleeping. I was thankful that my landlady had the good sense to purge her system before trying to feed her; such common sense was not my gift.

Coming down the stair, I smelled sausages frying and thought I was dreaming again. I had not had any sort of meat since arriving in Iiloskova. Almost everything on the hoof had been taken for the army, who must have been running short nonetheless. I thought of the reports of grave robbing for dead soldiers' boots and coats and such, and I wondered if cannibalism might be the army's next atrocity. I was reminded of my legitimate reason for coming north in the first place, to write about the war firsthand. It was easy to lose sight here.

Walking past the parlor entrance, I stopped all of a sudden. The woman was sitting on the sofa where the night before she had lain unconscious. A woolen blanket was draped over her narrow shoulders, a cup of something—probably tea—was on the side table to her right. And in her lap was my open valise: the woman had untied my manuscript and was reading my poems!

I stepped heavily into the parlor. "Madam," I said, startling her. She looked at me with those electric amethyst eyes, and I could not be angry.

"Mr. Pastrovich; I am so pleased to see you. I must thank you for . . . simply for everything." Her appreciation seemed genuine. "I hope you do not mind my reviewing your poetry. You offered on the train, so I did not think you would mind." Before I could respond—with what I did not know—she added, "It is wonderful . . . simply wonderful."

If she had limited herself to my bound manuscript, then she probably had not read "Beautiful Stranger"; I would have been embarrassed otherwise. I thought of the Prince of Ithaka's sketch too. How stupid of me to have left my valise in the parlor overnight. This strange city was draining me of my reason. The woman had probably overlooked the sketch as well. Not that it should matter, but I felt an unusual ownership regarding the so-called Prince. The bizarre man was mine—to research and write about, and to feel connected with. No one else could know these things. In short, my possessive feelings were inexplicably akin to jealousy.

"I am glad you like them," I said, "and that you are doing so much better this morning."

"Oh yes . . . Mr. and Mrs. Strubel have been simply wonderful. They are making sausages and porridge for our breakfast."

So their name is Strubel. How is it I had been there all along and did not know their name? I suppose I had not asked. For a journalist, my lack of curiosity was hard to fathom. In what other ways had I been slipping?

She continued, "I must confess that in addition to my curiosity about your poems, I hoped to learn something more of my savior himself. To no . . . avail, however. I do not even know your home city or town."

I had come into the parlor while she spoke then I sat in the narrow embroidered chair, which was still angled toward the sofa from the previous evening. "Yet you still have me at a disadvantage, for I do not even know your *name.*"

She smiled and placed my valise and manuscript to her side. "My true name is troublesome in your country's tongue. What do you think my name should be? I am most open to suggestions."

I wondered then if she was fleeing the authorities. The theory would explain her lack of resources and her coming to this edge-of-the-earth place. Perhaps I was opening myself up to trouble by befriending her. I had always been a cautious man, yet in this matter I did not care. I did not understand the game she was playing—for surely a game it was—but I joined in nonetheless. "Your name," I said, musing. When I was a child of eight or nine, I had a little girlfriend in the village; our parents enjoyed the pastime of predicting that we would one day be man and wife. I had not thought of her—or seen her—for many years. "Helena," I said. "Helena appears a fitting name." My little girlfriend had had eyes of iceberg blue, similar to the woman's only in their piercing and mesmerizing qualities.

The woman seemed to consider the matter seriously. "I am not certain I agree, but I will trust in your judgment, which has not failed me thus far. I shall be Helena."

And, like that, she was: Helena. We did not bother with a family name. I had not thought of it beforehand but together our names— Helena and Hektr—had alliteration, and a comfortable rhythm too. They sounded good side by side, like complementary piano keys, in a way that "Tasha and Hektr" never had. The "Pastroviches," "Tasha and Hektr," "Tasha and Hektr Pastrovich." The combinations were as musical as bowls falling and cracking on the kitchen floor.

Helena suddenly winced and put her hand to her forehead. "Are you all right?" I asked.

"Yes," she said in a moment, forcing herself to smile. "Just a lingering . . . twinge from last night's unfortunate episode."

I wanted to inquire about her activities since disembarking, especially what had happened the night before. She was no better dressed than when we were on the train. How had she survived these days and nights in the northcountry's bitter cold? I considered the woman's attractive features, and of the whorehouse I had run across my first night in the city—but I forced myself to let loose of the unpleasant, and unfair, line of thought. The smell of the sausages was quite strong and it was simple to concentrate on my growing hunger. Surely Helena was famished too.

I heard the other lodgers coming down the stair in a group and soon we were all at the dining table, which now seemed pleasantly crowded with the arrival of Helena, slight of frame though she was. The sausages were, in effect, rationed among us and no one ate his fill, but they were excellent and a most welcome treat. The steaming bowls of porridge were wholesome and filled in the space left vacant by the sausages; I ate mine with a bit of butter and milk mixed in. Two cups of tea, also with a splash of milk, and a half biscuit, and I felt ready for a productive day. The conversation at breakfast was superficial but very cordial. The female boarder, whom I suspected was a politician's mistress or a witch, appeared relieved that there was another woman among us. Females are unpredictable in this situation: Will they bond like sisters, or contend like life-long adversaries? Or some combination of both extremes?

I used the washroom after breakfast and looked at myself in the mirror, which was old and returned a somewhat distorted image. My beard was still not quite a beard yet, but it had come in enough to reveal its overall hoariness. But instead of looking like an enlightened sage, I appeared to be a sailor who had just arrived at port after a uniquely difficult crossing. My skin itched beneath the whiskers. Later in the day or perhaps tomorrow I would use my razor to cut the beard at my neck and cheekbones; then I would look less like a madman wandering between villages.

I was not at all certain how best to use my day. I had other reports regarding vagrancy and theft that I could pursue. But I had the sense that I was supremely lucky to have come across the story at the Hotel Slopek on my first attempt, and that I had emptied that well already. There was no word from Bushkov regarding conveyance to the front. The front. Was there truly a war being fought? Other than the shortages, especially of young men, in Iiloskova, evidence of war was not obvious. I believe, in the rest of the country—the south and west especially—the war had become such an abstraction it was easy to think of it as unreal, some mere tool of propaganda set up by the government for reasons that could not be divined. Perhaps a scapegoat explanation for the nation's faltering economy, or to draw attention away from corrupt leaders. Both contingencies felt more real than the repulsion of an invading neighbor.

So: If the front was unreachable and pursuit of the dispatches was unattractive, then the sanatorium remained. The Prince may have escaped its infamous halls and found his way south—stowed away on a train perchance. I changed my shirt in my room and put on my workaday brown necktie. I opened the door to find Helena standing there preparing to knock. "You should be resting," I said in greeting.

"I feel wonderful." She was smiling at me; she appeared wonderful. "You are going out?"

"Yes—I am pursuing a story. It is why I came here." Whom was I informing? Helena or myself?

"May I accompany you—" She corrected herself: "—assist you. May I assist you?"

"You appeared to be on the doorstep of Death himself only a few hours ago. Should you not fully recuperate here before venturing out?"

"I am stronger than I seem, Mr. Pastrovich. I will not be a burden to you any further."

"That is not my concern . . . I simply want to make certain you are well. What will you do for a winter coat?"

"Mrs. Strubel has offered to alter the fur coat—and to try to make it smell more wholesome. In the meantime, she has offered me an old coat and hat of hers. I shall be appropriately covered."

"Very well then. You are an adult; I will not treat you as a child."

In a few minutes' time we were on the streets of Iiloskova making our way to the sanatorium. Polozkov had told me of its location during our chess match. It was a large, old building with many windows, but—unfortunately, from Polozkov's point of view—they were all protected by iron bars. It was a walk of some three miles; I was hoping to find something horse- or mule-drawn on the way.

It was a sunny morning but cold of course. The sausage and porridge in my belly gave me an equally sunny disposition—or perhaps it was the companionship of Helena. I had been lonely for so long I often neglected to notice, like a long-standing debt that could be put out of mind, until the collector made his regular call and added penalty to the unpaid balance. I wanted a cigarette on this fine morning, so I stopped at a bench to roll myself one. I offered to fashion one for Helena but she said she would do it herself. Her fingers, which she freed from red mittens, were unpracticed at the art and her cigarette was irregularly shaped; but served its purpose nonetheless. I struck a match and lighted our cigarettes. She drew deeply—at this, she was practiced—before letting the smoke out in the frigid air.

We sat for only a moment before continuing on our way. She held one mitten in the hand of the other to leave her fingers free with the cigarette. The tobacco was good for her and put color in her cheeks. I carried my valise in my left hand so that it would not bump Helena's leg. We walked along, smoking and not talking, and studying the Iiloskovites we passed on the boardwalk. They were a sturdy people, many of Oriental stock, many others from the north—no doubt of the same bloodline as the invaders—evidence of some long-forgotten previous invasion, perhaps more immigration than invasion. What is the difference now? Why must we send a whole army to stop their advance? Why not welcome them as our ancestors did, let them settle in, then begin collecting their taxes?

I knew it was not so simple. But walking on this fine cold morning, with Helena at my side, my writing securely in my valise, pursuing an interesting story . . . peace almost seemed that effortless to achieve.

IX

She ran like a lunatic through the wide halls echoing her cry.

Iliad 22

OUR ROUTE QUICKLY LED US from a derelict business section to a derelict neighborhood. The houses appeared much older than my pension on Division Street. The boardwalk turned to uneven cobblestones then paths of packed snow and ice. Footing was difficult. We could not walk quite abreast of each other because of the narrowness of the path, so I stayed a stride ahead. Old trees, though leafless, blocked much of the sunlight, making the day feel even colder. It was quiet; no birdsong or dog barking. Just the wintry wind in the tree limbs and our crunching shoes in the snow. I thought of asking Helena some questions, like why she was here in Iiloskova, but it seemed the sound of my voice would be a violation of nature. We walked on in silence. Helena had finished her cigarette and put her mitten back on.

Suddenly a noise, an explosion, stopped us dead. It came from our left. Instinctively we looked across the cobblestone street. Another explosion as a window was blasted out of an old sideways leaning house; it was a gunshot, I realized, while Helena and I sought cover behind a tree trunk. We heard voices, a man and a woman, then the front door of the house was thrown off its hinges by an enormous fellow stumbling toward the porch. He was wearing a sleeveless undershirt, and his arms were as thick and as hairy as an African gorilla's. I had seen one in a traveling circus and everything about the man reminded me of the beast, his too-small head clamped tight to his shoulders, his round belly, the way his arms moved at his sides.

The man regained his balance and began shouting back into the house. I did not recognize the language. Helena must have sensed my ignorance and said, "He is telling his wife she is a crazy woman. 'The police will take you away and lock you up,' he is saying."

The wife, a small woman in a gray dress and greasy apron, appeared in the doorway pointing the hunting rifle at her husband. She did not shout but we could hear her fierce words nonetheless. Helena interpreted, "Police? There are no police. Otherwise you would have been locked up long ago, you—" She chose not to interpret the insult. I used my imagination. The woman stepped onto the porch, and her husband, in spite of his enormity, was obviously afraid of her. He moved backward and his stockinged foot slipped on some ice; then he tumbled down five creaky steps, smashing two of them, and lay motionless in the snow.

His little wife was doubled in laughter at the sight of her oafish husband's fall. She came to the edge of the porch, her rifle still in her hands, and looked down on him. I was surprised that none of their neighbors came out to see what was happening. Perhaps this sort of thing was a regular occurrence in this street. The wife quit laughing suddenly as if she saw what I did at that same instant. Blood was leaking from the back of her husband's head and turning the snowy ground a brilliant red. The wife navigated the broken steps and knelt by her husband. She put the rifle aside and tried to rouse him, saying his name—"Yoot," a nickname perhaps—and slapping his cheeks.

"I suppose we must help," I said and stepped out from behind the tree. I walked across the treacherous cobblestones. "Madam, may I be of assistance? I saw your husband's fall." Helena was close behind me and translated. I assumed she did so verbatim. The woman looked up and began chattering wildly, probably telling her side of the story. Her green eyes were ablaze, her tousled hair a mess in the wind that had come up. Helena and I were on the opposite side of her supine husband. The wife rubbed snow in his fleshy cheeks to try to revive him. I removed my gloves (I did not want to stain them) and lifted his enormous head to try to determine the severity of the wound. I turned his face away from me, and Helena observed, "It is only a cut of his scalp," first in my language then in the wife's. "We must stop the bleeding, though," she added, twice.

"Let us get him inside," I said. His lips were already turning blue. I dug my hands under his back and lifted as best I could, only raising his right shoulder from the ground. He must have been nearly twice my weight. And here I was with these two slight women who together did not weigh as much as I. Regardless, the three of us struggled for a minute or two to lift the unconscious husband; blood was smeared on my coat and trouser leg. We accomplished nothing. I was about to suggest that we try to find some neighbors when the wife went up the steps and into the house. She called a series of names, and children of various ages and genders began filing outdoors. There were six all together; the eldest two, a boy and girl, were teenagers. They came down into the snow to assist, and somehow the five of us wrestled the bleeding man back inside his house and onto a broken sofa in the nearest bedroom. I returned outdoors long enough to recover my valise and the hunting rifle.

Helena and the woman talked in the room while I stood looking stupidly at the taciturn children. The eldest boy had gotten the front door back on its hinges and was going about trying to cover the shot-out window. Next to the window, crumbling plaster was evidence of the first gunshot we had heard. The smell of gunpowder was still heavy in the air. The wife came out of the room and hurried up a set of unsafe looking stairs. I peered through the doorway and saw that Helena had removed her coat and hat and was rolling up the sleeves of her blouse. Momentarily, the wife returned with a pitcher and a basket.

I stepped inside the room to watch. The wife put her things down, and the two women rolled the husband onto his side. Helena proceeded to clean the wound with water and a sheet that had been cut into pieces. Meanwhile, she spoke to the woman, who reached into the basket and prepared needle and thread. It was coarse looking thread, perhaps even cat's gut. The lighting in the room was poor, so I lit a pair of candles on a small table next to the sofa. Then Helena heated the needle in the candle flame and went to work. I was impressed with how deftly she sewed the wound, parting the man's blood-clotted hair with one hand and using the needle in the other. In no time the bleeding was stopped and she tied off the thread. They rolled him onto his back and he was snoring, as if only taking a midmorning nap.

Helena used the pitcher and a wash basin to clean her hands; meanwhile, she gave some last instructions to the wife. I assumed she was telling her how to tend to the wound or how to eventually remove the stitches, but she could have been encouraging her to aim the gun more effectively the next time. The family's language was from the East, I believed, a mountain dialect. I wondered how many tongues Helena spoke with fluency.

We left the house, careful not to fall down the dangerous steps, and continued on our way to the sanatorium. In all, the episode had cost us less than an hour. After a time I said, "You were very good. You have some experience with the wounded?"

Helena did not look up at me. "I have been many places; one learns many things."

The sun had gone behind clouds now and the day was colder. "Are you doing all right?" I asked, realizing that fewer than twelve hours before Polozkov and I had carried her into the pension, nearly dead from vodka poisoning. Her recovery was bordering on miraculous.

"Yes, quite. The air is doing me good." So she said, but her face was crimson from the wind and cold, and her eyes were lustrous in a way that sometimes indicates a fever.

We soon left behind the old neighborhoods and were on open road; only snow-covered hillocks diverted the cutting wind. It was an almost unbelievable transition. I thought Polozkov had informed me incorrectly about the sanatorium, then we went around a bend and it loomed before us like a medieval fort; in fact, it may have been just that. It appeared to be four towers with supporting walls of stone in between. Each tower had pairs of narrow windows at intervals indicating the various floors, no doubt, but iron bars covered all of them. Had I been asked to sketch a cliché of a sanatorium for the insane, I would have drawn something very much like this one. It looked to be the residence of vampires and ghouls, even on a relatively bright and cheerful day.

There was a path of frozen footprints from the road to the sanatorium's entrance, which led through a tall iron gate in between columns of brown brick; the gate was not secured. I saw only the footprints as evidence of some communion between the sanatorium and outside world—no tracks from wheels, wheels of any kind. I wondered how they brought in food for the inmates and other supplies. Perhaps there were extensive gardens and orchards on the other side of the sanatorium; presumably there was a water supply, a lake or wells. In front there was only the field of snow and track of frozen footprints, the wandering line of which reminded me of the laceration in the husband's damaged scalp.

My companion and I walked up narrow steps cut into stone. A plaque next to the tall double doors said simply Iiloskova Sanatorium. I looked at Helena before turning the bell-key in the door. She was shivering; the trip had been a strain for her. "You can get warm inside," I said.

"I am not cold," she said, her lips trembling a bit. What then? Fright? The sanatorium was an unnerving place. Yet it seemed strange that she could so calmly sew a man's scalp together but become agitated at the sight of a mental-illness facility. I turned the bell-key and heard it rattling just inside the doors. It was a minute or more before someone finally responded and pulled back the oaken lefthand door. She was a middle-aged woman in a dark blue dress; her hair, brown with streaks of gray, was pulled into a tight bun. She looked like the headmistress of a grammar school. She said no words of greeting but stood looking at me expectantly.

"Hello, madam. My name is Hektr Pastrovich; this is my companion Helena. I was hoping to speak with the sanatorium's director."

The woman glanced down at my valise. "Are you a salesman? If so, I can save you some trouble—"

"No, madam, I am not a salesman, I promise you. I am looking for some information; I am a visiting journalist."

This news did not appear to make her feel any more at ease. "Doctor Zitch is our director. He is busy at the moment but you are welcome to wait—it could be a long wait though."

"I am a patient man," I said. She stepped aside and admitted Helena and me. When she shut and locked the door behind us, slipping the key into her dress pocket, I immediately detected an odd combination of smells: beeswax and ether . . . and cabbage maybe. It was most unpleasant. I looked at Helena and she seemed to sense it too. I listened for the sound of wailing inmates, tortured souls in captivity. But there was no noise, other than our shoes on the polished stone floor. The woman in blue led us along a side corridor to a small room with an oval table and chairs upholstered in leather. "I will let Doctor Zitch know he has a visitor," said the woman, closing the door as she exited. I set my valise on the table and removed my hat, gloves and coat. Helena put her hat and mittens in a side pocket of Mrs. Strubel's old coat but left it on. She looked unwell to me but it was hard to tell.

We sat, and I unlatched my valise. I got out my pencil case and notebook. I made sure the sketch of the Prince of Ithaka was in its place but left it inside the valise. "This place is very quiet," I said, making conversation.

Helena nodded. Something had come over her since arriving. She was nervous; she picked at the threads in her coat. It occurred to me that the sanatorium was an extension of the government's authority. If she was, in fact, fleeing authority, then just being here could cause her anxiety. I did not tell her our destination before leaving the pension. In retrospect, the omission seemed strange. Perhaps I wanted her to accompany me—assist me—and I feared she would change her mind if she knew where I was going. I waited until we were en route before mentioning the sanatorium. Yet I noted no trepidation at the knowledge.

"Helena, perhaps this is not the time, but I must ask: Why have you come to Iiloskova?" I was as surprised by the question as she. I continued, almost involuntarily, "You have no relatives here; it is not your home; it certainly is not a tourist destination."

She stopped fiddling with the coat threads but she did not look at me. "I . . . I am looking for someone. That is all." I noticed a tear form in her eye, amplifying its intense color.

I felt badly then—but I did not believe her, not entirely. Perhaps it was because of all the years of marriage to Tasha. We could not speak truthfully to each other. Every conversation was at least partly misdirection, the truth of the matter always veiled, either to prevent hurt or to cause it. I believed men and women could not speak in earnest with each other, only men to other men and women to other women.   Yet I knew of a homosexual couple in my city, two men who owned a textile business, and they were always at each other's throat—as vicious as any old married couple.   Perhaps then it was not a matter of gender but rather one of intimacy.   It was the pursuit of intimate knowledge that caused the truth to be smothered, like an infant beneath too many blankets . . . no . . . I do not know.   I was making my head hurt.

I used a sharpening stone to sharpen my pencils, killing time. Helena returned to picking at her coat threads.   It was cold in the little room, and I thought of the interrogation room where I had met the Prince of Ithaka.   This room was not so stark but there was something of the same feel about it—the impression that questions were asked in here and the wrong answer could have dire consequences.   I had collected the pencil shavings on my open notebook, so I stood and took the notebook to a waste bin in the corner of the room.   I brushed the shavings off but before I could return to my seat there was a knock on the door and it opened hesitantly.

In walked a fellow with bushy black hair, spectacles, and a severely pointed goatee, giving his face almost the shape of an arrowhead. He wore a threadbare brown suit; his shirt collar was open as he had no necktie.   "Hello," he said, "I am Sergei Zitch, director of the sanatorium.   May I help you?"   He stood in the open doorway, his eyes roaming between me and Helena, who had not looked up at him, so that her face was still in profile.

I introduced myself.   I introduced Helena merely as "my assistant"; I withheld her name, though it was silly, because I knew it was not really her name.   Yet another shovelful of subterfuge layered upon the truth.   Doctor Zitch and I took seats at the table. He was exactly opposite Helena, who did not toy with her coat any longer, but she did not make eye contact with him either.   I began.   "Doctor Zitch, I am visiting Iiloskova to write about the war for my newspaper."

"I am afraid you are not seeing our fair city in its finest light," said the doctor, straining, it seemed, to be convivial.

"Yes, I am sure it is quite different in peacetime."   I was willing to be polite but I wanted to get down to business.   "Has the war affected the sanatorium in specific ways?"

He thought for a moment. "There are the shortages of course. Our budget is not large even in the best of times."

I scribbled my notation system. "Yes, shortages of course. But in any other ways?" I waited a moment, then proceeded when he did not respond. "Are you treating any soldiers? Any shell-shocked young men from the front?"

Doctor Zitch removed his spectacles and cleaned the lenses with his suit's lapel. "The army has its own doctors, Mr. Pastrovich." He replaced the spectacles.

"So you have not treated any soldiers?"

"Many of our patients are old—they have long histories. There may have been some soldiers among them." His voice was all neutrality. I had no sense of his being overconfident or unsure of himself. I might as well have been reading a transcript of our interview.

"And you have been the directing doctor here for how long?"

"Nearly ten years."

"Do you keep patients until they are cured, or are there other considerations?"

"'Cured' is a relative term. Our goal in treating patients is to help them to be able to function outside these walls, so that they are not a threat to themselves or their loved ones."

"So, to paraphrase, sometimes patients are released without having been cured. Is that correct?"

"No, Mr. Pastrovich, that paraphrase is not correct."

Helena suddenly entered into the dialogue: "You mentioned 'loved ones,' Doctor Zitch. How do loved ones keep in contact with patients?" She pierced him with her eyes.

"Visits are permitted, of course. As long as they are in the patient's best interest. Best, long-term interest."

"And you make that . . . determination, Doctor Zitch?" she continued.

"Yes, visitations are part of my domain."

I wanted to ask if any patients had escaped in recent months but I knew it would gain me nothing. I opened my valise and removed the sketch. "Doctor Zitch, do you recognize this man?" I handed him the Prince's picture.

He studied it for a moment. "No. Who is he? Did someone say he was a patient of the sanatorium?" Suddenly, the doctor's voice was not purely neutral, some type of emotion had entered.

"Please look closely," I said. "He has been in Iiloskova and elsewhere."

"I have looked closely; I do not know him."

"How about other members of the staff? Are there other doctors who work with the patients?"

"No, I am the only physician. If I do not know the man, no one here knows him. I am sorry, Mr. Pastrovich, but being the only physician, I am very busy. I must see to my patients." He handed the Prince's sketch to me and pushed himself from his chair. "Good day, to you both." And Doctor Zitch marched from the room, as if late for an appointment. He left the door ajar.

"He knows the man," I said, giving voice to my thoughts, as I peered down at the Prince's rugged countenance. The police artist's sketch was not a perfect likeness but it did capture the Prince's weariness—world weariness perhaps—in his eyes, and the curve of his lips. I was thinking I could perhaps talk to the woman in blue, Doctor Zitch's assistant, or some other attendant at the sanatorium.

Helena uttered a sound, like a little cry and gasp, and rushed from the room. "Helena . . . ?" I took a moment to gather my things then went after her. Maybe she had become ill again. I followed the hall back to the main corridor; again my nostrils were assaulted by the pungent beeswax and ether odor. No one was in the corridor, not even the woman in blue, but the main door was left open. I went outside onto the stone porch and immediately I saw Helena on the frozen footpath, kneeling in the snow as if sick indeed. She was not far from the iron gates. I rushed to her, my heavy steps cracking the snow and ice, and I placed my hand on her shoulder. "Are you all right? I was afraid this would be too much for you."

Her head was lowered as if she might be about to retch but no sound was coming from her. I felt her trembling—from cold . . . nerves . . . illness? I did not know.

I heard something behind me, coming from the sanatorium's nearest tower. I looked up at a window that was being raised near the top of the tower. The process was noisy, as if the window had not been opened in a long time. Suddenly two white fists grabbed hold of the iron bars. I heard a man's voice, high-pitched and shrill, but masculine: "Gather your acorns! Winter is coming! Gather your nuts and acorns! Winter is coming!" The man's face was in shadow. I had the ludicrous notion it was Doctor Zitch yelling down to us. I expected to see his neatly trimmed goatee at the window. Of course it was not he.

Someone inside got to the man. His hands were being wrenched from the bars. I heard the scuffle. He called, out of breath, frantic: "Men of winter—gather your acorns—it is coming . . . !" His white fists disappeared and the window snapped shut.

I turned to Helena, who had been looking up at the man too. Her cheeks were inflamed, her eyes glassy. I helped her to stand. She pulled herself together, buttoning her coat and putting on her hat and mittens. She brushed the snow from the knees of her skirt. "I am fine, Mr. Pastrovich. Please, let us go." Her voice was quiet, tired. She began trudging through the snow, avoiding the frozen footprints and making her own path in the great whiteness.

I switched my valise to my left hand and began to follow. Our little rooms on Division Street seemed far away, as flakes started falling from the colorless sky.

X

'I ascended to a rocky vantage point looking for signs of life.'

Odyssey 10

I SAT AT THE TABLE IN MY ROOM, my writing things laid out before me, pen in hand. A leaf of paper was before me too. It seemed to occupy a great space, a void that could never be filled. I had scratched the Roman numeral "I." on the top of the paper some minutes before, indicating it was to be the first of something. I had thoughts of writing a piece for Mezenskov about the city of Iiloskova; I certainly had been there long enough to absorb its general atmosphere. It was not exactly what he was looking for, but I felt I could make it a good piece, a solid journalistic report. On the other hand, I believed I was truly on the trail of the Prince of Ithaka, and I could write about that as well. I was certain he had been at the sanatorium at some point. I also had the impression that Helena knew him, that she recognized his face. She was silent during our entire return to the pension. I did not want to press her and make her condition any worse.

How is it that so many could know the Prince? Old Golokov at the hotel, the mourning woman at the coffee store, Doctor Zitch … and Helena too? I wondered if Lieutenant Bushkov knew him and was lying to me. I sensed a conspiracy, but it was a ridiculous notion. I was just tired and far from home. Perhaps no one had had dealings with the man who called himself the Prince of Ithaka. They had all lost someone or something, and his face filled that emptiness. I could have shown them a sketch of any person, of myself even, and they would have reacted in the same manner—afraid, sad, angry . . . whatever emotion was near the surface, ready to leach out, like fluid from a scab.

I drew a line under my Roman numeral: "I." Perhaps it was poetry I wanted to write. I poised my pen and waited for the first line. My muse was not singing, not even humming absentmindedly. The empty leaf of paper seemed the size of a tablecloth, of a sail draped over the table. It hung down to the floor, and spread under the bed and beneath the door into the hall. I darkened the line under my Roman numeral, then the Roman numeral itself: "**I.**" It was as if something blocked my thoughts, dammed them up somewhere in my brain.

I took up the glass on the table but it was empty of vodka. I had let the final drop fall to my tongue shortly after writing the Roman numeral. Was it too late to go out and purchase another bottle? There was still murky daylight at my window. The landlord and his wife—Mr. and Mrs. Strubel, I reminded myself—would call us to dinner very soon. I thought about Helena in her room. For a while I believed I heard her pacing, a short journey to and fro in the tiny room. Then the sound stopped. Momentarily doors opened and closed and there were footsteps in the hall, more than one person. She might have been among them.

I darkened the Roman numeral further, until the nib had nearly pierced the paper. There was noise in the hall and someone knocked at my door: Mrs. Strubel spoke: "Mr. Pastrovich, supper will be on the table in a few minutes."

"Thank you, . . ." I called. I nearly said her name for the first time but the idea died at my tongue. Well, there was no sense in continuing to write now. I put my pen away and capped the bottle of ink. I left the paper out to dry; it would take a long while given the concentration of ink in the one letter, period and underscore. I buttoned my top button and tightened my tie, and went to supper in shirtsleeves and vest. The formality of a coat seemed superfluous. I was famished after the long walk to the sanatorium and back, and I figured Helena—so, so thin anyway—was also.

I came downstairs by myself and discovered that everyone was already at table. A place was left open on an end, flanked by Helena and Polozkov. I was reminded of a scene from a Shakespeare tragedy where the doomed king is unable to take his place at the banquet because his murdered friend's ghost is there before him. Or was it merely a trick of the guilty king's imagination as he had arranged the murder himself? My recollection was unclear. I hesitated a moment but no phantom took my place. I would not have been shocked if the Prince of Ithaka had walked onstage to play the ghostly part.

I pulled my chair up to the table and Helena immediately spoke to me. "Did you rest after all our exercise?" She smiled and electricity fired her amethyst eyes.

"Yes. I feel fine." I was not sure how to take her.

"Mr. Polozkov informs me you are an accomplished chess player."

I looked over at him, smiling beneath his hooked nose. "I would not use the word *accomplished*. If I remember, we played to a draw, so Mr. Polozkov must be of equal talent."

"Perhaps after supper you would do me the honor of a match." Helena's smile was radiant. "There are not games enough in this house. Mr. Polozkov informs me you all have been keeping to yourselves, other than your evening of chess."

"Pardon me," said the other woman from the opposite end of the table, "but I completely agree: games would be a very nice addition here." She smiled a pleasant smile of her own. Was her hair darker and silkier? She seemed younger than the mysterious female lodger I had known.

Helena put her child-size hands on the table to emphasize her point. "You see—I am not mad. Everyone is craving fun." She put her hand on my arm, which rested on the table. "Hektr, it would be selfish of us to play chess and leave everyone to watch or not. We will organize games for everyone." She was as resolute as a commander declaring his battle plan. "I will speak with Mrs. Strubel—there must be more than chess to play in this house."

Soon we were served fishcakes and steaming bowls of lentils and cabbage. We discovered that Polozkov had purchased wine for our supper, and glasses were passed from hand to hand. We toasted him for his generosity. I took a sip, and it was not cheap wine; it was strong and good, and I was most grateful for it. Helena began passing around the plate of biscuits. It was a lovely meal and everyone was in high spirits. True to her word, Helena inquired with our landlady about games that may be available. She seemed surprised by the question but said there were two old decks of cards, a cribbage board, and backgammon. She thought a moment then added "ball and jack-nails" to the list.

"Excellent," said Helena, beaming. "You and your husband must join us. You must not toil away in that kitchen all evening."

Not sure how to respond, Mrs. Strubel smiled politely before returning to her toil in the kitchen. After supper, more wine was poured and we retired to the parlor. Helena located the decks of cards, and Polozkov, Kritch, and the mystery woman decided they all knew the rules of "Queen in the Tower" and set about playing it. Meanwhile, I had readied the chessboard. Helena elected the white pieces and made her opening move, a knight boldly out in front. It proved not to be atypical of her style. She was very aggressive, yet kept her overall strategy concealed. I recalled that Polozkov was blind to diagonal stratagems but Helena did not share his weakness. We both drew blood very quickly—she by design, I by necessity. Pawns fell right and left, plus a rook, a knight, and bishops of each camp. She chased after my queen like a love-starved prince. It was difficult to concentrate because of the mirth of the card players. They were having a terrific time playing their game, laughing and beginning to banter back and forth like old chums. It got my attention when Polozkov called the mystery woman "Mirska"; she must have offered her name at last. Or was it as fictitious as Helena's? I felt a little like the only reveler in plain dress at a costume ball, embarrassed of my misreading the invitation.

I finally moved my queen into a position of relative safety, protected by a pawn and my remaining knight, only to have Helena put my king in check. I easily moved him out of harm's path, but I realized that is what she had been angling for for some time—pursuit of my queen was an elaborated ploy. I was in serious trouble and was thinking hard of a way out; Helena's king rested comfortably behind a fortress of pieces. The card players erupted in raucous laughter as Mirska won the game in a surprise flurry. Helena smiled at my irritation; I had to smile too.

The trio of card players shifted their attention to our game, Kritch moving his chair and Mirska moving herself to the sofa to watch. Polozkov retrieved the wine and refilled everyone's glass. Mirska encouraged Helena to put an end to me and make it a complete sweep for the ladies.

I attempted my own attack, to try to shift the game's momentum, but my ranks were too decimated and Helena easily took one piece after another. In my zeal I left my queen open and Helena's rook put an end to her black reign from the opposite side of the board—I was totally surprised by the assassination and knew then my situation was beyond hope. For a few moves the white army toyed with my king and a remaining pawn—or so it seemed Helena was toying with me, for the sake of fun-loving cruelty, then I realized she was not content for just any piece to end the game: she wanted her queen to deliver the death blow. I thought once again of the Shakespeare work, for I recalled suddenly that it was the queen who had set the tragic events in motion, events which ultimately led to the king's decapitation. I loosened my workaday necktie—the parlor had become very warm—and awaited Helena's final assault.

When Helena won the game, the spectators applauded her victory. I joined them and realized that the landlord and his wife were also there, applauding and telling Helena how wonderfully she had played. Polozkov wanted his turn, "at humiliation," as he put it. I eagerly gave up my place at the board. Mirska and Kritch convinced the Strubels to join them in cards. "Come, Mr. Pastrovich," said Mirska, radiantly, "we will show you the game too."

"Thank you. I will play a bit later. Right now I would like to go out for a smoke and to lick my wounds. The tigress was quite thorough in her attack." Everyone laughed.

I put on my coat and hat and went out to the side porch with my glass of wine. It had been snowing all day and evening, and the fresh powder seemed to cleanse the city. Though I knew it was just a superficial covering of the grime, the rug atop the swept-under dust, as it were. It was late in the season for such a storm, and the night felt relatively warm. I cleared snow from the porch railing and set down my glass. Then I fixed a cigarette; the smoke I blew from my lungs mixed with the falling snow. The world was supremely quiet. I felt at peace, smoking there on the porch, yet I knew the tranquility was mostly the result of the good strong wine.

Nevertheless, I smoked and listened to the falling snow. When I was a boy, my mother said the gentle little *plink-plink-plink* was not caused by the snowflakes, but rather by the footsteps of fairies who had come out at night to dance. Only when it snowed did our world resemble their own magical home-world. I sipped my wine and watched closely for the sight of fairies pirouetting in the snow. From inside, I heard raucous laughter again. Because of Helena, we had become like a family. If so, then the jealousy, the disappointment, and the fighting were just a matter of time.

After a while, the door behind me opened, and Helena emerged in her fur coat and hat. Mrs. Strubel had taken them in as promised and they fit quite nicely. "Hektr, what are you doing out here?" She closed the door and took the cigarette from my fingers and inhaled deeply from it. She blew out the smoke in a cloud that floated in the cold air, then handed the cigarette back to me. "Would you like one?" I asked. She shook her head. "No, that was enough, thank you."

"You made fast work of Polozkov; I presume you won."

"He is blind to . . . diagonal attacks; once I understood that, the game was a simple one."

"I am just enjoying the peace and the quiet," I said, finally answering her question.

She hugged herself in the bearskin and leaned against a post. There was a dreaminess in her eyes; the wine had worked its magic on her as well. We stayed that way for a time. I finished my wine and threw the butt of the cigarette in the snow. Helena said, "Peace yes—but quiet?"

I thought she was referring to the sound of fairie steps. "What do you mean?"

"Do you not hear it?" she asked, becoming a bit more awake.

"The snow?"

"No . . . the sound like thunder. Listen." We both peered into the snowy night as if our eyes might help us to hear more acutely. I stopped breathing. Yes, there it was: a distant rumble, followed quickly by another.

"It cannot be thunder," I said. "Not during a snowstorm—not unless weather in the northcountry is very different." Such a thing was possible, I supposed.

Helena listened until we heard the sound again. "No, it is not thunder. It is artillery; it is the war."

She was right. I had once visited the local garrison's artillery range, when I was a young newspaperman, and that was the sound—now at a great distance and altered by the snow. "How is it we can hear it tonight? Has the front drawn closer?"

"I do not know," Helena said. "A trick of the atmosphere perhaps."

I stepped off the porch and went into the street so that I could gaze toward the north and east, wondering if I would see artillery flashes reflected in the clouds. But there was nothing, except for the persistent sound, almost below perception. Snowflakes clung to my eyelashes, making it difficult to see anything after a while. In a moment Helena joined me in the street. She stood close to me and put her head on my chest. I hesitated then wrapped my arms around her. She had the bone structure of a wren beneath the big coat.

I thought of the soldiers fighting and dying and turning the new snow to crimson slush. I felt that Helena and I shared that vision. I believed I more than heard the distant explosions—I *felt* them. They reverberated through my skeleton and Helena's, like the aftershocks of earthquakes. In fact, I felt a bit unsteady, as if the next explosion may knock me off balance, sending us both toppling into the snow. It had been a long time since I had held a woman for comfort's sake. I could not recall the last time I hugged Tasha affectionately. And the prostitutes I had held—it was not for the sake of comfort, at least not theirs.

I thought: If Helena looks up at me, I will kiss her. But I saw only the crest of her fur hat, quickly being covered in snow. I heard the side door open, and a voice called from the porch. "Helena? Mr. Pastrovich? It is your turn to join us in cards." It was the landlord's voice, sounding strange with its undercurrent of camaraderie. I could see Mr. Strubel as only a shadow, a darkened figure leaning on the porch railing. "We will be in directly," I returned. I heard the door open and close.

I let go of Helena and brushed snow from her shoulders and back.

She was looking for someone, she had said. A man, I presumed. A lover? Was she imagining him in the war, under attack, and bleeding in the snow even as we stood there? Did the shudder of distant artillery in our frames correspond to the shudder of death in his? I looked into her face for an answer but I saw nothing in the dark. "Come," she said and took my arm. I led her to the porch and inside the house. Before shutting the door, I glanced behind: snow was already filling in, erasing where we had stepped. In the morning there would be no trace of us at all.

Later, in the wee hours, I was awakened by the lightbulb in my room coming suddenly to life. I put my hands up to block the piercing glare. The bed was still spinning from all the wine I had consumed. I was starting to feel sick, and my head ached. I unwrapped myself from the blankets and struggled to a standing position. I put my hand on the table to steady myself. I was fully dressed, even my tie. I had only managed to kick off my shoes before lapsing into sleep. I went to reach for the chain to turn off the lightbulb when it went out on its own. A final sputter of life then total darkness.

I was now awake enough to know I had to urinate, and I doubted I would be able to use the chamber pot. More would end up on the floor than inside the pee-pot. I felt I knew the house well enough to make my way downstairs without a lamp. So I did. When I was finished and making my way back along the hall, I heard a familiar sound emanating from Mr. and Mrs. Strubel's rooms. I did not have to investigate to know what they were up to. Good for them, I thought. I wished I had tablets for my headache, for surely it would be worse in the morning, but I had no doubt that I would be able to fall asleep again. My thoughts were all about Helena, and I knew I would dream of her, that I had been dreaming of her already.

XI

Repelled, the child turned toward the nurse's bosom,
wailing in terror.

Iliad 6

THE DAYS BEGAN TO PASS ONE LIKE ANOTHER. I did not go out, saying to myself the snow was too deep. When I was in my room, I stared at the blank leaf of paper. I had managed to doodle all kinds of designs around the Roman numeral—first geometric shapes, circles and triangles and even a rhombus, then birds and clouds, with a crescent-moon shape in one corner and a sun radiating from another. As a consequence, I did not spend a lot of time in my room. The parlor had become the heart of the pension, and the guests congregated there throughout the day and evening. Talking, playing games, reading—a trunk in the corner of the parlor turned out to contain all sorts of old books: romances, biographies, histories, folktales. The Strubels were the landlord and lady, but clearly felt as we all did that Helena was our queen. Not that we pampered her but she was the center of our world. We spun around her like moons in erratic orbits, sometimes bumping into one another in our efforts to be near her.

She did not act queenly. She seemed to see her role as more maternal. She had shown Mirska and Mrs. Strubel how to braid their hair. Theirs were not as elaborate as Helena's star-pattern braids (nor as fetching) but they were much pleased with them. And their corresponding hairstyles helped create a kinship between the three women. They chattered and laughed, and were even beginning to finish each other's sentences—like cousins who had grown up together. Helena and Mirska pitched in on the housework, so that they could spend more time with Mrs. Strubel, and so that she could spend less time working. I had the sense that life had never been like this for the landlady—that a childhood of drudgery had led seamlessly to an adulthood of the same.

Mr. Strubel did not seem to mind his wife's new friendships. He still had his chores out of doors, but the landlord found more time to sit with the men, talking about the weather and telling tales. The money I had paid for Helena's stay must have run out but Mr. Strubel did not bring up the issue. Then it occurred to me perhaps some of the others were subsidizing her stay with us. Or maybe it was because Helena had been helping Mrs. Strubel with housework.

For that matter, my own resources were diminishing. While I did not go out, I contributed to the fund that kept us supplied with vodka and wine. Mr. Strubel or Polozkov usually ventured out and procured our refreshments. Mostly, we drank the vodka straight but sometimes we would mix it with tea. The wine was for supper and our game playing afterward. We played late into the night: chess and cards, of course, but we had also added backgammon and charades to our repertoire. Helena was especially accomplished at charades. Her eyes were so expressive, it was almost as if she communicated her message through some extrasensory medium. By the same token, she could discern someone else's phrase with the slightest of clues. I got the impression that the only reason anyone else ever won at charades was because Helena let them.

Helena said she had come north looking for someone . . . but she would not find him at the pension. Indeed, she was as slothful in her pursuit as I was in mine. The difference, of course, was that I would eventually go home whereas Helena's quest was indefinite. I wondered what she would do when I had to leave—but I did not wonder very often. I still had a few days remaining and I refused to spend them in worry.

It was on our fourth or fifth halcyon day that we heard the shrieks from the kitchen. It was midmorning, and Polozkov and I were enjoying a drink and a game of backgammon in the parlor. As in chess, we were fairly evenly matched—though Polozkov had

won a few more backgammon games than I. The three women were
in the kitchen, doing whatever it was they did in there throughout
most of the day, and Mr. Strubel was out somewhere. Polozkov and I
heard the screams, and we rushed from the parlor, my knee clumsily
upsetting the backgammon board that lay on the sofa between us.
Polozkov threw open the kitchen door and the three women were
hugging each other and crying . . . and laughing. Apparently the
shrieks had been ones of joy.

"What is going on?" I said. "What is happening?"

It was some time before they could get hold of their emotions.
They were quite a sight, the three women in braids and aprons,
dancing around, breathless, tears streaming down their cheeks.
Once again I was reminded of that Shakespeare tragedy and of the
three strange sisters who began the conflict in the first place.

Helena finally calmed down enough to speak. "We will tell you,
but you must promise not to say anything to Mr. Strubel. Do you
promise?"

We agreed, irritated and anxious. What is it?

She continued, "Mrs. Strubel is with a child."

We were found dumb. With a child?

"You mean," said Polozkov, "she will be having a baby?"

The women shrieked again, and we took it as an affirmative
response.

"Congratulations," I said. "That is terrific." Polozkov offered his
good wishes too.

We left the women to their celebrating and returned to the
parlor. There was no hope of setting up the backgammon board as
it was before I knocked it, so we agreed to put it away until later and
start afresh. I took my vodka-spiked tea and went to the porch. I
did not bother with my heavy coat. The day was relatively warm
and the sun was out. In fact, I heard the sound of water running in
the house's eaves. The snow was melting; spring would come yet to
the northcountry. I wanted a smoke, but I had left my tobacco and
papers in my big coat. No matter. The tea would suffice. I wondered
if the Strubels had been trying for a child long—probably their
whole marriage, I guessed. If so, this pregnancy was like a miracle. I
thought of Tasha. Did she still pray for a child, or had she given up

on prayer? If one gives up on prayer, is that not the same as giving up on God? I wanted to talk with Tasha about these things but it was inconceivable. We could not have a civil conversation about supper, let alone theology.

To my right was a crash. An icicle longer than my leg had dislodged from the roof and fallen to the ground. It protruded upright from the snow, like a spear in its victim. I noticed Mr. Strubel coming down the walk carrying a crate. It was a crate he always took with him to hold whatever he acquired while out. Recently, the crate had contained empty bottles when he left the house. Apparently glass bottles were in short supply in Iiloskova and returning the empty ones allowed you a discount on new purchases. "Good morning," he called when he noticed me on the porch. I returned his greeting then waited so I could hold the door open for him. As he passed, I noticed two bottles of wine in the crate along with several brown bags—probably dried beans. I thought of the surprise that was in store for him.

I anticipated a new vigor in Mr. Strubel's step when I saw him again. Certainly, if the couple had been trying for a child for many years, they had long since reached the point of wondering whose fault their infertility was. Was the wife incapable of carrying a baby, or was the husband's seed too thin? I knew the question well. I took a drink of my tea and wished that I had seasoned it with more vodka.

I was getting cold in spite of the warmer weather, and I suddenly felt very tired. I was thinking about going in and returning to my bed when the door opened and Helena joined me. She stood next to me and breathed the air. "It is becoming a wonderful day, is it not, Hektr?"

"Yes," I said without emotion, "a wonderful day."

"What is the matter?" she said, looking up and piercing me with her eyes.

I shrugged. "Nothing is the matter. I was just out here thinking."

"Ah," she said, turning her head to look toward the street and the world beyond it. "Thinking can be bad for us. It can cause depression." She seemed to consider her own statement for a moment, then added, "We are better if we can live in the moment. It is the Past and the Future that tend to cause us worry."

"I suppose, but they are with us—all three—whether we think of them or not." It seemed to me her philosophy would have carried more weight if she was not someone who could just as easily be dead, if not for the generosity of strangers. I wanted to say something to the effect but it was too unkind. And I did not feel like being unkind. In fact, I wanted to hold her again but feared being rebuffed. There I was, recalling the past and worrying about the future, secretly proving her point.

Helena returned to her gay mood. "We must do something for the Strubels. This is a joyous day."

"Is it? Another mouth to feed, another soul living at the end of the earth, so near the front."

I could not deter her. "Yes, a new life is joyous—no matter the circumstances. Hektr, I did not suspect you of being a . . . cynic."

"Perhaps just today." I swallowed the last of my tea.

"Then I shall look forward to tomorrow," she said and took my arm. "Have you had baklava?"

"No, is it a drink?"

"A drink? No, it is a dessert, a wonderful dessert. I will not be able to make it precisely, but I think with some dried fruit and the correct . . . dough, I can come very close. Let us speak with the others, and 'pass the plate,' as you say here. Then we can go out and buy what we need."

Helena discreetly went to each of the boarders with her plan and collected coins from each. The Strubels were in their rooms. Undoubtedly, she was breaking the news to him. Then Helena and I put on our coats and hats and went out to buy the needed ingredients. I had been in Iiloskova long enough to know where certain commodities could be had. If I did not know the exact businesses, I knew the streets where to look. Mrs. Strubel had the basics—flour and cooking powder and lard—so we needed only the exotic ingredients.

The day was pleasant, a true harbinger of spring weather, but the boardwalks and streets were messy with melting snow and ice. At first, Helena held her dress to prevent its hem from becoming too wet but it soon was a lost cause. Many people were out, some in a hurry to get somewhere, others just standing about talking. Of course, they were older men, and women and children; Iiloskova's young men were gone, as if taken by some selective plague. In a sense, the war was a plague. It spread, it killed, its origin was unknown. Unlike a plague, however, no one seemed to be working toward a cure.

Helena led our expedition, as she knew what we needed. From place to place, she inquired about inventory, made decisions regarding possible substitutions, haggled with the shopkeepers, then bought the item or not. I carried the canvas bag that held our purchases. Vanilla proved to be the trickiest commodity to obtain, and eventually the most costly. Fortunately, we only needed a few drops of it. Salt was also difficult. The army had used incalculable amounts to preserve the meat shipped to the front. We heard this tale from several proprietors.

I did not know its exact cause—getting outdoors after days spent inside, the sunny sky, the anticipation of making something special for the Strubels—but Helena was positively radiant with happiness. Her skirt was soaked and must have seemed to weigh many pounds and we had spent literally everything she had collected from our fellow lodgers, including a pocketful of Mezenskov's coins I had contributed—yet nothing deterred her good mood. She even deviously made fun of people who passed us on the boardwalk, either contorting her face to exaggerate some feature or mocking the manner of their walk. I chided her insensitivity but it was only part of the game, and we both knew it.

Not just people were out, but animals too. Several horse- or mule-drawn wagons passed in the streets. I noted that most of the animals looked old or tired or sick, which was true of the people also. It had been a long difficult winter, and a long difficult war. The animal traffic added manure to the slushy mess in the streets. Helena was pointing out one especially poor creature, a badly swaybacked old horse, when a look of great surprise came over her face and her mood instantly changed, like the sun being taken over by a stormcloud. "Hektr," she said, pulling at my arm, "let us go in here." There was urgency in her voice. I glanced toward the street and beyond to the other boardwalk but I saw nothing to explain her sudden change in mood. It was only as the door was shutting behind me that I realized where Helena had dragged me: the whorehouse I had encountered on my first night in Iiloskova, when I was lost and afraid in the strange city.

Helena did not notice where we were, or care. As soon as the door was shut she turned and peered outside from behind the heavy shade covering the door's glass.

"Helena, what is it? What did you see?"

She had no interest in discussing anything at the moment. Meanwhile, I looked around inside; my eyes were having trouble adjusting to the subdued lighting. There were a couple of women sitting on sofas in a room just off the foyer. The whores may have been sixteen or sixty—my eyes could not tell yet. A man came forward in a dark-colored business suit; his heels were loud on the foyer floor. "Good day, may I help you?" he asked. I had the feeling it was Doctor Zitch from the sanatorium but it was not. It was just that this man also had dark hair, a goatee and eyeglasses. My brain made the combination form a picture of Doctor Zitch.

I glanced at Helena. She was still peeking outdoors. "My friend and I," I said, not knowing how I would finish the sentence, "are looking for the candlemaker." The sentence itself did not make perfect sense.

"The candlemaker?" he repeated.

"Yes, we are in the market for candles."

"This is not a candleshop."

"I see." And I did see better; my eyes were adjusting. This was a much older man that Doctor Zitch, and heavier. The two whores watching us, glad for a diversion perhaps, were fairly young women—in their twenties—but it was still difficult to tell because of their painted faces. "I apologize," I said, wanting to leave; however, as I looked at Helena, she did not appear on the verge of stepping outside. "Is the candlemaker next door?"

"I know of no candlemaker," the man said, beginning to sound irritated.

"That is strange. We were informed there was a candlemaker in this street. Were we not, dear?" I had introduced Helena as my friend, and now she was my wife: Lying was not my greatest strength. "Dear?" I continued.

Helena made some noise—affirmative or negative, it was

impossible to say—but at least I knew she was paying some attention to the situation.

One of the women spoke without getting up from the sofa: "In the next street over, there is a wax-man, I believe." She pointed nebulously with her red-painted finger.

"That direction?" I too motioned ambiguously.

"No; that way."

The man's irritation was mounting. His cheeks were becoming as red as the whore's fingernails. "Yes, that way," he said. "Now I recall, one street over, that way." He would say anything to make us leave the premises.

"Ah . . . that way. It is that way, dear," I said to Helena, who let go of the shade and opened the door. "Thank you," I said to the man and the helpful whore as we returned to the boardwalk. While one part of my brain was occupied with the ludicrous story about the candlemaker, another part was trying very hard to discern the meaning of Helena's actions. My suspicions of her being in trouble with the authorities came back to me full force. Then again, there was that missing time, between the train's arrival in Iiloskova and Helena's turning up at the Luminarium dead drunk, nearly literally. Had she made an enemy or two in Iiloskova in that little time? Of course, there is no requisite amount of time for making an enemy. Friendship usually takes awhile, days or even years; but enmity can develop in an instant.

Of the two possibilities, trouble with the authorities seemed more likely. The only problem with my thesis was that I had not encountered a policeman during my entire time in Iiloskova. Therefore, whom had Helena seen on the street? Outside again, and making our way back to Division Street, her mood had definitely been affected by the episode. Instead of carefree and comical, Helena was nervous. Her brilliant eyes darted back and forth. She rushed along, often bumping into people, her apologies quick and quiet. I wanted to ask what had happened but it was clearly not the time.

Then I realized her quandary. On the one hand, she was looking for someone; on the other, someone was looking for her, or so she believed. To accomplish the one, she must leave the sanctuary of our pension, but to avoid the other, staying off the streets was necessary.

I suddenly felt we were not equal in our slothfulness.

We were soon returned to Division Street. As we got to the pension's walk, I said, "What happened back there? Who was after you?"

At first it appeared she was going to ignore my query altogether, but then said, "I thought I saw someone from my past. It could not be, however. I am at the 'edge of the earth,' as you say. How could he be here too? It is just my imagination; I am more fatigued than I realized."

"If you are in trouble, I can help." It was more wishful thinking than truth. What could I do? Write a poem about her problems?

Helena smiled and patted my arm. "Thank you, Hektr, but I am fine."

We entered the pension. The others, except for the Strubels, were in the parlor. They asked if we were successful, and I held up the bag. Helena immediately went upstairs to change out of her soaking skirt. I went and sat by the coal-burner, propping my feet up close to the heat. Polozkov brought me a drink, which I appreciated. The others returned to their games and conversations; meanwhile, I thought about Helena. It was remarkable that she had traveled all this way, with no resources to speak of. Then I realized she did have a resource, a very valuable one: herself. The way she had captivated us must have been how she survived. She had arrived penniless and underdressed for the climate; now she had a roof over her head and food on her plate and proper clothing.

And in return, she had given us . . . a life, instead of mere existence. She had given us joy. All in all, it was a fair trade.

Shortly, the Strubels emerged from their rooms and came into the parlor. They were holding hands, looking as shy as newlyweds. Everyone congratulated Mr. Strubel. He blushed beneath his big mustaches. Helena appeared behind them, then she called Mirska and Mrs. Strubel into the kitchen. She could purchase the ingredients for the dessert in secret but she could not make it in secret. The three women would have great fun trying to coax the mismatched ingredients into baklava. We were all so starved for sweets that whatever they concocted would be much appreciated; besides, only Helena would know how close they came to the genuine article.

While the preparations were going forward, Mr. Strubel joined the men in the parlor. He and Polozkov played chess. I watched the landlord surreptitiously. How did a newly expectant father act? Pregnant women were said to have a certain radiance. What about fathers-to-be? Mr. Strubel did not seem especially happy. Of course, he was losing badly to Polozkov. He was drinking more energetically than usual, and the heat was rising to his face—providing him a certain rosiness, if not radiance, after all.

I too was feeling warm. And sleepy. I thought of going upstairs for my nap but I also thought of the task awaiting me in my room, of the leaves of paper void of my words. I decided dozing in my chair in the parlor until supper time was a good plan. And I must have done just that, as in no time Mirska was shaking my arm and telling me to wash before going to the table. My neck and back were stiff, reminiscent of my interminable train ride to Iiloskova. I did not look forward to the laborious return trip.

Supper was good: twice-boiled potatoes and a soup of turnips and carrots in a chicken-fat stock. Everyone ate heartily, but also quickly and did not ask for a second portion—we were all anticipating the dessert, which had filled the whole house with a lovely aroma in the late afternoon. When the dinner plates were cleared, Helena and Mrs. Strubel brought in the baklava on two large platters. I was not sure what to expect—something like a pie perhaps—and the dessert was not wholly dissimilar. It was a pastry with a pie-crust-like shell filled with sweetened fruit and nuts. It was topped with a glaze of some sort.

"It is not perfect," Helena said as everyone received a portion.

Mr. Strubel came from the kitchen with two steaming pots of coffee—another surprise on this day of surprises. The coffee was a bit weak but still a perfect addition to the baklava, which was very delicious. After so much time without sweets, the dessert was nothing short of ambrosial. We were all torn between the competing desires to bolt down the baklava and to slowly savor it which was not unlike, I thought, the twin desires of the sex act—proceed with gusto, or to hold back and prolong the pleasure.

Afterward, the metaphor continued, as I was overcome with a sense of euphoria. Bandits could force their way into the house and make off with all our valuables, and I would not care at all. We all thanked Helena profusely for the dessert. She actually blushed at the accolades.

Later, we all played charades in the parlor. Helena appeared off her game as others won time and again. I suspected she was allowing others to be first. I very much appreciated her deceit. We were drinking the last of the wine in the house. Helena had cautioned Mrs. Strubel against drinking too much. We thought her silly because we all knew the medicinal benefits of good wine. Perhaps expectant women avoiding wine was a custom of her strange homeland—wherever that was. Nevertheless, Mrs. Strubel heeded Helena's warning and drank very little. Mr. Strubel, on the other hand, was drunker than I had ever seen him. He was trying to teach us bawdy songs from his teenage years and hugging everyone, especially Helena, whom perhaps he considered like a sister-in-law.

Helena was good-natured about his pawing her, though she was starting to look a bit disheveled, like she had been wrestling with a bear cub. She excused herself from his grasp to use the washroom but then stopped at the parlor doorway. We were all looking at her. What?

"Listen," she said, raising her hand to silence us.

I thought perhaps she was hearing the cannonade of artillery again, then I heard it too—like a sputtering engine. The sound grew louder and louder until it was in the street in front of the house. We went to the front door, except for Mr. Strubel who had slid to a sitting position on the floor. We stepped out onto the porch and saw a truck in the street. It came to a full stop with a noisy backfire and puff of smoke. In the moonlight, the contraption might have been a funeral hearse. A dark figure came down from the steering compartment. The figure appeared to have a single red eye ablaze in the night.

The figure saw us on the porch, a group of silhouettes. "Hektr? Is Hektr Pastrovich among you?" he called.

I did not respond for a moment, though the voice was familiar. "Lieutenant Bushkov?" I finally said.

"None other," the navy-man responded, coming into the weak light that spilled from inside the house. The single red eye was in fact his ubiquitous cigar. He had on a heavy coat and hat which looked black but were probably blue. Piping on the coat appeared to be the color of moonlight. "True to my word, I said I would let you know when I had means to convey you to the front. I have means." He motioned toward the truck. His words came out in a cloud of smoke, as if spoken by a dragon. "Some dispatches arrived this afternoon."

I felt Helena's hand slip into mine.

"Will you not come in," said Mrs. Strubel. "You must be froze."

"Thank you, madam, but it is best not to let the Daimler rest for very long—it may never come to life again."

I noticed that there was someone else in the steering compartment, an assistant of Bushkov's no doubt.

The lieutenant said, "The driver is returning to the front tomorrow. You are welcome to join him, but I cannot say when you might be able to come back to Iiloskova."

Yes, I want to go—then I realized I had not said it aloud: "Yes, I want to go." Helena squeezed my hand.

"I am afraid I cannot come round to get you. The truck will be loaded with supplies. Can you get to the bureau office by midmorning?"

"Yes, of course."

"Good. Remember to be prepared for a considerable stay. And I am told winter is still very much in control at the front."

Lieutenant Bushkov touched his hat to the ladies and began to depart. He stopped in the moonlit yard and turned. "I nearly forgot, Hektr. I received a message from your editor this afternoon as well. He inquired of your well being—I can now say you are fine—and one other thing, but the telegrapher must have gotten it wrong. The boy who brought the message said the wires were fickle because of the snow."

"What is that?" I said to Bushkov's darkened figure.

"It merely stated, 'prince out.' Does that make any sense at all?"

"No," I lied. "It must have been garbled." Helena's hand was trembling, and felt like a chunk of ice in my palm. It was only a partial lie—why would Mezenskov bother with such information?

"Well, I will see you tomorrow." He reached the truck and pulled himself into the steering compartment. The motor belched to life, and in a moment Lieutenant Bushkov and his assistant were gone.

Only the putrid smell of the Daimler's smoke remained.

XII

'An ignorant soul shall inquire of your "winnowing fan."'

Odyssey 11

IN MY ROOM, I put the empty leaf of paper away in my valise. I did not want to take all of my possessions to the front, yet I did not want to pay for a room I was not using. I was sure the Strubels would store some things for me while I was absent. Surely it would be no more than a few days. I thought about packing but there was no need. I had very little to prepare and would have ample time in the morning. Besides, I was very tired. The wine had hit me quite suddenly after Bushkov's departure. Polozkov and Kritch helped Mr. Strubel to his rooms. The landlord was nearly as listless as Helena was on the night we brought her to the pension. Helena and Mirska assisted Mrs. Strubel in tidying the parlor and kitchen. Meanwhile, I had gone to my room.

I took off my shoes and my vest and crawled between the covers. Perhaps I lay there awake thinking, or I lay dreaming—but in either case my mind was on the Prince of Ithaka. He was at large, if indeed that was Mezenskov's message. Did the Prince escape custody or was he released? I had this view of him scaling walls and donning disguises and knocking guards over the head. But the authorities may have decided their jails were too full already and merely handed the lunatic a few coins and deposited him on the street, saving themselves some effort and money in the long run.

I had a strange feeling as I lay in bed, dozing or not. I could not identify it at first. I thought it should be fear; after all, in a few hours I was headed into a war zone. Or it should have been homesickness—I had been gone for several days, and it would most likely be several more before I returned on the train. Lust was a likely candidate too. It had been some weeks since I had been with a woman, and I felt an attraction to Helena. Her eyes captivated me. I thought, if we make love, I want it to be in the light of day so that I can see her electric eyes all the while. But lust was not what I was feeling either.

Then it came to me: I was feeling self-satisfaction. Mezenskov had sent me north to report the war firsthand and I was finally doing my job. My real job—not my underhanded, self-appointed job of writing for *The Nightly Observer*, to increase my name in circulation and fatten my wallet.

Speaking of which, how much money did I have left? I was definitely awake now. I had squirreled money away in so many places I had lost track of it. I got out of bed and lighted the oil lamp on the table. I went through my various pockets, my valise, and the hole in the mattress I had discovered a few days earlier. My money was in notes and coins, and I arranged it all neatly on the table as I counted. The total was not a lot but I had faith it would be enough. I only needed enough for the train ticket home, a bit to pay the Strubels for holding my things, and perhaps some bribe money at the front. I would be all right. I redistributed the money to the various pockets and the valise (but not the mattress), and prepared to sleep again.

I was about to extinguish the lamp when I heard a gentle tap at my door. Then I heard Helena's voice: "Hektr, are you yet awake?"

I opened the door part way. "Yes—are you all right?"

The hall was dark except for the light from the candle she held in a tarnished brass holder. "I am all right. May I talk to you, or are you too sleepy?" She still smelled sweetly of the baklava.

"No . . . I mean yes—please come in." I stood aside then closed the door.

She went to the window and looked out as if she could really see something besides her own occult reflection in the dirty glass. I pulled out the chair from the table, on which she had placed her candle, and sat. After a moment, Helena turned to me, wringing her small hands. "Hektr, I have a request to make of you—as if you have not done enough for me already."

I regretted that the lamplight was too low for me to see her beautiful eyes. "Yes, what is your request?"

"You know I am looking for someone, that that is why I am here. I believe this person may be in the war. May I accompany you to . . . the front? I will not be trouble for you."

"First, who is this someone, and why would he be at the front?" Tasha always complained that I could never just talk to people, that I had to interview them. Perhaps she had a point.

Helena said, "You assume I am looking for a man."

I waited. The room had grown cold while I dozed; the coals were nearly spent.

"I do not know why I believe he is at the front—I just have a . . . feeling."

I thought of her extraordinary abilities divining the answers to charades. "You want to risk your life going to the war zone because of a feeling?"

"Yes, very much." Her voice seemed to quaver. Was it from the chilly room, or did she fear I would deny her? I had a feeling of my own—that she would be going to the front one way or another. Helena had made it as far as Iiloskova; she would get to the front if she desired it enough. I said,

"I do not know what I can do for you. My resources are very limited."

"I understand completely. Help me to get to the front, then you can rid yourself of me. I will be . . . on my own." She was quite in earnest.

I envied Helena's pluck, if not her common sense. "I will not abandon you at the front. You know I will not."

She smiled. "Yes, Hektr, you are correct. I know you will not abandon me."

"You are a fool to ask, and I am a fool to say yes."

Helena came to the chair and hugged me around the neck, pressing my cheek into her bosom. "Thank you, Hektr. You make me want to believe the gods are watching over me after all."

I squeezed her arm. "We need our rest. I have no idea where we will be sleeping tomorrow night."

"Quite so." She released me. "I will be ready in the morning. Just let me know when it is time to depart." She took her candle and left my room.

I no longer felt tired. I fixed a cigarette and lighted it with the lamp before blowing out the flame. I lay in the dark smoking and thinking, trying to relax. But my mind was running so, I thought a game of chess with Polozkov might slow its wheels. I listened intensely in the dark; I detected no movement in the house whatsoever. I heard only a periodic gust of chill wind that threw snow- and ice-dust against my window. I recalled the pixie dust I once mused the soldiers were using at the front. I would find out, firsthand. I waited for the feeling of self-satisfaction, of achievement, to come again. Instead I now felt foolish and weak for agreeing to take Helena there. It seemed that women always managed to dampen my spirit—though not always through their own fault. I was unnaturally susceptible to their charms. Here I thought of *charms* in the occult sense too, not simply as *charming*. My mind ran to images of Tasha and of her black art, for surely there was something malignant at the core of her womanly magic. I inhaled the smoke of my cigarette and forced my memory to find Tasha the young village girl that I courted and wooed and asked to marry me with my heart quite in my throat for fear she would deny me. Yes, I desired her, Natasha Alexandra Korunova, in her peasant dress tight at the bosom and her wooden-soled shoes that clopped along the street like horses' unshod hooves. She had come to the city to study to be a typist, to become mistress of the highest of business sciences. What were her hopes? The topic never seemed to come up in our conversations—perhaps I was too intensely focused on the roundness of her breasts beneath the simple blouse to engage in anything more than small talk. Wait . . . that is not true. I talked of my hopes; I told her about my desires to become an important writer, a poet especially. Of giving readings in the great halls of Europe, of having myopic university students discuss the workings of my mind and publishing erudite papers about my words. Yes—there is the truth finally. I thought only of my desire for greatness and of Tasha's lovely breasts.

Hm . . . here I am, not too far from being an old man, and I have neither desire of my youth. My cigarette had burned down to my fingers. I put it out against the wooden floor. Then I fell asleep listening to pixie dust against the window.

At least my sleep was not restless. Tapping at the door woke me and I had not moved during the night. Gray light came through the window. I tried to call out to my visitor to wait a moment but my voice was thick. I went to the door stiffly and heavily, trying to clear my throat. I thought it would be Helena but Polozkov stood in the cold hall. He said, "Mr. Pastrovich, I was asked to rouse everyone. The ladies are preparing a feast for your departure. It has snowed somewhat heavily in the night, so you may want to start your journey all the sooner." Polozkov was holding a cup and saucer, and he handed them to me. "Mrs. Strubel has made some tea for you."

Taking the tea, I thanked him and turned back to my room to finish packing my things and readying myself. The tea was very good, though not especially hot; Mrs. Strubel had sweetened it with drops of honey. It helped to clear the thickness from my throat. A feast, eh? Of course, what counts for a feast in the northcountry is only a moderate meal elsewhere. Still, my stomach rumbled at the thought of it. In a few minutes I was ready. I had packed an extra shirt and undergarment in the pouch pocket of my valise. I found my red tie on the back of the chair where it had hung since the night we brought Helena to the pension. I folded it loosely and placed it in the pocket inside my coat. I doubted that I would need a formal tie but who could tell? I wore my heaviest trousers, vest and jacket—though they were the shoddiest of my apparel. Where I was going, warmth was more important than appearance. The remainder of my clothes I folded and placed in my suitcase, which I would leave with the Strubels. I considered leaving behind my manuscript of poems. I knew it was silly to drag the heavy sheaf of papers to the front but I could not part from them.

In the hall I could already smell the sausages that had been fried. I went downstairs with my overweight valise in one hand and my heavy coat folded over the other arm. I heard all the excited voices in the dining room and kitchen. I left my things in the parlor, next to a small canvas bag that I presumed to be Helena's. She did not arrive with luggage, so it must have been a bag given to her by Mrs. Strubel. They had become fast friends, and I was certain the landlady would be sorry to see her go, especially now that she was expecting. The Strubels' baby was due before the end of summer. I had difficulty imagining Iiloskova in its summer finery, surrounded by green fields and dotted here and there with beds of wildflowers. I also had difficulty imagining the Strubels as parents. But the baby and summer were coming—I did not feel so sure of my own future, nor Helena's.

"There you are at last, Hektr," said Helena as I came into the dining room. "I did not know you were such a tired-head."

Everyone laughed, and Mirska corrected her good-naturedly: "You mean 'sleepyhead.' You did not know Hektr was such a *sleepyhead.*" Mirska's hair was braided just as Helena had taught her.

"Whatever," said Helena, trying to sound irritated. "Now everyone sit down before breakfast becomes of ice."

I sat at the table with the other men, including Mr. Strubel, and soon the ladies were bringing out plates of sausages, griddle cakes, and fried potatoes and eggs with chopped onions. There were also biscuits and canned jams and jellies. Perhaps the greatest delight of all was steaming black coffee that Mrs. Strubel poured from a heavy glass pitcher. Extra chairs were set at the table so that everyone could eat together. The table was crowded with plates and cups and active hands as we ate and passed items back and forth. It was a feast as promised.

Kritch, brushing crumbs from his beard, asked, "So, Hektr, how long will you be away do you think?" Everyone was wondering but no one had said it until now. It was a moot question really, because as soon as I returned to Iiloskova I would be leaving for home, leaving for good. Besides, what they really wanted to know was when I would be bringing Helena back to them. In her absence they would mill about like termites in their queenless termitary. I thought for a moment what it would be like to stay here in the northcountry, perhaps to find work with Lieutenant Bushkov, to be with Helena, to stay in touch with the Strubels, and Kritch, Polozkov and Mirska. It would not be the same, of course. After all, we were all just lodgers at a pension—travelers who would go our separate ways inevitably. Was the world not one large pension? And were we not all temporary lodgers there? I was becoming philosophical, as if drunk on good food and strong coffee.

"I cannot predict," I answered. "Transportation is irregular to say the least."

"True," said Kritch, drinking down the hot coffee, his eyes watery, perhaps from the warmth of the dining room. "True," he said again, after setting down his cup, as if the word warranted repeating.

Breakfast went too quickly. Helena and I offered to help clean up but we were told we must hurry to the news office; they were right of course. There were hugs and handshakes and kisses on our cheeks and good wishes for us. Then we were outside the pension, crunching through the new-fallen snow, fogging the cold air with our breath. Our shoes in the snow was the only noise we made. We did not talk; there was nothing to say. I wondered if a cart would come by that we could commandeer for a few coins. But it seemed no one was out, and we walked the whole way to the news bureau in silence.

On the way, I wondered who would be our driver—certainly not Lieutenant Bushkov. I suspected he had no desire to go to the front. Iiloskova was close enough for him. I imagined a grizzled veteran of the war, with a wiry beard, a scar upon his face, maybe even missing an eye. The news bureau office was just as before, except that the truck sat in the street, its motor rumbling in the cold. The snow beneath its tailpipe was black. Early in the war there was a newspaper story about the specially built Daimlers the army had purchased, with totally enclosed steering compartments, metal plates affixed to the wooden bodies, and speeds that exceeded twenty miles in one hour. Here was one such mechanical marvel. A sheet of canvas had been fastened tight over the back of the truck, thus hiding its contents. I imagined it to be full of supplies for the war effort; yet I could not think what those supplies might be, or where one would obtain a full supply of anything in Iiloskova.

I directed Helena toward the bureau door with a wave of my hand. Bushkov must have been listening for the door, for as soon as we were inside he called from his office. "Hektr! Come back here!" We put our cases in the cold foyer and went to the navy-man's voice. I let Helena enter his office first. Lieutenant Bushkov, in a cloud of cigar smoke, was visibly surprised to see a woman walk through his door. There was another fellow in his office, a white-faced boy with white-blond hair. He wore a dirty army coat and had a corporal's insignia on his sleeve, though it half hung by a few threads as if someone had tried to tear off the patch; this child must be our driver.

I introduced my companion and said she would be traveling with me to the front. Bushkov and the young corporal were obviously curious but asked no questions. The corporal's name was Smenov. Bushkov said he was a "local boy," meaning he was from Iiloskova originally. All I could think was that "boy" was right. Bushkov insisted we have a drink "for the road." I figured I would have to swallow some of his poisonous vodka, but he went to a cabinet in the corner of his office and brought out a large crystal decanter. He blew dust from it as he brought it back to his desk. There were four mismatched glasses upside down on a bureau by the window, their upside-downness implying they were clean. "Cognac," Bushkov said as he poured the golden brown liquid into the glasses. He handed Helena and me each a half-filled glass, then one for the corporal and one for himself. Bushkov offered us a toast of "god's speed" and we drank the cognac, which was very smooth and good. It warmed me immediately, only the way that quality liquor can. With the second swallow, my ears began to buzz pleasantly, and the lovely smell of the cognac lingered in my nose. Helena's fair skin flushed pink; so did Smenov's cheeks, where not even a hint of peach fuzz grew.

Lieutenant Bushkov handed me a folded sheet of paper that had been on his messy desk and said it was a letter of introduction for the commander. Then he wanted to refill our glasses, but this time it was my turn to insist. "Thank you, my friend, but we must be going. I want to arrive at the front in full daylight." I put the letter in my coat.

"Of course, of course." He took our empty glasses and saw us out the door to the waiting truck. "Travel well," he said as Smenov took his place at the wheel and Helena climbed in too. There was a narrow seat behind the front seat, and Helena claimed it for herself. There were old army-green blankets piled on the half-seat, and Helena immediately placed one around her legs. I waved to Lieutenant Bushkov as I closed the truck's heavy door with a rusty squeal. I positioned my valise and Helena's bag on the wide seat between Smenov and me. The young corporal wrestled the truck into its first gear and we began bumping along the frozen street. The truck had a mirror on my side, another innovation of German engineering, and I looked to see if Bushkov remained on the boardwalk, perhaps waving to us or even saluting us, but the mirror was angled for the driver's view and all I saw were the upper windows of buildings that we passed. They appeared empty of course, in spite of the noise the truck made as it jolted its way along the rutted street.

Helena offered me one of the old blankets. At first I started to say no thank you but changed my mind and she handed it forward. I then wondered if these blankets had ever been used for the wounded or the dead. The blanket now on my lap was so mottled with stains it was impossible to tell what was what. The blanket was frozen, so I suspected that as my body heat thawed its fibers, it would begin to emit all kinds of unpleasant odors. For some reason the blanket symbolized in my mind where we were headed, more than the beaten-up truck and more than young Smenov even. The "northern front" had been an abstraction in my mind for so long, like fairyland, like heaven, or like hell . . . that it was difficult to believe I was on my way there. But the old green blanket, with its frayed edges and cigarette holes, made it real. My stomach began to turn, and I wondered if the Strubels' good-intentioned breakfast was such a sound idea after all.

We were passing out of Iiloskova and into the countryside; the transformation was immediate and distinct. The buildings and city streets ended abruptly and we were on a narrow country lane cut into the snow. A dead-looking tree plunged out of the snow here and there, and in the distance there would be a tumble-down farmhouse etched on the white horizon now and again. Otherwise, the three of us in our noisy truck were alone in the world. I searched the bare tree limbs for crows at least but even the rooks had abandoned this place of ice and death. I shivered, though I do not think from the cold.

After a time, I noticed that Helena was asleep. The skin of her face was so pure and pale it was almost literally white; she appeared to be a thing related to the snow that stretched in all directions. For a moment, before I could keep my brain from doing so, I imagined that if Helena were lying naked in the snow she would be virtually invisible. The image was too weird and macabre, and I forced it from my mind's eye. I willed myself to think of some other picture . . . of a honeybee in a yellow blossom, then of a brown scorpion in the sand. I shut my eyes against the pure white light, the reflected snowlight, and tried to think of nothing at all.

Then I slept, thanks to my full belly and the good cognac. I dreamt of an ocean that appeared to stretch to infinity toward every compass point, and of a ship that bumped along on the waves, and of believing I had spotted land but it was just the clouds in my sleepy eyes. I blinked my closed eyes, and time after time the mirage disappeared like smoke on the wind.

I awoke because I felt the pressure of a hand on my shoulder. At first I thought it must be Smenov, the young driver, getting my attention for some purpose. Then I realized it was Helena's delicate hand without its wool mitten. I looked back at her and she appeared to be sleeping still. She had felt the need to be comforted, or to comfort me. I slipped off my right glove and placed my hand over hers. Helena's fingers were icy and rigid, like crooked sticks protruding from a frozen pond. We stayed that way for some time, until the truck hit an especially deep rut in the road and we were all jostled violently for an instant. When we settled, Helena, only partially awake, drew her hand beneath her blanket.

I spoke to Smenov for the first time since we started our journey. "So you are from Iiloskova, eh?"

He nodded once, keeping his eyes stitched to the wide road that wound out before him.

"It must have been a bustling place in your youth." In your youth—I may as well have said "last year" or "last week."

Smenov nodded once, but kind of at an angle, indicating "kind of bustling" perhaps.

The journalist in me was drawn to the challenge of a reluctant interview, but I felt too anxious to summon the necessary focus. Just then the truck hit another severe bump in the road, and something heavy shifted noisily in the back of the truck. Smenov seemed unconcerned, so I suspected it was not explosives that we transported to the front.

I began thinking about that phrase: "the front." In fact, "the northern front"—as if there were others. It sounded forward and progressive, as if we were pushing out, moving on. But there was no sense of progression. It was a defensive front. Probably "the trench" would have been more accurate—"the northern trench." My mind wandered: "the northern imaginary line," "the northern state of mind between us and them," "the northern self-deception regarding our civility and their barbarity." Or simply: "the northern fantasy." And for that matter, it was more northeastern, but that certainly did not roll off the tongue. Besides, there was civility and high culture in the East: art, music, philosophy, literature. We would not want to imply such pedigree, or even near-pedigree, for our enemy. They were just from the north: tree-choppers, blubber-chewers, and seal-fuckers. I recalled a poem by a Greek which translated to something like "Waiting for the Barbarians"; I edited, "Waiting for the Seal-Fuckers." It, admittedly, did not have the same ring.

I tried to envision the front physically. What would it be? Tents, trenches, and rough-hewn cabins for the officers? I remembered seeing a painting in a geography textbook at school, an American painting titled *Valley Forge*. I realized that I imagined the front like that—cabins and kettle fires and freezing soldiers dressed in rags. The long-suffering but resolute looks on the soldiers' faces made the picture stick in my mind.

XIII

Quieting themselves, they took their seats.

Iliad 2

ON GOOD ROADS—though the concept of *good* roads may have been foreign in the northcountry—the front should only have been about three hours from Iiloskova. I checked my watch and discovered that we had been traveling for nearly six. I did not want to seem an impatient child by asking how long before we reach our destination, but I could tell nothing from our young driver's demeanor. It had not changed throughout the trip. He continued to stare straight ahead at the rutted white road, his lower lip slightly agape. He only changed position and expression for an instant as we encountered an especially deep pot-hole.

"To whom will we be reporting?" I finally asked, reaching a compromise with myself.

Smenov roused himself from the road's enthrallment to answer. "The commander." He blinked at the white road as if aware for the first time of its brightness.

"And who would that be?" I felt myself becoming irritated at his idiotic response.

Smenov looked to the snow and ice for an answer, then: "Commander Zlavik."

"Commander Zlavik himself." There had been surprisingly few reports about the supreme commander of the army, Anton Zlavik. I did not know how to take this fact, as an indication that he was a man who valued his privacy, or as some sort of government subterfuge. I was about to inquire about Zlavik, the man, when my eye caught something strange on the horizon, which had become blue-white. It seemed to be a farm of some sort. Even though it was some distance—the snow made gauging nearly impossible—I could discern a tall house, probably two levels; and a large barn with a conical roof. There also appeared to be several smaller structures around both the house and barn. Who would live out here . . . virtually on the rim of the Arctic continent? And what could one farm? Fields of summer tundra and herds of minks to care for in winter? I dubbed the place "Mink Farm." We passed by the tiny settlement, which appeared to be cut off by the snow. I was surprised the army had not taken it over as an outpost of some sort. As I took one last glimpse of Mink Farm I discovered there were wisps of smoke coming from the house's chimney, so it was not abandoned. The hearty Mink Farmers were still hard at work.

My mind wandered, my thoughts like ghosts cavorting on the snowfields beyond the truck's frosty window glass. I wondered about our friends left behind at the pension on Division Street, about Tasha and even about Mezenskov back home ("home" seemed to be becoming a meaningless abstraction), and I thought about the Prince of Ithaka, imagined him trudging through the snow—traveling, forever traveling, he said. I glanced out my side window believing, for an instant, I would see him there along the road. Of course I did not. The unabated white was affecting my reason. I had heard of "snowmadness"; now I was starting to understand it.

My thoughts were interrupted by Smenov braking the truck. There were two sentries in the road. A sawhorse barricade painted in red and black stripes stood between the soldiers, who carried long rifles—P57s, I believe the model was called. The "P" was for Pachrov, the gun's inventor; I was not sure about the "57"—perhaps it was Pachrov's fifty-seventh version. The barricade was a mere prop. It was of so little substance it would have snapped like a twig under the truck's tires. The army was apparently unconcerned about a rear attack. The sentries themselves appeared to be twins: ill-kept beards on sunken cheeks, eyes wild from the wind and ceaseless white. I suspected their frames were skeletal but it was impossible to say because of their layers of army clothes. Instead of hoods, they wore strips of green-gray cloth wrapped around their heads, like an infidel's turban. The headgear was no doubt fashioned from discarded pants and shirts.

Smenov opened his door to speak with the soldier who came forward, his P57 held casually in his gloved hands. "Supplies," said Smenov nebulously. The soldier was about to routinely nod when he realized the driver was not alone. At first he saw me next to Smenov (I smiled ridiculously), then his ice-bitten eyes noticed Helena in the back half-seat.

Smenov, a boy of few words, said, "Journalists," as if that made it all perfectly clear. And he shut his door with a rusty and impatient-sounding crunch. The sentry signaled his twin to move the old sawhorse aside. Smenov found his gear and we rolled ahead. After a minute or two we rounded a bend in the road and the army encampment appeared before us, a collection of crudely constructed shelters—all part tent, lean-to, and shack in varying degrees. The structures were all of white canvas, like sailcloth; or of wood that had been washed white—so, spread among the thin forest of spruce trees, the makeshift shelters appeared as ghostly domiciles in the northern wilderness. I imagined that if I blinked and cleared my vision, the shelters would vanish like mirages.

I expected there to be more soldiers milling about but only a few figures, dressed in brown or dark green or gray, could be seen. Perhaps their inconspicuous color scheme was working and I could not discern them in the forest of spruce. Smenov maneuvered the big truck among the spectral tents and brought it to a halt next to two other similar vehicles. "Here we are," he said, cutting the truck's laboring engine.

"Home sweet home," I added before looking back at Helena, who was gazing through the truck's dirty side window. I climbed down from the truck then helped Helena do the same. Bags in hand, we went to the rear of the truck where Smenov was undoing the knotted straps that secured the canvas flap. The boy-soldier was engrossed in his occupation and paid no attention to Helena and me. After a moment of standing there in the packed snow I said, "Thank you for the ride, corporal. Where can we find the commanding officer?"

134 ～ Men of Winter

He gestured to his right, not taking his eyes from the Oriental-puzzle straps, and said, "Command is about a quarter mile." I noticed that the effort to untie the straps had bloodied his raw fingers.

Helena and I began following a footpath in the snow that seemed to lead more or less in the direction Smenov indicated. There was an array of intersecting paths, like the workings of a net—or like Helena's intricately braided hair, which was now hidden beneath a hat of black wool. The day had grown cold. The tall spruce and a gauzy layer of clouds blocked the sunlight. Plus, I reminded myself, we were farther north. Farther north than Iiloskova! It did not seem possible: Iiloskova had always marked the end of the world for me, for everyone, except perhaps the Iiloskovites. I was in the fairyland, but there was no pixie dust and no magic—unless it was a dark magic.

Helena and I approached a group of soldiers going in the opposite direction. Their heads were down but they noticed us and stared strangely. No doubt they were not used to civilian visitors, yet they said nothing as we passed each other on the path of ice. Beyond their earshot, I said to Helena, "I feel the foreigner for certain."

"I always 'feel the foreigner,' as you say it." She did not look up from the path.

It reminded me of how little I knew this woman with whom I had entered the war zone. Perhaps I should have refused her and come to the front alone. But that would have been impossible; she had a strange power over me. Over everyone it seemed. I wondered briefly what they were doing at the pension on Division Street. I suspected, in general, they were missing Helena.

Helena touched my sleeve. "I am just thinking: our friends are having their afternoon tea and playing games."

The queer timing of Helena's observation unnerved me and I did not know what to say. Fortunately, I lost my footing on the path for a second and it altered the course of the conversation as Helena advised me, mother-hen-like, to be careful. "Yes," I said, "a sprained ankle would not do out here." I realized that I had not known what to expect *out here*, at the front, but this was not it so far. Where is the fighting? Where does it take place? Where is the enemy? Where are the wounded? I supposed all would be clear in due course.

We had been walking for what seemed to me an appropriate

distance to reach Command, yet no structure presented itself as such. A soldier happened by, a boy looking not much older than Smenov, and I asked for directions. Without speaking, he waved his hand, wrapped in strips of brown wool, at a tent-shack of modest size tucked between two giant spruce. We thanked the young soldier, who continued dumbly on his way. The path dipped a bit, making it difficult to keep our footing, as we completed our walk to Command. It occurred to me: all the stories I read about the war, all the rumors I heard—and some that I helped spread—originated, in a sense, from this one haphazardly erected structure in the snow. All that was the war and the front and death and deprivation resided in this tent-shack, whose angled white roof I could see now was speckled with spruce needles that tinted it blue. Perhaps the meager daylight, filtered through the living needles on the trees, added to the effect: for the more I looked at the structure the more it seemed to emit a bluish glow, an almost otherworldly radiance. No doubt some optical trickery of the snow contributed to the effect as well.

I glanced at Helena to say something about the phenomenon but held my tongue when I saw that her face had taken on the bluish cast too. I tried to clear my vision but her corpselike complexion remained. She noticed my gaze of course. I just smiled and said, "Almost there" as I returned my sight forward.

I imagined there would be guards posted in front of Command or at least the bustle of officers in and out but it was as lifeless as Bushkov's newspaper bureau. We reached the structure and I was surprised to find a heavy and ornately carved door at its entrance. I wondered that the flimsy framework could even support the ponderous door. A fishing scene was depicted in the carved wood. First the sea, the rippling waves rendered in two dimensions, then men launching a boat. My eyes skimmed over the wooden tableau . . . no, not a fishing scene . . . whaling. The creature they hunted dwarfed the fishing boat. Water erupted from its blowhole in a shape that, carved by itself, might have evoked the full bloom of a snapdragon. I recalled a book from America, something about a gigantic, white-colored whale. Chapters had appeared erratically in the literary papers, submitted by an amateur translator, probably a language student at the university. The basic plot of the whaling story was of interest but the poorly done translation made the narrative plodding, and almost scientific sounding.

I knocked on the door but I suspected my rap was lost in its ornate thickness—in essence, blown about and dissipated on the oaken sea. No one responded of course. I suppose I might have sought the commander elsewhere—there had to be a dining hall, for instance—but Helena simply pulled back the door and we stepped inside. It was not well lighted and therefore seeing was difficult, especially since my eyes had been dazzled by the snowcountry for so long on the road, if our path of conveyance could be honorably called a "road." Moreover, the queer blue light outside was further filtered indoors by the white sailcloth stretched over the structure's skeleton. I had the sense of being underwater. I forced my lungs to inhale at that instant to make sure I could breathe.

"Hello," I called out to the empty corners of the tent. We set our bags down, glad for a rest from that burden. I had little in the way of extra clothes but my papers and writing utensils were weighty. I wondered that I should have left them on Division Street; meanwhile, I surveyed the interior of Command. There were three trestle tables set up in a horseshoe shape. Maps and books and stacks of papers covered the tables in orderly rectangles. There were also pencils and compasses and rulers—the cartographer's tools—and, of course, pens and glass bottles of ink. The ink took on a different hue in the weird light—more purple than black, like blood drained from royalty is supposed to look. The color of privilege and superiority. There were also wooden chairs placed here and there on the uneven planked floor, and three army cots with small pillows and woolen blankets folded on them.

"Nobody home," said Helena, stating the obvious for emphasis.

I nodded and went to the middle table. I picked a book from one of the stacks. I expected it to be about tactics of war or a code book or about techniques of interrogation. But the title surprised me. I did my best to pronounce the German: *Kalypso, Bedeutungs Geschichtliche Untersuchungen auf dem Gebiet der Indogermanischen Sprache.*

"Kalypso," said Helena, "Investigations into the history of meaning in the area of Indo-Germanic languages, or Indo-European." She added, "It sounds very . . . dry."

I had the impression I had stumbled onto an encampment of the Naturalists' Youth Club, or "Wilderness Scouts" as they were called informally. Perhaps further poking around may locate boxes of homemade cookies sent by some of the Scouts' mothers. Indeed, only the maps here and there, some spread out and others rolled up and standing upright in what seemed an overlarge umbrella stand, gave Command a military look at all.

"Do you think we should wait, Hektr?"

Helena curtailed my reverie of snooping. "I am not sure what else to do. I—" The sound of footsteps crunching in the snow interrupted me. I replaced the book and stepped away from the table and stood erect, something like a soldier myself, though I had no military training whatsoever. My stance was more an attempt at mimicry.

The ornate door swung open and white light replaced the blue. Two officers—one older, one younger—entered the tent structure. They must have been somewhat snowblind and were not expecting us, so nearly walked into Helena standing with our bags.

"The devil . . ." said the older officer, stopping just short of Helena. He was around my age but a head taller and with a neat black beard dotted with white (now blue as the door swung closed). He wore the falcon insignia of a commander on his coat and the rank's eight-pointed gold star on his fur-trimmed cap.

"I am Hektr Pastrovich . . ." I fumbled my coat open pawing for the letters of introduction Mezenskov and Bushkov had provided me. I found them with my gloved hand and offered them to the commander somewhat crumpled, especially Mezenskov's. He read each quickly, after unfolding them by holding an upper corner and snapping downward.

The commander looked to Helena.

"My assistant," I said, "Helena . . ."

She offered her hand to the commander, who received it and identified himself as Zlavik. He politely removed his cap, revealing thick black hair with brushstrokes of white over each ear. I tried to read his expression, which retained a mixture of surprise and annoyance from his stumbling onto us in his tent. But there was something else too. Disbelief that I had brought a woman into a war zone? A military man's natural distrust of journalists?

Zlavik nodded to the young officer and motioned toward the stove in the tent. The whey-faced lieutenant went to the cast-iron wreck, pulled back its door and began stoking the embers in its black belly. Meantime, Zlavik continued, "I am afraid we have little in the way of amenities. We receive few guests as you can imagine." He began undoing the gold-tinted buttons on his coat as if the tent was already becoming warm. "The mess sergeant has space in his pantry—that may be the best place to put you. There is ample room; supplies are quite short. Perhaps, Mr. Pastrovich, you could begin by writing that."

I did not know if the commander was completely serious; I did not know if I should get out my pad and pencils and make a note of it.

Zlavik went on, "I will have the lieutenant here show you to the mess. After that, you can move about as you will. Remember, however, this is a war zone. I cannot be responsible for your safety."

"Of course," I said.

"Join me this evening, in my quarters. You can dine with myself and other officers."

"Thank you, Commander. You are most hospitable." Helena and I took up our bags and followed the lieutenant out into the snowbright day. I listened for the sound of artillery or of rifle fire but heard nothing, save for our crunching footsteps. The lieutenant was slightly ahead of me. I looked down at his boots and they were well worn. In fact, one sole was loose and his heel flopped a bit as he walked. For that matter, his green-gray uniform coat was ripped and hastily sewn in three places I could see. It also was too big for him. Only the tips of his gloved fingers appeared below his coat cuffs. I thought of the shabby dress of the Prince of Ithaka, of his oversized shoes, one with a hole in the toecap.

We had left the aura of bluish light and the day was white again. Indeed, through the roof of the spruce forest patches of sky were white—as white as the snow beneath our feet. Perhaps I was only tired and anxious but for a moment I seemed to lose my orientation, my sense of up and down, which it must be like for someone twisting through the sky in an aeroplane on such a day, not certain at all what is *above* and what is *below*. I looked toward the tree tops thinking I just might see a flying-machine but it was an irrational idea. Maybe in the skies over Paris or Brussels or Berlin (the Germans love their machinery!), and one day soon Moskow or Saint Petersburg. . . .

It seemed we had passed the dining tent on our way to Command. Perhaps because it was so small—for a dining hall—I did not recognize it as such. A rectangular structure, of course, with a blackened tin chimney to one side disturbing its symmetry and releasing greasy gray smoke into the cold air. The lieutenant opened the tent's weightless door—something more in keeping with the style of the tent city—and we stepped inside. The "mess" was vacant except for one man at a bench scraping an enormous iron frying pan, large enough it appeared to cook a small child. Rows of tables and benches, more or less in order, filled most of the space, save one quarter where cooking and serving equipment had been erected.

"Ah, Botkin, there you are," said the young officer. Botkin went on scraping uninterrupted. Botkin had long dirty-looking mustaches and matching side whiskers. There was a sergeant's special insignia on his sleeve. His rank allowed him to feed troops but not to lead them in battle. "Botkin," continued the lieutenant, "do you still have cots in the pantry?"

He continued to scrape intensely; we had come close enough to see the charred black matter that he chipped at, like the topography of an unwelcoming beach. The black crumbs fell onto a cloth on the table. "Who's asking?" he said at last. I noted the area covered by the charred crumbs was greater by far than the surface of the cloth he had put down.

"Commander Zlavik wants room for these two visitors." I heard annoyance in the lieutenant's voice, perhaps at the lack of respect shown by his supposed underling.

Botkin ceased his scraping and looked up at us all. He studied Helena and me for an uncomfortably long while—as if more discerning than the supreme commander of the army. "The cots are there."

"Please show us," said the lieutenant.

Botkin set his pan down in the circular pile of scrapings and led us through another door to a medium-size tent. On the door to this tent—"the pantry," Zlavik called it—was a padlock but it was not latched. Botkin offered, as if an explanation for the slipshod security, "Not much worth stealing these days."

A half-sour, half-rotten smell greeted us as soon as he opened up the pantry. I expected a rat or some other vermin to come scurrying out of the dark. We followed Botkin inside; he appeared oblivious to the stench. The sergeant lighted a lantern hanging on a pole. There were several rows of shelves but very little on them. There were open crates and empty canning jars collected here and there. Straw and other grime covered the planked floor. Botkin went to some cots that were stored on their sides. He set them upright and slapped them a few times to disturb the dust. He picked some blankets from a pile on the floor. They were old and tattered (and probably soiled) but I suspected tonight I would not mind.

Botkin inspected a stove. "It'll work," he declared. "I'll fetch some wood—that's the one thing we have plenty of."

I found it hard to believe this was the best Zlavik could do for us. Perhaps it was because of Helena—he could not very well have her stay with the troops. For a moment I was irritated that she had insisted on coming but it was a selfish notion and I put it out of my head.

Sergeant Botkin exited the pantry and the lieutenant prepared to the do the same. He said, "The commander dines at six; I shall retrieve you here fifteen minutes before." He bowed slightly then left us alone. The lieutenant's exactness further irritated me but it was no doubt what made him a good choice for the commander's aide.

XIV

His secret would be out if she touched the telltale scar.

Odyssey 19

'Here we are," I said to Helena. "We have come all this way and now I am not certain what to do next."

"At least I am quite certain. I cannot live in this filth, even for a day or two. There is an old broom in the corner and some rags and a pail. I can make this horrid place a bit more livable."

Yes, I thought, but said, "What shall I do?"

"Get me a pail of snow that I can melt on the stove once the fire is raised, then go amuse yourself for a time. Here you will just be in the way."

I got her pail of snow and went out as she had instructed. I decided that, if nothing else, I could get the "lay of the land" so to speak. I had already been west, at Command, and I knew that the line of battle must be to the northeast; hence I wandered in that direction. The forest soon became denser and the air colder. There were no more ghostly tents strewn among the trees. Yet there must be troops somewhere. The snow was no longer trampled down, so I sank in it to my ankles. My toes were becoming of stone, as were my fingertips in spite of my gloves, especially the fingertips of my left hand because of rigidly carrying my valise, which I had left in Helena's care.

The forest was quiet, except for the wind in the tree tops and an occasional glob of snow that would fall to the forest floor with a surprisingly heavy thud. In fact, one such accidental projectile struck me on the shoulder and startled me severely. I continued walking slowly northeast trying very hard not to lose my bearings. I had no desire to be lost in the woods, only a few miles from the enemy encampment. I wondered if at night I would be able to see their fires—probably not, due to the trees.

The woods were oddly illuminated, as if from the ground up; or as if there were no light source whatsoever. The light was simply *there*, like the air and its frigidness, like the scent of spruce. These things were all around me, reminding me of the gathered elements of a terrarium. Perhaps that is why the pieces of sky appeared so queer through the forest canopy: the sky was made of glass; and we all acted our parts inside the terrarium for some child-giant's amusement. I stole a glance upward to catch an enormous eye peering at me from above the glass lid, from the heavens. But only the monochrome sky was there; perhaps I looked at the wrong instant, just missing the eye before it focused elsewhere in my contained environment.

Then I felt the loneliness of the forest pressing in on me. The emptiness, an almost tangible element, added to the light and air and smell of spruce. Where were these great armies that had been clashing for these many years? I thought a moment: nine years! The forest's desolation was so complete I believed the sound of artillery would be welcome—a sign of life, or at least of death, somewhere in the world. I felt like running from the forest, back the way I had come, to the army's camp and beyond, all the way to Iiloskova maybe, or at least as far as Mink Farm. It was a foolish thought. Exhaustion was getting to me.

I would not succumb to my childishness. I leaned against a tree trunk and began preparing a cigarette. I would smoke a cigarette here in the lonely wood before returning—that would prove something about me. Another ridiculous notion, I realized, as I finished rolling my cigarette. I lighted it and flicked the spent match into the snow. The earthy taste of the smoke and the feel of it in my lungs were a comfort, and I could sense my mind becoming more lucid with every breath.

Standing perfectly still, my hands in my pockets, the cigarette in my lips, I could detect things that had escaped me before. High above, the canopy made a swishing noise as the wind caused the needled limbs to brush together. I could hear the snow scraped from its resting place before falling to the ground with strange impact. (I thought of the River Vulpa back home and of the serene walks I had taken there.) Behind me, a clicking sound must be a small animal— squirrel or chipmunk—on a tree limb. I turned slowly. The clicking ceased . . . but there only a few yards from me was an enormous buck, a bona fide lord of the forest, wearing a majestic crown of twelve or fourteen points. He stood as stock still as I had been and was again. Brown and white, he was nearly invisible in the wintry wood. I began to wonder if he was there at all—if he was some creature of my imagination, like the giant eye I had tried to spot just minutes before. The only thing at work on him was his black nose, which moved ever so slightly from side to side, like a rabbit's. His lordship was trying to pick up the scent of something. I hoped my cigarette would not give me away. In my dark coat and beaver hat, I imagined myself his equal phantom in the woods. If I did not move he would not see me. I thought that if I could somehow glide noiselessly through the air, I could touch his great muscled back before he realized I was there. Perhaps even then he would not move, believing me a thing of the forest too—not his peer but not his enemy either.

I thought—

Suddenly the buck bolted and at the same instant tree bark exploded into the air just at my shoulder. An arrow protruded from the trunk. My first crazy thought was that the tree had pushed the arrow out at me but I knew the arrow had come from out there, from among the trees. Also, my sense of hearing told me there had been multiple arrows—a half-second before the explosion of bark and a half-second after I heard them cutting the air . . . and the light and the scent and the emptiness . . . the arrows especially cut the emptiness.

My initial shock left me and I fell to the ground for cover. At some distance I saw a trio of phantoms moving through the trees. I crawled on my hands and knees to where the buck had stood, the reflex of some weird brotherly bond (not brothers of the forest, but brothers of the attack, brothers of the moment). There was blood bright on the snow. The lordly buck was hit, and the hunters were chasing him down. A shame, I thought. Then I had another thought, more or less synchronous with the whistling sound of arrows cutting the air again: I thought, here I am on all fours wearing my dark coat and beaver-fur hat, and the woods are lousy with bow hunters. . . .

An arrow sliced through my hat and shoulder of my coat before lodging in the ground by my foot. A second arrow passed so close to my head I felt its wind on my cheek. A third stuck in the ground near my hand. I describe them in succession but they each hit their mark in the same second stroke of time.

I rolled to my left and emitted a little shriek—probably more animal sound than human. I just kept rolling and heard more arrows strike the ground behind me. My graceless escape was halted when I rolled into a fallen tree. I scrambled to the other side of the trunk for cover and lay panting on my back. An arrow lodged in the fallen tree; I heard the wood crack. I realized my right eye was crimsonly cloudy. I blinked and my lid and lash were sticky: I was bleeding. Instead of escalating my panic, the knowledge seemed to calm me, or focus me. I reminded myself that head wounds, even superficial ones, bleed profusely.

Another arrow zinged above me. I tried to suck in my belly, which protruded just beyond the trunk. I felt blood trickle warmly into my ear. What can I do to call off the attack? Then I remembered the red necktie in my pocket. I carefully unbuttoned the top of my coat and groped inside. The tie was folded with my notepad and letters of introduction. I pulled it out just as another arrow crashed into the fallen tree and bits of wood and bark hit my face. I spat a bit or two out of my gaping mouth.

I wrapped the red tie once around my hand then flopped the wide end over the tree trunk, where I made it dance jerkily. The tie was immediately pinned to the trunk by an arrow. "Fuck!" I began whipping wildly the narrow end of the tie in the air, and shouting, "Stop! . . . Stop! . . ."

A voice called from the wood: "Who's there?"

"A friend! A friend from the camp! From *your* camp!"

"Stand, and let's see you!"

I was somewhat dizzy but got to my feet. I held onto the tie, seemingly for support. I squinted into the woods and tried to clear my vision. "I am hurt," I said calmly. "One of your arrows." I felt myself swaying from side to side, as if blown by the wind, or intoxicated.

Figures materialized from the trees. They were soldiers, with P57s on their backs but homemade bows in their hands. One had a captain's insignia on his sleeve. He said, "You shouldn't be out here. Who are you?" He had smudged his face and his yellow-blond mustaches with mud.

"Hektr Pastrovich. I have reported to Commander Zlavik. I have papers." Blood was running down my cheek like tears, soaking my beard.

Instead of asking to see my papers, the captain removed my hat and examined me. "Just a scratch. You're lucky. Another inch or two." He did not have to finish his thought.

"Yes. I was just having a look around. I am a journalist. I did not realize it was hunting season."

"When fresh meat is available, it's always hunting season," said the blond captain. He handed me my hat and I put it on. The "scratch" stung more exposed to the air. "Let's get you back to camp. The wound isn't bad but it should be tended to." Then he worked the arrow out of the fallen tree, unpinning my necktie. The cut in the fabric was more or less where my heart would be if I were wearing it.

I folded the tie and returned it to my coat pocket. From my pants pocket I took a white handkerchief and held it near my eye to soak up the blood that was running freely in and out of the socket.

The captain noticed the tear in the shoulder of my coat. "Are you cut here too?"

I moved my shoulder and felt it with my hand. "No, I do not believe so."

"Very lucky," repeated the captain. His two men were hanging back, like schoolboys who had perhaps misbehaved. The captain began leading us all to the army camp.

Shortly we came across a group of soldiers who were tying the great buck's fore and hind legs to a long pole; the deer did not have my luck. Soon he would be properly dressed and in a few hours someone's supper. The buck's black eye, still moist with life, stared at me as our group passed. The men working with the buck watched me strangely but did not say a word.

I tried not to think of the buck as we continued our walk through the woods, but I could not forget his staring eye. It seemed accusatory. Perhaps it had been my scent that caused his reckoning, that caused him to stop at that exact place, where the hunters spied him and took their deadly aim.

As we walked along I dabbed at my eye and tried to clear my vision but it seemed I would need water for that. I knew I would receive a talking to from Helena for not being careful. But unlike the shrewish talking-tos of my wife's, I looked forward to Helena's good-natured chastisement. I would sit on a bench, secretly happy, while she clucked around me and dressed my wound. Perhaps I would embellish the story just a bit, to make the woods seem more menacing and my actions more heroic, or at least more athletic. Tramping through the woods behind the blond-headed captain, I had the urge to take out my notepad and begin practicing my embellishment . . . instead I stared straight ahead with my good eye, trying to discern a trail but seeing none.

The spectral tents of the camp appeared again. I informed the captain I had been placed in the cook's pantry and assumed he would take me there directly but we veered west. I thought perhaps I was disoriented and had lost my sense of direction. The camp appeared busier now; more soldiers were milling about on the icy paths. One could not see the sun but the sky was less luminous. A northern night was coming on. I recalled thinking of the northcountry night as a great baneful beast—I felt that way again.

I tried once more regarding our route: "My things are in the pantry. I am with a friend who can dress my wound."

"We are almost there," the captain said without turning his face toward me.

Almost where? I wondered. The path dipped down and my shoes slid a bit before I regained traction. We had come to a tent with a long narrow frame. Unlike other tents I had seen, this one had a hand-painted sign nailed above its double doors: no words but the serpent and staff of the camp surgeon. I thought of protesting—I simply wanted to go back to Helena. But, on the other hand, this could prove an informative visit, journalistically speaking. The captain's men pulled open the surgery's doors and he and I entered. As one would expect, the surgery was lined on both sides with beds, with only a long narrow aisle between the foot of each. I sensed a rotting smell not unlike the one in the pantry. Many of the beds were occupied—I assumed by wounded soldiers, but my eye had not adjusted from the white outdoors. It seemed too quiet for a place with so many people but I guessed the wounded and the dying were not inclined to be chatty.

The captain led me to the far end of the surgical tent (his men had remained outside). I detected a dripping noise somewhere in the tent; however, I decided I preferred not to know what was dripping from where. We came to an army-blanket partition on one side of the aisle, and the captain looked behind it. "Colonel Slivania? Colonel?"

I looked too. There was a bald man seated in a wooden chair that appeared too small for him; he was sound asleep at his desk, his head in his folded arms. Instead of a medical man's white smock, he had on regular army clothes, with the addition of a black scarf around his neck.

"Colonel Slivania?" repeated the captain as he shook the doctor's arm.

This roused him and he slowly sat up. He appeared to be a man who was wholly used to sleeping at his desk and being unceremoniously awakened. There was no sense of surprise whatsoever in his demeanor. Slivania did not bother to ask what was the matter, confident I suppose that he would be enlightened soon enough. He let out a deep sigh and I smelled the vodka on his breath.

"Colonel, I am sorry to disturb you but there is a minor medical emergency."

"If it is minor," said the doctor, his voice rough with phlegm, "then why do you not disturb my assistant?"

My eye had adjusted and I noticed a painting above the doctor's desk: a beach scene with colorful wildflowers growing on a knoll before the roiling surf. It seemed familiar but I could not place it at first.

"There is no assistant, Colonel."

Colonel Slivania blinked and looked up at us for the first time. He had enormously bushy gray eyebrows which were all a-tangle from sleeping at his desk. "Tell me," he said, "is there a man asleep in the first bed, on the opposite side of this blanket?"

Both the captain and I looked. "Yes," he said, "like a baby."

"Bastard," remarked the Colonel. "Duly noted," he added, tapping his bald pate. "What is it then?" He was fully awake now.

"We have a civilian, with a cut on his head."

The doctor paid attention to me for the first time. "Hm," he said. "Sit down here." He traded positions with me then lighted an oil lamp on the desk.

I removed my hat and held it in my lap. The doctor took the bloody handkerchief from me and used it to dab at the arrow wound itself. It seemed to be just at my hairline, almost a finger length from my left ear. "Not too bad," he said after a moment, of course this coming from a man who had probably spent his career removing shattered limbs and stuffing the guts back inside of people. "A stitch or two would be useful I think."

He went to the tall cabinet next to his desk and removed a metal bowl and a clean white cloth. There was already needle and thread stuck in the cloth. I suppose it was time-saving to pre-thread needles. That level of preparedness bolstered my confidence somewhat but when he took the needle between his fingers I got a sense of its size. It looked like a needle one would use to reconnect the large bowel—of livestock!

I spoke my first words to Doctor Slivania: "Is such a large needle necessary?"

"Absolutely not . . . but it is all I have. Do you prefer to bleed all night? Your decision."

"Absolutely not," I grumbled. I suspected Helena had brought needle and thread—though I was not certain—but, regardless, it had become a matter of honor that I sit for the doctor's mammoth needle. On the bright side, there would be no need to embellish my story now.

From his desk the doctor took out an unmarked bottle and poured some of its contents into the metal bowl. I knew then the source of Slivania's breath. He wetted a corner of the cloth and proceeded to clean the wound. He did not bother with my eye, no doubt thinking I could attend to it myself in due course. He placed the blood-stained cloth on the desk, then dipped the needle into the vodka. "Take the bowl," he ordered, "now drink it down. It will help."

I swallowed the recently stilled liquid in two gulps—and I had no doubts as to its usefulness as a disinfectant. The doctor took a drink directly from the bottle and went to work on me. As the needle passed through my skin it felt more like a pencil or a music conductor's baton. But surprisingly it did not hurt, much. The doctor adroitly put two stitches in my scalp. As he was tying off the thread, I recalled where I had seen the painting before, or one very much like it: in the interrogation room at the police station back home. I recalled seeing it the day I met the Prince of Ithaka, who, in a sense, had convinced me to come north, to finally accede to Mezenskov's wish that I report on the war firsthand. The Prince's sketch was in my valise. I wished that I had it with me to show Colonel Slivania and the captain. No matter—I would have ample time. It appeared the armies were at a standstill. What word do the French have for it? *Détente.*

The doctor snipped the loose ends of the thread with scissors he kept on his desk. He was not especially careful and several strands of hair fell onto the hat in my lap. The hairs seemed more silvery than before I left for Iiloskova. Coming north had aged me. Perhaps returning home will shed the time, I mused.

I thanked the doctor, and the captain led me out of the surgery and toward the pantry. The adrenaline that had coursed through my arteries during the attack had totally subsided, which seemed to magnify the effects of the unripe vodka. My head did not hurt per se, but I could feel my pulse against the new stitches. I wanted to sleep, yes; but mostly I wanted to dream, to dream of someplace else, someplace warm and sunny—perhaps of the beach in the painting.

The captain did not take me all the way to the pantry. He pointed me in the direction once we were close and left me to complete the journey alone, already beginning to sleep—and to dream—on my feet, like soldiers on a long march . . . or so I have heard. The cold, and maybe too the bad vodka, made my eyes tear up, which helped to wash the blood away. In spite of my dreamy state of mind, I took note that smoke rose from the pantry's tin chimney and at a distance it could indeed pass for some couple's cozy nest.

Pensive, the queen emerged from her chamber.

Odyssey 19

I HAD NOT CORRECTLY JUDGED HELENA'S REACTION to my mishap in the woods. Instead of clucking, as I had anticipated, she was mortified at my condition. I have been trying to imagine my "homecoming" from Helena's perspective: I, Helena, am relaxing a bit after cleaning the pantry. It still smells bad but not so intensely and at least I am confident there are no vermin hiding in the tent. To my amazement and delight, I have found a jar of black tea on one of the shelves and have made myself a tin cup of it. I am thinking Hektr will be most pleased with my discovery too. I have made a chair of old crates and have put one of the less soiled blankets over my legs—and with the nice warm tea the afternoon is most pleasant. I hear footsteps in the snow and smile as the door is pulled back. I expect Hektr to be apple-cheeked from the cold and tired and I think of how grateful he will be for my tidying up and for the little writing desk I have fashioned him from two crates and a sheet of wood and for the unanticipated hot tea. But what is this? Hektr's face is smeared with blood, his beard matted with the gore on one side. More than apple-cheeked, his whole face is flushed and he is perspiring copiously. His legs appear of lead and I am afraid he will faint before I can get him to a cot. . . .

But this scenario does not explain Helena's shock—her surprise, yes—but not her utter shock. Her complexion turned from white to true white—to virgin white, to snow white . . . choose your modifier. It is an old-saw in literature but I shall invoke it nonetheless: Helena reacted as if she were seeing a ghost walk into the tent—and not any ghost . . . the ghost of her father or mother, or child, or husband . . . a ghost who is made all the more fearsome because of familiarity, because of bonds forged while the ghost was not a ghost but rather walked and lived and loved among the quick. Helena's shock was the Scottish king's shock, in the Shakespeare play, when the ghost of the king's friend comes to dinner—thus was Helena's shock. There was something else about Shakespeare's scene, something to explain the magnitude of the king's shock—oh yes, the king had murdered his friend! Thus was Helena's shock!

She rose from her makeshift chair so suddenly she spilled her tea and the army blanket fell to the newly-swept floor. She opened her mouth as if to speak but said nothing. The shock even seemed to dull her beautiful eyes, which appeared more muddy gray than electric lavender in the lamplighted tent. Helena was unsteady, as if *she* might faint. Her obvious distress enlivened me somewhat. At the same instant, she got hold of her emotions, and we rushed to each other with mirrored intent: to steady and support the other. But Helena was stronger—I was, after all, the one who was physically injured, who had lost blood—and she guided me to my cot, on which she had placed the best blanket and pillow.

She finally managed to speak: "Hektr, what has happened?"

"An accident, that is all. I am fine." She helped me remove my coat and hat and lie down. Helena got some hot water from the stove, water she had been keeping for my tea, and she began cleaning me up. I lay on the cot and sleepily told my tale—too listless to embellish, much. I noticed some color returning to Helena's face but something of the great shock lingered in her eyes and around her mouth.

Pondering her inexplicable reaction, I drifted off to sleep. I tried to will myself to dream of someplace warm and pleasant . . . but it seemed the relentless snowcountry and the eye of the dead buck and Helena's shock were to be the pictures of my dreamworld. So it was.

In spite of the disturbing thoughts, I slept hard and Helena woke me just minutes before the lieutenant was to call on us for dinner.

My head was aching but not too badly; I figured it was more from the vodka than the arrow. Hm . . . vodka and arrows, an intriguing pair of images for a poem. I would have to remember to scribble it down. Meanwhile, I thirsted for Mrs. Strubel's medicinal tiger-root tea.

My beard, fortunately, had absorbed most of the blood, so my shirt and jacket were reasonably clean. At Helena's urging I replaced my brown tie with the red one. She said the arrow slit gave the necktie (and me I suppose) character. I hoped my vest, when fully buttoned, would cover the hole but it was just above the vest's v-shape. I realized, looking down, how my white shirt formed something of an arrowhead shape. I was thinking abstractly tonight—perhaps because of my near-death experience. It was a night to write poetry.

Helena continued to wear her gray skirt and white blouse. She took the purple wrap from her bag and draped it around her shoulders. It was the same wrap she was wearing on the train when I first saw her. And the same wrap she was wearing as her only protection against the cold when I found her again in the Luminarium, nearly dead from exposure and vodka poisoning.

We were in a festive mood, Helena and I, as if we were dressing for a night on the city. There was a tap on the flimsy door of our tent just as Helena was putting on her great bearskin coat (how lucky, I thought, that Helena had not gone into the woods). It was the lieutenant and he was holding a bull's-eye lantern with the flame very low. Helena blew out the lamp in our tent and we followed the young officer out into the snowy camp. No one had spoken.

The night was heavily dark in spite of the utter whiteness of the world. The lieutenant led us through the camp more by recollection than sight, I thought. Maybe one's eyes adapt to the snowcountry after so many years. Maybe the soldiers, after all their time in the northern wilderness, were becoming a new species—they would grow thick hair on their bodies and their blood would learn to cope with the constant cold. A new language would be next, or a new way to communicate altogether, something akin to whalesong. It occurred to me these were all slurs we had for our enemy: they were hairy as baboons, they were incapable of intelligent speech, they were less than human.

I noticed a strange light reflected on the snow. I looked up and thought at first I was seeing the enemy's fires after all, but it was the northern lights. I had never seen them so spectacularly displayed, looking so much like the handiwork of divinity. Luminous red and green dust swirled among the broken snowclouds. I touched Helena's arm and pointed out the dancing lights. I believe she smiled in the dark night but was generally unimpressed. Perhaps in Helena's native country she saw them often. But I doubted it. I realized Helena's accent, which at first had been so distinct, was almost completely gone; for all practical purposes she spoke like one of us, totally blended into her environment, like a fox whose coat turns white with the first snowfall. Helena had adapted her language and her dress but she kept her unique braids and there was nothing she could do to alter the otherworldliness of her strange beauty, her magnetic eyes, her flawless white skin and her frame, so thin and lithe it was almost more floral than human.

We came at last to a tent that appeared to be dark until the lieutenant opened the door and yellow lamplight spilled onto the snow. We three stepped into the commander's tent and Zlavik welcomed us gaily. "Ah, Mr. Pastrovich, Miss Helena—please, come warm yourselves by the stove." Zlavik was standing at the head of a rectangular table of medium size and he motioned to the opposite end where two chairs were unoccupied near an ornate wood-burning stove. In between, Colonel Slivania stood smiling, a red napkin in his hand. Beyond the table was Zlavik's personal living space, a bed with an iron frame, a writing desk and chair, a small wardrobe.

The lieutenant took our coats and hats and we went to our places at the table. There were several other chairs, and the lieutenant took one opposite of Doctor Slivania, leaving an empty chair between himself and Helena. I would be across the long table from Commander Zlavik. Food was already on the table but in covered dishes. A large silver platter and matching cover were near Zlavik. The aroma of the food was quite evident and my mouth began to water so much I feared I would drool. I had not realized the profoundness of my hunger but it had been many hours since the feast on Division Street. I imagined Helena was famished too.

Each place at the table was set with fine china depicting peasant haymakers in a field, all rendered in blue. The forks, knives and spoons were polished silver. I had not eaten with such finery in my life. There was a crystal goblet, empty, at each place, and a small glass filled with what I assumed was vodka. "Please, before sitting, let us toast to whet our appetites." Zlavik held up his glass. The rest of us followed his lead. My nose told me it was a spiced vodka, expensive. The commander continued: "To the war's quick conclusion."

"Indeed," said Slivania and we all drank down the clear liquid. It was very good and warmed me instantly.

We sat. Zlavik had Slivania fill our goblets with a deep red wine while he filled our plates, which we passed to him boardinghouse fashion. The silver platter held a venison roast—I thought of the buck of course but it was not for sure my majestic brother. There were also roasted black potatoes with vinegar and boiled wax beans that had been canned. There was pepper relish for the meat and freshly baked pumpernickel bread. Commander Zlavik was generous with his portions.

Everything was delicious and I exerted great power of will not to eat ravenously. I thought of that adverb, in fact, related etymologically to the black bird of evil portent who feeds upon dead things. No matter—I had the urge to eat as a raven eats. The wine was strong but very good also.

When we had had enough to take the edge from our hunger, Commander Zlavik began the conversation. "Tell me, Mr. Pastrovich, do you write exclusively for one newspaper?"

I stopped chewing. The commander's direct question had recalled my moral dilemma. Do I respond with Mezenskov's paper or do I tell the truth, that I am half working for the tawdry *Nightly Observer*? I swallowed and chose a new version of the truth: "I am somewhat of an independent journalist. My work may appear in various places."

"Ah," said Zlavik, putting down his wine glass enthusiastically. "That is very modern—very much of the new century."

"Hmph," said the doctor. He had finished his first glass of wine and was pouring himself a second.

Commander Zlavik laughed. "This is a debate my old friend and I have had many times: the merits of the new century versus the good old days. The doctor would just as soon we return to our caves and bearskins."

Colonel Slivania defended himself. "That is an exaggeration of my view—but it is true that I could more easily treat the bite of a dagger-tooth cat than the wounds our own time is able to inflict."

"But what of modern medicine, doctor?" said Zlavik. "Would you give up your drugs and surgical tools? Regression would have its price, no?"

"The ancients had their healing techniques—do not underestimate them. But medical men have not been able to keep pace with the militants' methodology."

"Well put, doctor," said Helena, holding up her glass as if toasting him. The doctor smiled and tipped an imaginary cap.

"Yes," said Zlavik, "my old friend can wax eloquent. What is your view, Mr. Pastrovich? Should we reverse the sands of time? Would you prefer a room of scribes methodically copying your words for a mostly illiterate world?"

I considered for a moment, swallowing a bit of potato. "It is a moot question. We can only live in the present and it is there we must focus our energies, to improve the world as it is now."

"Oh my," said Zlavik, "I have a crusader at my table, someone who wants to improve the world! Tell me, how do we do that? If you could *improve* something, what would it be, how would you go about it?" Meanwhile Slivania had stood and refilled everyone's wine glass.

I nodded my thanks to the colonel, stalling. I did not know what to say—and Commander Zlavik knew it. He waited, sipping his wine, relishing the silence—not malicious, just glad to have a fresh sparring partner.

"The aged," I said finally, "the state must take better care of them."

"All right, the aged . . ." Zlavik was anxious to play. ". . . a group worthy of respect. So how does the state do it? What program will you establish? How will it be paid for? Out of whose pocket?"

I wanted to bring up the cost of the war—it had depleted all the coffers—but it would not be a prudent topic. "The pockets of the well-to-do." It was a pat response.

"The well-to-do," said Zlavik, more mockingly than I would like. "Precisely how deep are their pockets? And how do we pry our hands into them?"

I was tired of the game; my king was in check; everyone knew it. The silence inside the tent derided me and my headache was returning full force.

"Hektr is a poet!" We all looked at Helena, surprised, I most of all. "A wonderful poet."

"Indeed?" said Commander Zlavik, relinquishing his prey, for the moment at least.

"Yes," said Helena. "He has brought some of his work with him. He must share it with you some time."

Suddenly I missed the conversation about assisting the aged. Though I was also quite flattered by Helena's good opinion.

"Yes, Mr. Pastrovich, I would very much enjoy seeing your work. What sorts of poetry do you like to write?"

"I am not devoted to one form. For a time I was interested in the sonnet."

"Italianate or English?" asked Zlavik, a formally educated man.

"English," I said.

"Some of Hektr's sonnets have been published," offered Helena, sounding wifely in her promotion of me. Did I tell her of their publication? I thought back to our meeting on the train and other conversations. No, I had not told her.

"It was nothing," I argued. "Just some small literary papers."

"Do not say poetry is nothing, Mr. Pastrovich. Do not allow your modesty to denigrate your literary forebears," said Zlavik in dead earnest. "For one, how would we know of the great conflicts in history without the poets to keep them alive for us? Indeed, how would we know the world at all without the poets?"

I was surprised by Zlavik's opinion but I agreed wholeheartedly.

"A toast to poetry," said Doctor Slivania, his glass raised.

"Forget the wine," said the commander. "Poetry deserves better." And he passed around the bottle of spiced vodka. When our glasses were full, Zlavik said, "To the poets . . . may they survive this and every war . . . to tell the tale."

"To tell the tale," repeated the doctor, then we all did and drank our glasses empty. The liquor set my heart nicely ablaze, the way poetry can, and I felt sentimental toward Commander Zlavik, warrior yes, but lover of verse too.

The lieutenant had remained silent, except for our group toast. He was busy admiring Helena; I believe she had noticed too. I had been amused by the young man's mute attentions but the potent vodka—or perhaps the talk of poetry—altered my disposition: the lieutenant's fascination with Helena's beauty angered me, and it was not the anger of a companion beginning to burn in my chest, nor that of a protective brother, but rather the malevolent anger of a jealous lover. I thought of cutting out the young man's eyes with my table knife. It was an ugly idea and I tried to will it out of my mind.

Commander Zlavik interrupted my black musing. "Who is your favorite poet, Hektr?"

I blinked hard at my plate of food—a half potato remaining, two bites of meat—to reorganize my thoughts. "My favorite," I repeated. "The sonnets of Tolstayov were very important to me at one time, and Pushkin of course."

Zlavik nodded enthusiastically.

Helena volunteered more information about me. "When Hektr was a boy, his father told him the stories of Homer. He says he does not recall them but they must have . . . affected him, at such an impressionable age." My murderous thoughts about the young lieutenant shifted to a mild irritation toward Helena, who was very generous with my life story but still shared nothing about herself—not even her name.

At this new detail Zlavik became even more animated. "Homer is my personal hobby," he said, rising from the table. "You must see this." He went to a trunk at the foot of his perfectly made bed and retrieved two small books with red leather covers. He sat again, the books in each hand. "I picked these up in Paris, before the war of course: *The Woe of Penelope* or *The Woeful Penelope*, some such, in two volumes. The verse translation is not wonderful—the French you know—but endlessly fascinating nevertheless." Zlavik passed a book to Slivania and the lieutenant.

"Another drink then," blurted Helena, "to Penelope's woe." The bottle of vodka had come to rest near her, so she filled her glass to the brim and passed the bottle to the lieutenant.

I recalled the character of Penelope from Homer's second book; her woe had to do with her long-absent husband. I thought of Tasha back home, alone now for several days. Is she woeful tonight? No more than usual I concluded as Slivania handed me both the bottle and volume one. When my glass was full I joined the others in raising it.

"To Penelope's woe," said Helena, "and the woe of all women," she added bitterly.

We men mumbled something about Penelope and drank. I handed the book to Helena, who opened it to a random page and read the French to herself, her electric eyes darting from side to side, then she said,

> And the first suitor placed a silver bowl at her
> Sandaled feet. The Queen thought—no—thoughts of
> Kicking it aside came to her. But she considered it
> Better, More—no—Further and merely thanked the young or
> youthful Prince. There was no feeling in her words. . . .

Helena wiped a tear from her cheek. "I am sorry, gentlemen, my French is out of practice."

"No, not at all . . . it was quite wonderful," said the commander, who I am sure did not know what to make of Helena's emotions; I did not. "*Merci*," he concluded as both leatherbound volumes were placed before him.

"I wonder that we should call it an evening," said Slivania. "Our guests have traveled much today. They must be exhausted."

"Quite," agreed Commander Zlavik. "Though, Hektr, I was wondering if you and I might have a word. Lieutenant, would you be kind enough to escort Miss Helena to her tent."

"Of course, sir," he said, standing and placing his napkin by his plate.

I wanted to protest but the words did not come, and Helena and the lieutenant were quickly in their coats and gone from the tent. The doctor also said his farewell, and the commander and I were alone.

$\mathcal{XVI}$

'Thrice you circled it, touching it everywhere,
tempting the fighters to foil their own design.'
Odyssey 4

W HEN EVERYONE HAD GONE I noticed the wind, which had picked up and was vibrating the sides of the tent. The fuel in Zlavik's stove had been depleted and the tent was growing cold.

"There is no reason to shout to each other, eh?" The commander moved to my end of the table and sat where Helena had. He refilled our glasses, emptying the vodka bottle. He undid the collar button of his uniform jacket. We sipped the vodka, then Zlavik spoke: "Hektr, do you believe in fate? In destiny?"

"I . . . I am not sure." At the moment I was only sure of the vodka, the spice of which was heavy on my tongue.

"Well, I do, Hektr, I believe in fate. Twenty-five years I have been in the military. When you have been around death and disease that long, you begin to believe in destiny. Why does one man survive the field of battle and another lose his life? Training plays its part of course—I must believe in that too—but it does not explain why the most skilled warrior falls while the greenest novice lives to fight another day." Zlavik stopped to sip his drink.

I filled the silence with "I suppose," an incongruent response to Zlavik but the best I could do.

"I believe your coming here today, this day of all days, was destiny, Hektr. I did not know it until Miss Helena spoke of your abilities as a poet."

"Why today? What is special about today?"

"You have arrived on the eve of the greatest battle our country has known."

I did not know what to say.

Zlavik went to his bureau and came back with a map-size piece of paper tied with black ribbon. He cleared space on the table, unrolled the paper, which *was* a map, and used objects at hand to hold down its uncooperative corners. "Do you recognize this place?"

My eyes had trouble focusing; I sipped the vodka to clear them.

Zlavik laughed. "You should know it—you are here." Zlavik's finger came to rest on a series of Xes drawn in pencil. "Here then is the Great Northern Forest—with which you have some familiarity— then this is an open expanse, approximately three miles, then here is the opposing army, where they have been camped throughout most of the winter."

I stared hard at the map and tried to see them there—the barbarians, the seal-fuckers—but all I saw was faded white paper, just like where our army camped, amid their penciled Xes.

"And here is the key, Hektr, the key to our great victory: Lake Aurora. Mark that name—it will go down in history. Schoolchildren will sing songs about the Battle of Lake Aurora. They will draw pictures of its blue waters to keep by their beds at night—to keep away the bogeymen, just as Commander Anton Zlavik had kept them away, had defeated them for good."

I stared at the uneven line that ran perpendicular to the great forest. Its waters ran beyond the borders of the map.

"Do you know the story of Genghis Khan and his defeat of the Shah of Khwarizm?"

I knew of Khan of course but not the battle; I shook my head, gently.

"The Shah took refuge in the high-walled city of Otrar, on the edge of a desert so hostile not even the stalwart bedouin traversed it. Khan divided his army, which was already outmanned two to one, in half. One part he left under the direction of his second in command, who arranged his forces before the walls of Otrar as if to lay siege. Meanwhile, Khan himself led the other half of his army into the desert, intending to loop around and attack Otrar from the desert, from its unprotected side. Weeks passed and the Shah gained in confidence; he expected the remainder of Khan's army to pack up and go home any day. Then, one morning, Khan's second began what appeared to be a futile assault. The Shah planned to crush his enemies. Then, out of the desert, swept Genghis Khan—every man and horse alive, every weapon of war in working order. Bewildered and believing Khan to be a phantom, the Shah of Khwarizm surrendered his city and his kingdom."

"A marvelous story," I said, sincerely.

"Surprise, that is the key, Hektr—do the impossible and you surprise your enemy. Khan at Otrar, Washington at Trenton, Bonaparte at Bard." Tired of sipping, Zlavik drained his glass. Then the commander smiled, almost mischievously. "Throughout the winter I have dispatched the better part of my army across Lake Aurora—they have camped here." He pointed to a spot on the table near my vodka glass. "You have no doubt noticed, Hektr, that the camp here is mostly deserted and several of my officers were missing at dinner."

I nodded; my head was pounding.

"For the past few days, my men have been making their way along the lake. Precisely at thirty minutes before sunrise—in just a few hours—I will launch a frontal attack, my army pouring forth out of the forest. Simultaneously, the larger part of my force will cross the lake and mount a rear assault—just as the great Khan had done."

I sat there in silence trying to absorb it all. Finally something popped into my head and I said it aloud: "Spring. It is springtime."

"That, my friend, is why it will work—why it will be more than a surprise attack, but a complete shock. They will not expect my army to be crossing the lake at this time of year. The ice is too capricious."

"But—"

"No 'but'—for great gain, one must take great risk. Khan at Otrar, Washington at Trenton, Bonaparte at Bard. They rolled the die for their countries and won just I am doing. Zlavik at Lake Aurora."

I could tell it was a phrase he had repeated to himself many times. Was this calculated risk or snowmadness? Another phrase bubbled up from the recesses of my brain and I spoke it aloud, almost involuntarily: "The Greeks at Troy."

"Yes, exactly, the Greeks and their horse at Troy. I knew you would understand." Commander Zlavik patted me on the shoulder, one comrade to another.

"And my part?"

"That is where fate comes in. Every warrior needs his poet and here you arrive on the eve of my finest hour. It is destiny, Hektr, that you will tell my tale, that you will be the witness of history. It will be from your account that children will sing their songs, that historians will make their judgments about me and the great battle." Zlavik's face was aflame with passion . . . and vodka.

I wanted to decline. I wanted to say I had come looking for information about a ragged vagabond who called himself the Prince of Ithaka. I hardly felt up to the task of being history's eyewitness. Yet . . . if it all plays out as Zlavik has foreseen, it could be the turning point of my career: Commander Zlavik's biographer, the author of *The Battle of Lake Aurora* . . . these glimpses of a possible future passed through my head.

The wind rattling Zlavik's tent seemed to also rattle my brain, intensifying the pain. In fact, for an instant the pain spiked so dramatically a tear slipped from my eye.

Zlavik, staring at me intensely, noticed the tear and wiped it away before I had time to react. He must have thought I was overcome with the enormity of the moment. I could not tell him it was simply because it felt like the only thing keeping my head from bursting was Doctor Slivania's two thin stitches.

"You must get some rest, Hektr. Tomorrow will be here soon. There is a road of sorts east of the camp. . . ." He pointed to the map. ". . . it goes through the woods and comes out here." Zlavik indicated a spot near the shore of Lake Aurora but still some distance from the enemy. "I have been using it to move my artillery into place. There will be a medical caravan headed by Colonel Slivania leaving at four. You can ride with the medics. From there you should get an overall sense of the battle as it gloriously unfolds. Observe but do not get too close until the battle is won. Remember, you are every bit as important as my cleverest captain."

I gathered my coat and hat and left Zlavik's tent. I braced myself for the frigid north wind but the breeze came from a different direction and there was a hint of warmth in it. It soothed my head a little as I made my way through the black camp. My brain was so full of thoughts—all merging and spinning, kaleidoscopically—I had trouble sorting out a single idea but I knew I must inform Helena as soon as possible that the army was about to be on the move. I did not know what that would mean for her; I could not focus long enough to begin to speculate. I blinked at the sky but found no moon. I tripped over a tent stake and fell to one knee on the path, which had become exceedingly treacherous. The knee of my pantleg was wet and uncomfortable when I got to my feet again. For a moment I thought the tent just in front of me was Commander Zlavik's, that I had traveled in a circle—but it was not Zlavik's. However, the incident confirmed my disorientation. I did not know where the pantry was located. I sniffed the air for the smell of greasy smoke from the mess tent . . . no scent on the whipping wind.

I continued in what I hoped was the correct direction. I strained to see in the dark, which accentuated the pain in my head. My surging pulse threatened to pop my stitches. I tried to extend some extra sense out before me. I recalled reading a scientific article that suggested sightless insects use the vibrations of their body hair to navigate. I wondered if my mustaches and beard might direct me. I considered calling Helena's name—perhaps the wind would carry my voice to her. Then I considered just thinking *Helena* very hard, to send out my message of distress from my mind to hers, on some sort of invisible telegraph wire.

I shook my head to try to conjure a lucid thought but I would have had more luck pulling flowers from my coat sleeve. It only made my brain hurt worse. I realized tears were streaming down my cheeks, matting my lashes and soaking my beard. Maybe it was the wind, or the terrible headache, or the stress of knowing what I knew. Maybe my tears were a kind of pre-mourning for the soldiers who would fall tomorrow: whether Zlavik's plan was the result of genius or madness, men were going to die. Men who had survived to the last day of the war would survive no further. They were one final assault away from home—from wives and girlfriends and children— yet it would be one assault too many.

I wiped my eyes on my coat sleeve and blew my nose, one nostril at a time, into the snow. I must find Helena, I must find my way home. The wind swirled and I detected a putrid smell—not unlike the pantry before Helena's cleaning efforts. I determined the direction as best I could and headed out.

It surprised me that no one was about. Zlavik had said most of his men were across the lake or gathered in the woods, but still…. There was an English novel by a female author—I saw it in a bookstore— and the title translated to something like *The Final Man* or *The Last Man*. That is how I felt wandering in the dark camp, so far from home (from reality): the last man on earth, the last man alive.

Following my nose, and a wished-for sixth sense, I slowly meandered between tents, trying almost to ski on my shoes because the path was so slippery. I would feel as if I had lost my way then the wind would whip around and the stench would be stronger. In fact, now it seemed too strong—too powerful to be the pantry—but I had no other plan so I stayed with it. My ability to reason was severely hamstringed by the shards of broken glass rattling to and fro in my brain.

Quite suddenly the rotten smell struck me so hard in the face I stopped completely. I squinted in the night to see what lay before me: the ground was a mass of darkness, like a giant crater in the snow. I tried to discern it but it became no more distinct. Even the northern lights had ceased their celestial dance. Should I go forward or back? Before my mind could decide, gravity did it for me. My foot slipped, no more than an inch, but it was enough to begin my descent down a severely sloped wall of ice and snow.

Out of instinct I leaned back but I continued sliding feet first— until I reached the bottom in just a few yards and the force propelled me forward so I came to full stop on my hands and knees. Damp things hit me in the face and sprayed my coat. I realized immediately I had discovered the camp refuse pile. What sort of refuse? Food certainly, but medical refuse too? I raised one hand and something leafy clung to my glove for a moment before dropping off into the filth. Was it potato skin or human skin? It was impossible to say in the dark. I quickly added profound nausea to my list of woes.

I scrambled, slipping and retching, out of the crater of garbage and sat on its edge, my ass getting wet, but not caring. Tears flowed in earnest now. I cried as I had not cried in years, since I was a boy. Everything I had held in all those years of adulthood—every stubbed toe, every brutal argument with Tasha, every insult from strangers on the street—everything came gushing out in high-pitched childish sobs. I sat there, next to the crater of waste, wailing uncontrollably in the wind for I do not know how long. I hung my head and tears rained into my lap.

I might have stayed that way all night except that for a moment the wind ceased and I heard a voice, a female voice: "Who is there? Is something wrong?" There was music too; a band was playing. It seemed impossible that Helena had found me but I did not imagine the voice and the music. "Hello!" I called, my own voice muffled by my tears. "It is I, Hektr!" I got to my feet and saw that ahead a door was partly open and feeble yellow light shone on the snow. The voice must have come from there; Helena must be there.

I staggered and slid up the path to the tent—the music growing louder—and tapped on the door. "Hello," I said meekly, "Helena?" I tried to see inside but the lamplight, though not strong, dazzled my eyes and my head hurt so much I fell to my knees, blind and sick.

"What's the matter, love?" I heard the female voice say. Then another: "Who is he, with no uniform?" The music was coming from a scratchy gramophone—a jolly tune with a tuba and an accordion and violins. "Take your gal by the hand, go upon the ice, and skate your love to the band," sang the gramophone voice. The two women, one on either side of me, began helping me to stand and come farther inside. A third female voice said, "By god he stinks, this one. You have to bring him in?" All I could smell was tobacco, heavy in the close quarters of the tent.

I was led to a cot; I kept my eyes shut to the ferocious lamplight. Fingers began to undress me. "Time is come for your figure-eight love," sang Gramophone Voice. I thought of my wallet in my coat which contained all of my money, except for the bills tucked into my wet socks. I did not care—they could have it all if I could just rest here until my head stopped pounding and my stomach quaking.

Third Voice said, "I thought we was done for the night." First, Second and Gramophone Voices did not respond . . .

. . . . the fingers bathe me, my face and neck, my hands and arms, they help me to use the pee-pot, the fingers steadying me . . . are there nurses at the front? the fingers are expert . . . I lie naked on the cot, under a blanket but shivering nevertheless . . . more accordion and violin but Gramophone Voice is silent . . . the hellish lamplight is out and sweet merciful darkness fills the tent . . . I feel better but am so cold my teeth chatter . . . "the moon, full moon lights our love, love," it is Gramophone Voice . . . someone is slipping under the cover too, "there now, shhhh," First Voice says softly . . . she is naked too, warm and soft . . . she holds me and in a while I quit shaking . . . an oboe and a cello . . . my head is resting between First Voice's breasts . . . they are full breasts and they pillow my head in warmth, my headache is subsiding . . . more cello, and the accordion again . . . I wake somewhat, in the dark tent, I am suckling First Voice's breast . . . "up up up the path we go, baby and me, the sun sinking low low low" . . . I am working the hard nipple with my teeth, it must be painful but First Voice gently strokes my head and face . . . I feel her fingers between my legs . . . oboe viola sad . . . she is lying on top of me, her warmth bathing me, gently rocking . . . my lips kiss her neck, her ear, earring, First Voice's feathery hair is in my face . . . the scratchy music is over, the tent silent . . . I think it is Helena, I know it is not, the hair is not Helena's nor the body, but I think it is she . . . I may say her name in the dark . . . "Helena" . . . someone is snoring softly . . . we stay this way, Helena and I, for a long time, Helena not rushing . . . then I feel her shudder, all along her spine, even her jaw, and this releases me too . . . we kiss in the dark, Helena is missing a tooth, another is jagged, and I fall asleep, deeply asleep. . . .

XVII

His shade fluttered forth, bound reluctantly for the wintry underworld.

Iliad 22

I DREAMED OF OVERSLEEPING, of being late for my big day—a wedding, the birth of a son, the first day at work—something important, and I just missed it, that was all there was to it. My time had come and I was not there. So I was in despair, from my dream, when I woke suddenly and completely, at first not knowing where I was.

Then it all came to me, an avalanche of awareness.

I bolted from the cot and pushed open the door, expecting and fearing full daylight, but the sky was only a silvery predawn hue. I instinctively reached for the pocketwatch in my vest and realized I was stark naked, except for my wedding band. I rushed to find my clothes and left the door open to provide some light to see by. I was aware there were three bodies sleeping in the tent but paid little attention to them in my panic to find my things. Blankets and ladies undergarments and so forth were strewn upon the floor. I pawed through them but could not locate my belongings.

A sleepy voice, too sleepy to identify, said, "Shut the door, it's cold."

"I cannot find my things." I was frantic.

"I tossed em," said Third Voice. "They was stinkin the place."

"Outside?" I was too shocked to move.

"Don't have a hysteria," said Third Voice, sitting upright, her dangling little tits pointing straight at me. "Your wallet and watch and such is on the table." She nodded tousled brown hair toward a corner of the tent.

I saw my things in the shadow light. I pulled a blanket around me at the waist and stepped outdoors. There were my clothes and shoes in a pile, half soaking wet and half frozen. My bare feet were becoming like ice so I hopped back in the tent.

"Don't worry, love," said another voice, First Voice. She got up from a mound of blankets on the floor. "We have plenty of slough off." She turned and went to a trunk against the wall. Her ass was as round and as white as the moon. She came to me with an armload of clothes, all army issue. We picked out pants and a shirt, wool socks and army boots. The pants were a bit short and the boots a bit loose but otherwise all right. There was even a long gray coat with captain's insignia on the sleeve. I ended up with a left glove and right mitten. I would be dry and warm at least. I wondered at being in a uniform, mismatched though it was, but I would be far from the fighting.

I filled my pockets with my possessions. Before putting my wallet away I opened it and looked at First Voice. She was my age. A strand of hair with a touch of gray hung in her face, which still told of the prettiness of her youth. She smiled a little: "On the house, love." I noticed a purple bruise on her right breast and wondered if it was from me.

"Thank you," I said, meaning it. She kissed me on the cheek and patted my hindside then went to the cot where I had spent the night. I hoped it was still warm for her.

Outside, I grabbed my hat from the pile and put it on. I noticed the red tie poking from the debris like a serpent tongue. I took it too, as a keepsake. I briefly imagined giving a lecture on Anton Zlavik and the Battle of Lake Aurora and theatrically wearing the red tie as a sort of prop.

Though the sun was not quite up I could determine east by the brightness of the sky, which enabled me to get my bearings. Walking through the silent camp, I soon spotted the dining tent—I had not been so far off the mark after all—and then the pantry. I felt great relief and rushed to speak with Helena. It struck me then that I was missing her. We had spent so much time together it felt strange to be apart from her.

I approached the pantry from the rear and noticed a figure in gray lying in the snow. From the man's half profile I could tell it was the young lieutenant. My first crazy idea was that he should be more careful because it was dangerous to sleep outside in wintertime. Then I noticed the thin trail of blood and the path where he had been dragged. Incredulous, I rolled him over and saw the crimson patch on his uniform where he had been stabbed in the chest. The blood had soaked into a perfect heart-shaped pattern. It was so ludicrous I almost laughed. The lieutenant's face was vivid blue and ice crystals had formed in his lifeless eyes. It looked like he was wearing a bogeyman's mask.

I followed the body's trail and knew where it would lead. The pantry door was ajar. I opened it all the way and quietly said, "Helena?" It was difficult to see but things had been upset and there was a black stain on the floor that marked the lieutenant's original resting place. I am ashamed to say, but I was worried about my valise and manuscripts as well and was relieved to see the case on the floor unopened. "Helena?" I said again.

She did not respond but I detected the slightest sound in the back of the pantry—as quiet as the footfall of a mouse. I walked along the standing shelves, losing light as I went. I kicked something metal with my boot; it was a gory bayonet, which spun like a compass needle for a moment. There were items on the floor throughout: empty grain sacks, the top of a crate and so on. In the farthest corner of the tent there was something black on the floor and I realized it was a bearskin. I picked it up slowly. Helena lay fetal, her face and hands aglow in the dark tent.

I leaned down. "Are you hurt? Did he injure you?"

Her eyes were open but she did not acknowledge me. I helped her to stand—she weighed nothing—and more or less carried her to a cot, which I had to set upright. I knelt before her and examined her as best I could. She seemed to be in order. Her hands were bloodstained and there was a spot of it on her cheek which I tried to wipe away but was unsuccessful. Her eyes glittered in the doorway light yet seemed vacuous too. They recalled for me the lieutenant's crystalline eyes and I tried not to think of it further.

"I am sorry. I should have been here—but Zlavik kept me, talking and drinking, then I was lost in the dark. . . ." For whom was I confessing, for Helena or myself?

Suddenly there was the sound of a massive explosion, then another: artillery.

I stood so fast my head swam for an instant. "I have to go. Zlavik is attacking. I must be there." I reached over and took my valise. "I will be back for you. I promise." I started for the door.

"Hektr. I am coming too." A single tear had rolled from Helena's eye and when she brushed it away the blood spot disappeared too. She took her coat and bag then we were outside rushing east—to find the road Zlavik had talked about. The sounds of exploding mortars were virtually continuous. When they did pause, you could hear the far-off percussions of P57s. The great battle had begun and its destined historian was miles away!

How long? I wondered. Once Zlavik initiates the attack, how long before his forces cross Lake Aurora? I supposed timing was everything. Too soon or too late both meant disaster for his plan.

Helena and I were more or less running through the ghost camp, our breath smoking in the morning air. It seemed no one had been left behind, save for the whores and Helena and me and the lieutenant's half-frozen corpse. It was an inauspicious beginning for my career's turning point.

We came across the ruts from the trucks and horses and mules that had been used to move everything into position for the final battle: the troops, of course, but also the long- and medium-range howitzers, and the cannons left over from the previous century. Following the ruts, we easily found the clearing in the woods that Zlavik euphemistically called a road. The sounds of war grew louder. Every so often I thought I even heard the screams of the dying but it was just a trick of the wind in my ears. Or so I hoped.

I glanced at Helena. She still looked dazed but otherwise all right. She had no problem keeping up. In fact, I had the sense at times that she was holding herself back, that she could have left me quite far behind. My head was throbbing dully. I was beginning to feel winded but I must keep going. I must *see* the fighting; I must be there when the day is won. The sun was fully up now and I was starting to sweat from the exertion. I smelled the spice from the vodka seeping from my pores. It was unaltered. It had traveled through my system, had encountered my chemistry, and emerged unchanged. I suspected I could piss a glassful of the vodka, pure as from the bottle, right now.

Snap out of it! I scolded myself. History is unfolding and I am indulging ridiculous reveries about urinating vodka! I must take in all of the experience so that I can record it perfectly later. Every mortar explosion, every pistol pop—I must etch them all onto my brain. I thought of a stonecarver chipping a tableau of the battle into granite: chip chip chip chip for mortar, chip chip for pistol. . . .

Damn me! I was doing it again. Wandering aimlessly inside the catacombs of my own mind!

I did not know how long the road was. But we could not be too far from the battle. I looked up and thought silvery predawn had returned to the sky but realized it was smoke. The road became softer with the rising of the sun, which made the going more difficult. Helena and I had slowed to a trudge. My recently acquired boots were good for the task but Helena's shoes were not. Her feet were sliding from side to side almost as much as they were moving forward. Also her skirt had become soaked and had to feel as though it weighed several stones. Yet she soldiered on, glassy-eyed and taciturn. Her hair was still braided beneath the wool cap but several raven-black strands had come loose and danced in the wind, which was still strong in spite of the trees all around us.

The woods became less dense and without fanfare we came to a clearing and immediately saw army trucks and a series of white open-air canopies with tables beneath them. It looked like someone was set up for a large picnic but I realized this was a medical post. There were soldiers there, the early wounded perhaps.

As Helena and I got closer, I recognized Colonel Slivania, who was working on a soldier's leg. Though the smoke was all skyward, the sulfurous smell of explosives filled the air. We reached the medical post and no one paid us any attention at first. Doctor Slivania's patient had been hit below the left knee, shattering the shin bone and turning the calf muscle into raw meat. The colonel was clamping the artery and trying to stop the bleeding. He looked up for a moment and recognized me, in spite of the change of clothes, but said nothing. The sleeves of his army coat were soaked in blood. The intensity of his work was a contrast to his eyes, which had a far-away look beneath their bushy brows.

There were a dozen or so wounded, and a handful of doctors or medical assistants were tending to the worst cases. One young man had been hit in the face with flying bits of something and the man working with him was trying to extract the debris from his bloody eyes. The other wounded were not so severe, and Helena and I (or just Helena) had attracted their attention.

"I have to go farther," I said to Helena, raising my voice above the blasts. "Closer to the fighting."

"Go on, Hektr, I will wait for you here. Soon they will need as many hands as they can get."

I recalled the drunken husband whose wounded head Helena had mended; she could no doubt be useful to Slivania. And I thought of the young lieutenant, bayoneted in the chest; Helena could no doubt take care of herself as well. "All right—but be vigilant." I thought she might return the advice but she went to one of the wounded men, one who apparently had been shot in the hand.

I continued on. The sounds of battle were louder and louder but I already had grown accustomed enough that I did not flinch at every exceptional explosion. I had begun to detect an almost musical pattern in the artillery blasts and rifle fire, as if it was an *avant-garde* composition for some radically new opera. If so, the stage was grand and the theatrical effects groundbreaking. My ridiculous costume certainly added to the illusion. But the soldier with the destroyed leg and the blinded one—they were real. The armies were definitely using real weapons, not the pixie dust and incantations I once fantasized.

Still, I had the feeling that I was watching myself trek toward the fighting—that *I* was the enormous eye looking down on everything, charged with observing and judging all but so far only able to focus on myself, an infinitely minor player, as significant to the outcome of things as a squirrel in the forest or a fish beneath the frozen crust of Lake Aurora. I wished for a divine view of the battlefield, as I had last night when looking at Zlavik's map. But if I had divinity would I be content to merely watch? Would I not lift one side to victory while annihilating the other? Was that the sort of god presiding over this battle? I decided that I hoped not—because I did not know which side was mine, the one deserving victory or the one destined for annihilation. Better to let some other forces decide the outcome than a thinking, judging god.

For some time the ground had seemed to be shaking with artillery percussion, but really I think it was more that the vibrations were affecting my inner senses. Suddenly, though, a shell exploded so close that I truly lost my balance for a moment, as if I was trying to walk in a pitching boat or a moving train. I put my arms straight out, like a tightrope performer, to steady myself. I leaned to compensate for the heavy valise in my hand.

The country was somewhat rolling and I was approaching the crest of a hill. From over the rise came a group of soldiers, not running but walking unnaturally fast. They startled me and I began to get close to the ground, to take cover where there was none, then realized it was a pair of soldiers with a stretcher carrying a wounded man, who was moaning loudly. As they passed I tried to discern his injuries. He looked directly at me and reached out blood-covered hands imploringly, maybe believing I was a doctor. The stretcher-bearers knew better and went past me without hesitation. Stupidly, I waved my mittened hand at the fellow; it was a strange sort of wave, more like a priest bestowing a blessing, a farcical mittened blessing.

I continued forward and was at the top of the hill when another blast unsteadied me, this time enough to make me fall to the ground. I lay there feeling the vibrations in my gut and chest and groin and traveling through my arms and legs. I settled my face in the snow and felt the explosions tingle my cheek. It was an oddly pleasant sensation and I stayed in that prostrate manner longer than necessary.

When I rose I discovered I could see a great expanse of Lake Aurora, as frosty blue as the sky was supposed to be. I thought of my father, long deceased, and his love for ice fishing. He was able to pass down the technique but not the affection. At first I thought Lake Aurora was much smaller than I had led myself to believe, for the far shore did not appear that far, then I realized the shore was not a shore at all but our army, dressed in obfuscating white, pouring across the ice executing Zlavik's master plan. I stood, thunderstruck, watching the wondrous sight, believing for the first time I was to be history's eyewitness. Soak it in, I told myself, every detail, every nuance.

Thousands of men were running, their weapons in hand (I supposed—I was some distance away), but the horde was eerily quiet, not even their boots making much noise on the snow and ice. They appeared to flow as a single organism—one massive creature of war. At that moment the sun broke through the clouds and smoke and shone upon the heroic throng—a sign from the heavens that our cause was right, that Zlavik was ordained to be the savior of the people and I the voice of the great battle. It flashed across my mind that Zlavik could even be prime minister one day and I his righthand man. I saw myself living in a wing of the state palace, not too far from Prime Minister Zlavik's ear when he needed my sage advice—

My daydreaming ceased the instant the ice cracked.

It is difficult to describe, the sound, a great and awful splitting like granite shattering, but not a slab of granite: a whole mountain of granite, splitting from its highest peak to its base. That was the initial ear-shattering crack, then there were the cascading rivers of splitting—an entire range of mountains toppling, one after another or several at one time. And the sound of the men, not screaming so much as shouting, all their bodies going into the icy water in the same moment—all those bodies weighed down by heavy clothing and army packs and P57s and extra ammunition.

It was very noisy for a minute or two then deathly quiet, not even the artillery firing. A spectral mélange of all the noise rang in my ears. A seeming handful of soldiers scrambled off the lethal ice to "safety"—but almost all of Zlavik's surprise invasion force had drowned. There was an awesome jagged opening of the bluest water I had ever seen. One would think there would be pieces of ice floating here and there but there was not, as if a giant had cut out the ice as one cuts the top of a pumpkin and had removed it somewhere. Sunlight streaked across the lovely blue surface in a golden line. The sight was worthy of an oil painting by the eye and hand of a master.

I did not know what to do. Human instinct said to do something.

I began fumbling for my notepad as if I was going to write it all down, as if I was ever going to forget the sight and the sound of it. There was even an unusual smell in the air, something mixed with the artillery smoke, something released from the depths of Lake Aurora—a little fishy yes, but also startlingly fresh, like it came from a distant time when human beings, or human-like beings, first roamed this frozen plain, a time when the gods were still alive and walked among the earthbound creatures. But for me, ironically, the odd scent became the very smell of Death—Death palpable and real and personified and smelling like this.

Then the calm was shattered as both sides resumed the battle. It was intensified to a genocidal pitch. The enemy realized their advantage and wanted to finish us off once and for all. We fought merely for our lives now. The artillery fire was beyond thunderous— it could only be compared to the wrath of an enraged deity. The ground quaked and I became sick with its shudderings.

Something struck the ground near my foot. My eyes had remained on the broken lake; now I looked down the plain before me and groups of soldiers were headed toward me. I felt glad to see them as if these men were the very survivors of the Lake Aurora disaster—hm, not *The Battle of Lake Aurora* after all, but *The Lake Aurora Disaster* (I doubted the new book's popularity). I actually began to wave to the quickly advancing soldiers, welcoming them.

Then something flew past my head, faster than on fairy wings. My mind processed it all very slowly—or so it seems in retrospect: There were soldiers aiming their P57s at me, the soldiers appeared angry, things were hitting the ground at my feet and flying past me. Holy merciful shit! I have it: They are shooting at me!

I turned and ran. I had some yardage on the soldiers and from their perspective I disappeared over the crest of the hill. Why would they be trying to kill me, a mere journalist, history's eyewitness? Could they somehow know of the young lieutenant's death? I remembered my mismatched uniform. Were these enemy troops then? It seemed unlikely, given the geography of the battlefield. But why would our troops be firing upon their own officer?

I discovered it was more difficult to keep my footing running downhill than it was walking uphill. I was more or less out of control, my arms flapping, my valise banging against my leg. At last I reached level ground and saw the medical post before me, except it was half torn down and people were running in every direction. One of the three Daimlers was on the move headed into the forest. Word of the calamity must have preceded me.

I went to the one white canopy still standing, the one under which Slivania had worked on the destroyed leg. The wounded were gone. I was still in a panic: the soldiers firing at me could not be far behind, unless they had been distracted and delayed by something. I looked around for Helena among the men who ran back and forth. Meanwhile, a second truck found its gear and lurched forward.

I did not know what to do. I thought of running into the forest but a tiny rational part of my brain told me I would not survive long there. I considered simply staying put and allowing the soldiers, ours or theirs, to shoot me. Before I could decide, a small hand touched my arm, so light I could barely feel it through my thick sleeve. "Hektr, this way," said Helena and she led me to the remaining truck, its engine rumbling, its tires partially disappeared in the soft snow.

"Are you able to drive?" asked Helena.

"I have never tried. I suppose I understand the mechanics of it."

"Then drive, please. The doctor is afraid of machines." We had reached the truck and I saw Colonel Slivania seated inside. His face was ashen but he smiled hello to me before returning his gaze forward. Helena sat next to him and shut the noisy door. I was hurrying around the front of the truck when something struck my valise with great force, and my valise struck me and I the truck. I looked down to see a neat hole in my valise. For a moment I thought the bullet must have passed through the case and struck my leg but that did not appear to be what happened.

I leaped into the truck behind the wheel and imitated the movements of the boy corporal who had driven us from Iiloskova. I worked the foot pedals and the gear shift and to my great relief the big truck jumped forward and kept moving.

"Follow the other trucks," said the doctor. "The wounded are being evacuated. We have equipment and supplies."

These were not poetic final words but they were final nevertheless. For as I was maneuvering around to get the Daimler rolling in the right direction, a bullet punched through the front glass and hit Doctor Slivania precisely between the eyes. Neither Helena nor I reacted very much. It was too quick and too shocking and too much chaos reigned around us. I got the truck pointed toward the woods and started coaxing it to its top speed. I heard other bullets strike the truck's metal-plated body. Strangely, Slivania's corpse remained perfectly upright staring straight ahead with its three eyes, two blue and one black.

We entered the woods with the other trucks completely out of sight. The sounds of artillery still filled our ears. I wondered where Zlavik was. I wondered if he did what leaders of old were said to have done and fell on his sword, so to speak, in disgrace. I wondered if the murderous soldiers would pursue us into the forest. I wondered if the truck had enough fuel to get us all the way to Iiloskova. I found I could offer an opinion on none of it—only watch the road and go faster.

I looked up for a moment through the dirty truck glass, hoping to see an eye peering earthward, but there were only tree limbs and patches of pure blue sky. I noticed Helena was staring toward the heavens also.

XVIII

In form, the figure of a young girl,
the gray-eyed goddess approached him.
Odyssey 7

I ANTICIPATED HELENA ASKING ME what had happened, why all hell had broken loose, and I wanted to tell her—I wanted to tell everyone, to fulfill my predetermined role. But neither Helena nor Slivania was asking. I concentrated on the road and getting used to the truck bumping along unpredictably, and invested myself in controlling its headstrong course. After a few minutes, a bump caused Doctor Slivania to fall to my side, his head coming to rest on my shoulder. Helena tried to wrestle him upright again but it seemed a lost cause and I told her to leave the colonel be. Blood trickled from his fatal wound into his left eye then onto the captain's insignia on my sleeve.

Wind whistled through the hole in the front glass and sounded like a teapot, or a flutist warming up. In either case the sound was both mournful and merry and only increased my anxiety.

I negotiated a bend in the road and caught a glimpse of the truck ahead of me. I was overjoyed and began to have a sense of safety. Tension released in my arms and shoulders that I did not even know was there. I swiveled my head on my neck to release even more and that is when I saw an image in the side mirror for the briefest instant: a truck following us. But there had only been three trucks at the medical post.

"There is someone behind us," I said, as much to the doctor as to

Helena.

Helena, out of reflex, looked out of her window but could see nothing. "Are you certain?"

"Yes." Here I was, though, with a dead man resting on my shoulder driving an army truck through the Great Northern Forest, closer to the top of the world than I ever imagined I would be, wearing a discarded uniform given to me by a whore—perhaps I should not be so certain of my perceptions.

I continued on, trying to see behind as much as ahead. The road was serpentine, which helped create the illusion that Helena and I were quite alone. I wished again for the omniscience of that overhead eye—to know what was what, and where. I was thinking about the giant eye, in fact, when the deer bounded in front of the truck. I swerved instinctively to avoid it but did not; nor the tree which brought the truck to a sudden dead stop. The three of us pitched forward. The doctor, not able to catch himself, slammed hard into the front glass, face first.

"Are you all right?" I said to Helena.

"Yes, I believe so." At the very least, we were both stunned.

The engine had quit and I knew there was no restarting it. Smoke or steam rose up from the truck's broken engine.

"Come on," I said as I pushed open my door and grabbed my valise. Helena exited from her side. If she had her bag, she left it behind.

On the road I noticed the deer struggling to get his legs under him but the hind two were broken. I figured he would not be suffering long. The same was not necessarily true for Helena and me, unless the soldiers had adopted cannibalism. We ran into the woods, I wishing they were thicker and hoping they were thick enough. I heard the other truck rumble up the road. We took cover behind a trio of close-grown trees and I heard the whine of the truck's brakes. I listened intensely. The rusty doors were opened. There were boots on the road—how many I could not say. The soldiers did not speak to each other, at least not with words, so their role as friend or foe remained unknowable—not that language would have assisted much with this determination.

I looked down and saw Helena's and my tracks in the snow.

They were not obvious—the forest floor was naturally uneven—but were discernible. I heard a twig snap and it was all the motivation I needed. "Run," I said to Helena quietly and we did . . . loudly.

We crashed through the woods, sometimes tripping, sometimes catching our clothes on tree limbs. I thought I heard gunfire but it was hard to say with all the noise Helena and I were making in our mad escape. How long we ran is also hard to say; but we came ultimately to the shore of Lake Aurora. Except for the sheen of moisture on its surface, the ice appeared midwinter solid. Farther north, though, I knew the lake was open and water lapped with frustrating gentility at the edges of the jagged ice. We stood catching our breath and listening for sounds from behind.

"Hektr, are you injured?" whispered Helena as she pointed to the side of my coat where a dark stain had formed near my thigh.

"No. It appears my valise is bleeding ink. One of the bottles must have broken." I thought of my manuscripts and hoped they were unblemished.

I looked at the sky. There were still several hours of daylight but the night would be bitterly cold, especially near the lake. How long would it take to hike around to the south?

I never had the chance to ponder the question because something snapped in the woods and Helena bolted onto the ice, her bearskin coat flapping behind her. "Wait!" I whispered loudly, like an actor on stage. Helena was already well ahead of me and not looking back. Then there was another snap and I too was running and sliding and boot-skiing across the lake. I braced myself for the impact of a bullet in my spine and hoped I would die instantly if shot. I was also preparing for the ice to give way beneath me. I was not a small man, yet I was not a whole army either, I reminded myself.

The lake was perhaps a half mile across at this point. I found a form of locomotion that worked on the unusual surface. It was as if a goose had taken polka lessons from a Norwegian skier. I knew with each bizarre step the chances of being shot decreased, so I stepped quickly. Helena, light as a bird, had also improvised a method of movement and was well ahead of me. I thought she might allow me to catch up to her but maybe she sensed the instability of the ice and figured some distance between may be safer for us both.

I felt an urge to look around and see if we were being pursued but did not want to risk the time. I would look back from the far shore if I managed to reach it. Ahead of me I watched Helena scramble onto solid snowy ground. I continued my invented gait, confident now I would make it. Helena stood on the bank watching me. I reached the edge and smiled up at her, out of breath but happy. She reached out her hand, more for ceremony than actual assistance. Before I could take hold of it the ice cracked beneath my feet. I lost my balance and fell. My valise flew from my hand and slid a few feet on the splintering ice. The surface had not completely broken but was threatening to.

I looked at my valise; a thin trail of black ink traced its path.

"Hektr, do not be concerned with your case. Come to the edge and take my hand." Helena was kneeling on the bank reaching out to me. I looked at her and at my valise, alone there on the ice, and back again.

"Hektr," said Helena imploringly. There was genuine fear in her eyes.

However, I could not help myself. I scooted out farther on the ice, wiggling on my belly like a serpent. The hairline fractures in the ice spread around me, a web spun by a drunken spider. But I was within inches of reaching my poems and bits of stories. It was as if my child lay helpless on the breaking surface. I wondered, If it was Tasha lying on the dangerous lake, would I crawl out to her and risk my own life? I wanted to think yes, in spite of the misery, in spite of everything.

Got it. I wrapped my mittened fingers around the handle.

It cannot be correct—but I believe I heard Helena scream before I felt the ice give way. I plunged into the frigid water and released my own burbling yell. They say one's life flashes before one's eyes. I do not know that I agree. I thought of the Prince of Ithaka and his crazy laugh. I thought of the whore I had slept with and of how I imagined it was Helena. I thought of Mezenskov as he was opening his cashbox. And of Tasha and a fight we had once about adopting a child—not a specific child, just adoption in general. . . .

Then my knees hit the rubbery mud on the bottom of the lake and the gloved hand sank in it too. I was still burbling when I realized the water was only a couple of feet deep next to the shore like this. I looked over my shoulder at Helena, icy water dripping from my beard and off the tip of my nose. Helena began laughing— harder than I had ever heard her laugh, even harder than the day Mrs. Strubel told Helena and Mirska she was expecting a baby.

I had saved my valise from the frigid "depths" of Lake Aurora. I got to my feet. I had not perished but I was miserably cold and wet—possibly even dangerously so. Helena stopped cackling and helped me onto the shore after all. "Let us get away from here," she said, "then build a fire to warm you."

I silently agreed and we began to head more or less east and south. Apparently no one was following us, at least not across the lake—the hunter is rarely as desperate as the hunted.

The woods on this side of the lake were dense and the going difficult, but at least the trees blocked the wind. We walked for a long time and I was adding hunger to my list of discomforts. Helena was amazingly strong for someone so slight. She had to be as tired and hungry and nearly as cold as I but raised not one word of complaint. I suspected her strength was more spirit than physical attributes. I recalled how wan she was that first day, on the train, and her sickness the night I found her again in the Luminarium—it was difficult to imagine her sinking so low, letting life get the better of her. Maybe she was strong for me and others around her—but on her own, with no one to encourage and protect, she was less resourceful, more willing to succumb to the vagaries of life.

It was a minute or two before I realized the noise I had been hearing was my teeth clattering. Helena heard it too. "Poor Hektr. We must stop and make a fire." She looked around for a suitable place. Fuel would not be an issue, nor matches—I had a pocketful, tucked safely inside my coat. Getting warm by a raging fire and smoking a cigarette were very pleasant thoughts. The tobacco would even take the edge off my hunger. I began looking around also. For some reason I glanced at the sky, where I saw an odd vertically formed cloud. No, not a cloud . . . smoke from a fire.

"Look," I said to Helena, my voice trembling from the cold, and pointed.

The possibility of enjoying someone else's fire, already blazing, and maybe a bite of their food was very tempting. Yet we did not want to come across a camp of soldiers either. I had lost my bearings somewhat but believed we had been traveling away from the front and back toward what remained of civilization.

We crept through the woods and discovered that we had been very near the edge of the forest. We peered from between the remaining trees, and across an open field was a large white farmhouse situated by a circular barn with a conical roof and several other outbuildings. Smoke came from two of the house's brick chimneys.

"I think I know this place." I was almost thinking aloud. "It is Mink Farm."

"Mink Farm?"

"That is just what I call it. I saw it from the road on the way to the camp. If I am correct, the road leading back to Iiloskova is a mile or two east." I motioned in the direction I believed was due east.

"Is it safe to ask for assistance?" Helena stepped out of the forest. "Never mind—we have no choice."

I thought of stopping her but she was right. We must take the gamble. I shuffled after Helena, my feet completely numb from the cold. I waited for a rifle barrel to poke from a window or for a band of soldiers to pour from the barn, but nothing roused at our approach. Helena and I might as well have been accepting our invitation to Sunday dinner, especially the way she ascended the rickety front steps and tapped on the door. Not so much a door, I realized, as a sheet of wood that had been placed there against the cold. The thin wood had been attached to three overly massive iron hinges. A very heavy door had once stood there. I thought of the out-of-place door with the whaling pictograph at Command. Perhaps Zlavik and his men had visited Mink Farm after all.

No one responded to Helena's knock, so she pulled back the door by a piece of rope that had been nailed to it for that purpose. "Hello?" she tried as we stepped inside. It was probably not warm but compared to outdoors it was heavenly. There was a large front parlor with only a couple of sticks of furniture. I shut the door against the cold and the room became dark as the windows were covered by heavy draperies. There was a staircase to our right then a long narrow hall leading to a room that was better lighted. We stepped cautiously and called out our greeting again.

The room we came to was the kitchen and it was illuminated by a combination of daylight from small uncovered windows and the fire in the belly of a black stove with its fuel door open. I took off my wet glove and my mostly dry mitten and warmed my hands by the lovely fire. Helena removed her large coat, the hem of which had become wet and heavy, and spread it over a chair.

On the table in the corner of the kitchen some canning jars were open and I smelled spiced apples. The scent immediately started driving me to madness. I went to the table and picked up one of the jars. There was spiced apple syrup in the bottom of it, so I cleaned it out with my finger and sucked it down, nearly taking off the fingernail in my zeal. I offered one of the other jars to Helena and she accepted it.

I removed my hat and placed it on Helena's coat. The kitchen was nicely warm with the fire going in the old stove. It was a homey kitchen, with tall pine cabinets and dishes displayed on the walls, which were washed a summery pink. The notion of pulling up a chair and having a smoke was becoming quite appealing. I thought of the old tale about golden-haired Masha who happens upon a cottage in the woods belonging to a gruff bear.

Helena was just finishing her jar when we heard a crash upstairs. It began my heart racing. Helena looked at me as if to say, What was that? I said, I do not know. I took her hand and we crept to the stairs.

"Hello?" Helena tried. "You have visitors!"

There was no response.

"Perhaps someone is injured or sick," whispered Helena.

"Or perhaps it is an old farm cat getting into things." I was more optimistic.

Helena started up the stairs and I followed, one creaking step at a time. "Hello?" Helena said again, but again nothing. We reached the second floor, which was a dim narrow hall with four doors—two on each side—and a curtained window at the far end. I slowly opened the first door to the right and peered inside: it was a bedroom with an ancient bureau and a musty odor. Helena checked the door on the left: nothing. I opened the third door. It also was a bedroom but not an empty one. A figure lay in the bed. The room was so dim and the figure so completely covered I could not determine man or woman, young or old, soldier or civilian. Helena squeezed me a bit aside in the doorway and observed the sleeper too. On the floor was the source of the crash, a broken washing bowl which apparently had been knocked off the night table by the person in bed. He or she must have been ill or drunk to have slept through breaking the bowl. A small wood-burner in the room was emitting some heat and a smoky smell that mixed with the smell of sickness.

We carefully closed the door and stood looking at each other in the hall, not certain what to say or do. I noticed on the wall several framed images of family members from the early days of picture making. I could not make out the faces in the poor light but I was quite certain they were all long dead. They were of another time and I found myself hoping theirs was happier.

My musing was stopped by an explosion downstairs, a rifle shot maybe, but louder. I stooped down and steadied myself against a wall. I began to smell the flinty stench of combusted gunpowder. Going downstairs seemed a bad idea but we could not stay put indefinitely. Helena started us moving toward the stair.

I took one, two, three cautious steps down, straining to see beyond the railing. Smoke was thick in the air. My nostrils burned and my eyes watered. Step number four. There was a figure in the hall, a small person . . . and wearing a dress beneath a red wool coat? With my eyes adjusting—and the smoke clearing—I saw it was a young girl holding an antique rifle at least as tall as she.

"Do not be alarmed," I said.

She spun and looked up the staircase, the impossibly long weapon more or less pointing at me, smoke still rising from its barrel. I was not concerned however. I doubted that the old gun could hold more than one shot at a time.

"We mean you no harm." I motioned to Helena to come closer to me on the stair. I figured the sight of Helena would have a calming effect on the girl.

She said nothing but lowered her weapon somewhat—perhaps her arms were growing tired—and she seemed less wary. There was a large wooden pail of water next to her that she must have been out fetching. The girl was blond and made me think not of Masha, of "Masha and the Bear," but rather of Snegurochka, the snowmaiden. It seemed my half-frozen head was filled with nothing except old stories.

Helena said, "We are travelers and have come in from the cold."

I smiled and nodded but I suspected I looked more like a lunatic than a happy, harmless wanderer. The girl's attention seemed fixed on my uniform. "I am not a soldier—anything but, in fact—my clothes were ruined so I had to take these." She must have been wondering how bad the others were.

"Where are your parents?" asked Helena. "Is one of them upstairs?"

The girl, ten or possibly younger or older, lowered her gun entirely, picked up the pail and went to the kitchen. We followed her. The girl's shot ripped Helena's coat and broke the chair beneath it. I picked up my hat from the floor. The poor girl must have thought a wild animal had wandered into her house. She was an excellent marksman as she had shot Helena's coat exactly where its heart should have been.

The yellow-headed girl, whose glacial blue eyes were almost as remarkable as Helena's, went about preparing tea with the water from the pail. Helena at first tried to lend assistance but it became clear the girl was used to none. In time, she told us her name was Yadnina but her grandfather and mother always called her Nina. They each had disappeared, first her mother then her grandfather— just went out to get food or wood and never returned. Nina was not clear when it all happened but it seemed many months had passed since her grandfather's disappearance. She never knew her father or anyone else in her family.

She was a very resourceful child to have survived so long on canned food and whatever she could shoot with that ancient gun. She was so thin I thought if she stood in front of the sun on a clear day one could see through her, watch the workings of her skeleton and the pumping of her organs.

I asked about the person upstairs. He was also a stranger who came to her farm, in worse shape than Helena and I. He was so weak Nina could barely get him up the steps to bed, where he had remained for three days.

The tea Nina served was a homegrown concoction, not too different from Mrs. Strubel's tiger-root tea and just as satisfying. Nina went upstairs to take some tea to her other guest. As soon as she was beyond hearing us, Helena said, "It will be dangerous here for a young girl, with soldiers fleeing every which way. We must take her from here."

"Yes, but how? We appear marooned ourselves."

Helena had no response, other than a flash in her eyes. She was determined to help Nina, I could tell. Life seemed to work itself out for Helena and she no doubt believed it would again. I hoped she was right. For the time being, our fates were wrapped up together, like the red and white stripes of a confectioner's stick, and that was my only comfort.

Beyond the kitchen's small windows a twilight sky was forming. It would be a long night—but in the darkness there was some security. I closed the inside shutters, rendering the house completely black, I believed, and thus invisible. At first light the soldiers could find us—a woman and a girl who together did not weigh one-hundred-fifty pounds, an unconscious fellow, and me. Perhaps by some miracle the gods would hold back tomorrow's dawn, giving us more time. But more time for what?

XIX

'Consider the plot of the conniving gods —
to separate us, in the splendor of our youth.'
Odyssey 23

I HAD REPLACED MY THINGS with a pair of pants and stockings left behind by the grandfather. He was thinner than I, so I could not button the pants completely, but rather held them up via a pair of red suspenders. I felt quite foolish but there was no helping it until my own pants were dry. The grandfather had a sort of study or library off the kitchen. I lighted a candle, after making certain the draperies were closed tight, and looked over the books on his shelves. When I handled the draperies, a heavy aroma of pipe tobacco was released into the study. In addition to being a pipe smoker, apparently the grandfather was multi-tongued. There were books in German and French, and even a book of verse in Polish. I picked up a dusty old volume in my own tongue, a collection of folktales about Ulas Ulasovich and his whimsical wanderings. I flipped at random to a tale titled "Ulas in the Land of the Polar Bear King." It was a Ulas tale I had not heard. Like everyone, I was familiar with "Ulas in the Land of the Giants" and "Ulas in the Land of the Dancing Light" and "Ulas in the Land of the Mountain Witch." I read a couple of pages about the Polar Bear King but the poor light was making my eyes sting, so I returned the book to the shelf and continued browsing.

The shelves were on three walls. As I went around the corner, perusing the titles on the spines of the books, my foot kicked something that clattered heavily to the floor. In the candlelight I saw an enormous bow, and lying in a chair was a quiver of arrows. Grandfather must have been a hunter—though the bow looked like too much for an old man to handle. Then I recalled Nina and her gigantic rifle: perhaps the people of the far north are unusually fit and hardy. In my mind I nearly exchanged *unusually* for *abnormally*, or *freakishly*. I leaned the heavy bow against the chair.

Helena called me to supper and I blew out the candle. I went to the table in the kitchen where Nina and Helena had placed our slender repast, which consisted of a few strips of dried turkey, a spoonful or two of canned mincemeat, and a half coffee cup of warm cider. Though small, it was the most hospitable feast Nina could provide and I appreciated it very much. I thanked her and made over the meal, as did Helena, but I sensed the girl was embarrassed that she had so little to offer. When we were nearly finished, her eyes brightened as if she suddenly recalled something. Nina went to a cabinet, dug through it a moment, then produced a large ceramic jar. She brought it to the table and removed its stubborn lid with the aid of a knife. Instantly the smell of vodka rose above the plates, which had been picked clean. Nina filled everyone's cup. I was not sure it was proper for such a young girl to drink but surely her experiences had promoted her to the status of adult.

We toasted each other and drank the vodka, which was well aged and strong. My fingers and toes were still slightly numb from the cold and I thought the vodka might just finish warming them all the way. I poured the second round and we drank again. I could feel the blood rise to my cheeks. Helena and Yadnina were truly aglow.

Nina told us her grandfather had made the drink long ago for a special celebration that for some reason never took place. She could not retrieve from her childish memory what the event was supposed to be and her failed recollection appeared to bother her. I could imagine why: her family was gone and all that remained of them was her memory; if that were to vanish as well she would be left nothing.

I changed the subject to brighten her mood. "Your grandfather must have been—" I immediately regretted my choice of tense. "—a bow hunter."

Nina looked puzzled, maybe afraid she had forgotten that detail too.

"The bow and arrows in the other room," I said, helping her and motioning toward the study.

She shook her head and said that the man upstairs had them when he arrived.

Helena put her cup down with a loud *plink*, took a candle from the table and went into the study. I noticed her face was no longer crimson but rather reflected the yellow light of the flame. She was in the study for only a moment before emerging suddenly and walking through the house to the staircase, then up. Her pace nearly extinguished the candle.

I got to my feet to follow her but was slow. By the time I reached her she was standing next to the stranger's sickbed, his face cradled in her hand. In the candlelight I watched enormous tears roll from her lavender eyes and rain upon the bed sheets. I suspected she was quite drunk. The stranger, whose face I saw in shadowed profile, remained profoundly unconscious.

"Helena, what is it?"

She spoke but did not take her gaze from the man whose face she lightly held. "I lived on an island, in the warmest part of the world. I was happy in my relative isolation, with my serving women and my weaving and my interest in the wild things the gods had placed upon my island. Then one day a man came to my island, a castaway washed up there by an angry sea. This man was near dead, encrusted with salt, battered bloody, starving and choked with thirst. My maidens and I took him into our caves thinking that he must die soon and we would provide him the proper rites. When we bathed the man and began to care for him, I discovered he was beautiful and had been powerful before his battle with the sea. In time, he recovered and I grew to love him. And my man from the sea loved me too—I know he did. We lived as husband and wife for seven years, during which time the word *happiness* became new to me."

Helena paused. The tears continued to dampen the sheets; she had been saving them for some time.

"But my man from the sea was a wanderer and a warrior and had a lawful wife at home and a son whom he had not seen since infancy. It was the first day I knew cold, knew winter, the day that he left me as he had come, upon the sea."

Helena looked at me. "Hektr, I did something terrible—because of a grief I had never known, a grief so profound I could not conceive of moving beyond it, but that is no excuse. Before he launched his boat into the surf, I secretly wished my man eternal life. I wished that he would outlive his wife and his son and all of his people—so one day he would return to me and we would renew our love. I waited and I waited, every single day spent upon the beach watching the sea. Once a dead porpoise washed upon the sand and I rushed to it, not knowing what it was, not knowing it was a cruel prank by the sea god, repaying me for loving his enemy. The disappointment nearly crushed me. I was patient until I could be patient no longer. I left my island in search of him. I made my way in a strange world, not knowing where to look but knowing that look I must."

I peered at the fellow in bed. "And now you have found him?"

She let go a great sob and said, "I have searched such a long time, such a long, long time."

The last forty-eight hours have been too much for her, I thought. She is having a hysterical breakdown. I recalled how little I really knew of her. Perhaps she was escaped from an asylum, or was a murderess, or both—and that is why she concealed her identity. Then I thought better of her and that maybe the last two days had been too much for me as well.

I went to Helena's side. "You must rest now," I said gently and I hoped not condescendingly. I looked down at the fellow in bed, my first good look at him, and a tingling ran along my backbone. It could not be! I hurried downstairs, passing Yadnina in the hall, and retrieved my wounded valise in the kitchen. I hastily cleared space at the table and began going through the valise's contents. As I already surmised, the bullet had broken one of my ink bottles. I carefully removed bits of broken glass, my fingers becoming black in the process. I took out my poetry manuscript, *Songs of the Poet*, and discovered the bullet had pierced the title page and the first few sonnets. As I jiggled the string-bound sheaf, the bullet itself fell upon the table with a leaden thud. Other than a slightly off center hole ringed in black ink, my manuscript was all right.

I removed some loose pages of notes, all of which were ink-stained to a degree. Finally I found what I was really looking for:

the sketch of the Prince of Ithaka. It was soaked in ink. Only the Prince's left eye and a patch of forehead could be seen. I found a rag in the kitchen and attempted to wipe off the sketch but most of the ink was already set.

Nevertheless, I returned upstairs with the damaged picture. Helena had not moved. I held the sketch near the fellow's face, which I then partially concealed with the bedsheet, leaving his left eye and a bit of forehead exposed. Helena did not question what I was up to; she seemed to be somewhat in shock. I looked hard at the drawing and the man's obscured countenance. I tried to retrieve his image from the police interrogation room, and I tried to recollect the sketch before it was damaged. It was fruitless. Maybe the unconscious man was the Prince of Ithaka. Maybe not. Logic told me that it was not. Still . . . the resemblance. . . .

I reached down to uncover the sleeping man's face and his eyes fluttered open for a moment then closed just as suddenly. I felt Helena, or whoever she was, waver against me for the instant that his eyes were open, though it was mainly the whites that had shown.

My brain could take no more. I returned to the kitchen, where I wadded the worthless sketch into a ball and deposited it in the belly of the stove. I added some sticks of wood and closed the fuel door. I could stay awake no longer. Let Nina and Helena and Helena's lost love sleep upstairs, I thought bitterly. I took the bearskin coat for a cover and went into the study, where there was an antique sofa.

The sofa smelled of undisturbed dust and pipe tobacco and was too short for me but it did not matter. I curled myself up as an infant does and soon was as dead to the world as the fellow upstairs. I dreamed of a lonely stretch of beach dotted with wildflowers. A strong wind was removing the petals and the surf was washing them out to sea in parti-colored trails.

XX

'Now the giant raised up a gigantic stone,
and spun round for the murderous toss.'
Odyssey 9

I FELT AS IF I HAD SLEPT FOR YEARS but in a beneficial way. I was refreshed and revitalized. In short, I felt good. I was hungry but not weakly so. In the kitchen I discovered my clothes were dry or in some cases dry enough. I gladly exchanged my clownish suit for the mismatched uniform. I opened a shutter and saw the silvery hue of early morning. We would need fresh water so I decided to volunteer my services. I suspected little Nina had more of her homegrown tea stashed somewhere—that would be a nice way to begin the new day. I was feeling benevolent toward Helena and her supposed love. I was convinced her bizarre soliloquy was the result of stress and exhaustion and too much vodka and too little food.

I heard movement upstairs and the muffled sound of voices behind closed doors. I looked forward to bringing Yadnina and Helena and the stranger cups of hot tea. Perhaps if I poked around I would find a bit of dry biscuit to include with breakfast. Maybe there was even a little jam or honey in the cellar, something Nina had overlooked and would therefore be just as surprised and tickled as Helena.

I took the pail and opened the makeshift door. I did not know where the pump was but figured it would be easy enough to follow Nina's tracks. I stopped on the porch for a moment to make a cigarette. I had to remove my mitten to do so. Soon I was inhaling the heavenly smoke. I felt strong enough to wrestle a bear—ha, two bears, one with each hand!

I took up the pail and descended the loose steps. Yadnina's path led toward the circular barn; perhaps the pump was behind it. I took the cigarette from my lips and began whistling a jolly tune. At first I could not recognize my own repertoire, then I recalled it from the gramophone in the whores' tent. I tried to think of different songs but my brain could only produce the ones from my strange night of lovemaking. So be it, I decided, and whistled gaily.

I did not concern myself with the tracks that intersected Nina's, horse or mule hooves. I suppose I thought they were old tracks, if I thought at all, until I stepped in the fresh manure. I stood frozen, my boot still squarely in the shit, and followed the tracks with my eyes. They led to the barn. I tossed my cigarette in the snow and crept toward the old structure, which had narrow vertical openings spaced along its curving exterior. I went to one such opening and cautiously peered inside. I first saw the five animals in various stalls, three horses, it seemed, and two mules. I could see blankets and bedrolls scattered here and there around a nearly exhausted fire. I crept to the next opening in hopes of a different view and seeing the men themselves, who I assumed to be soldiers. But whose? Ours or theirs? And did it matter?

Meanwhile, my mind was racing. I must warn the others. Should we escape into the woods? All right maybe for Helena and me, and Nina too, but the unconscious fellow? Perhaps we could make a stand, with Nina's thunderous gun and the bow and arrows. Nina was an amazing shot but I doubted she was taught to load the weapon at field combat speed. And who would use the bow? I probably could not hit the barn at fifty paces, leave be an armed man.

Maybe the soldiers were friendly and would assist us. I was peering in my third opening, to no avail, when I heard the rusty arm of the water pump, more or less directly behind me. I turned suddenly, too suddenly—it is what caught the attention of the soldier who was just about to have a drink.

My instinct was to run, and the soldier's was to chase. I wanted to escape to the house but knew it was not the right thing to do, so I continued to run around the barn. I went past an open door . . .

and three more soldiers, who were holding tin cups. They joined the chase too. It continued that way—I running for my life and the soldiers pursuing, seemingly on my heels, for two or three revolutions until one of them figured out to go the opposite direction and cut me off. I stopped and hit the ingenious soldier with the pail, which I had stupidly clung to, but just in the arm—only enough aggression on my part to anger him. Then the others were there, five in all, and I was manhandled into the barn.

"Why are you running?" said the soldier who was at the pump, a corporal, with shaggy hair hanging from beneath his cap and a patchy unkempt beard.

"You were chasing me," I stammered, out of breath, as much from anxiety as from exertion.

"Only a guilty man runs. What are you guilty of?" The soldiers had placed a barrel in the center of the barn and they persuaded me to sit.

"Nothing. I am guilty of nothing. You startled me, that is all." Above my head a lantern hung on a chain suspended from a rafter. In spite of the open door and the narrow windows, the inside of the barn was mostly in shadow.

"Guilty of nothing. I am sorry to have startled you," the corporal said, mock affably, smiling. Then he struck me so hard my head snapped back and I flew from the barrel. I was stunned, lying on the barn's dirt floor. Two soldiers jerked me to my feet and sat me on the barrel. "Oh dear," said the corporal, "I must have startled you again."

I felt blood trickling down my chin from a split lip and there was a stone under my tongue. I expectorated a tooth and a string of crimson saliva.

"Perhaps you are a deserter, eh?" The corporal's face was close to mine. His breath reeked of wartime death. He seemed to be winking at me, then I realized it was just that he was missing an eye and the lid was sunk in its socket. Saying I was a deserter, I wanted to tell him he was like the frying pan accusing the kettle of being cast iron. Instead, I managed,

"No, I am not a soldier. I had to put these clothes on."

"Pretending to be an officer then. That is the cause of your guilt."

"No, my own clothes were ruined." I had bitten my tongue too and it was becoming difficult to speak. Sticky sweet blood ran down my throat. "I had to put these on. . . ."

"Liar!" snapped the corporal, looking as though he was going to strike me again.

"I am a journalist. I was reporting the war. I have papers . . . in my coat." I removed my mitten and reached into my pocket. I dug around but the only thing I found was the red tie. Helena must have removed the papers when she hung my coat to dry or I lost them somewhere along the way. I felt like vomiting but there was not enough in my gut to get the job done. "I seem to have misplaced them," I said meekly.

"Of course, of course," said the corporal, mocking again. "It has been bedlam. It is perfectly understandable how you would lose your identification papers." The corporal stood back looking at me with his single orb, enjoying his role as interrogator. "I have it: you are a spy. Who but a spy would have a borrowed uniform and no papers?" He considered further. "Who else is in the house? More of your traitorous friends?"

I did not know what to say; I was grasping for anything: "Commander Zlavik knows me—we dined together. . . ."

"Zlavik! Where is the butcher?" The corporal took me by the coat so firmly he was strangling me.

"I do not know," I croaked. "I have not seen him."

"Lying bastard!" He tossed me to the ground, knocking over the barrel. He delivered two sharp kicks to my ribs then left me there in the dirt.

I was out of wind and it was agony to try to recover it. I lay curled in a fetal position as the soldiers conferred together. I thought about begging for mercy but knew it would do no good. I watched one of the soldiers go to a stall in the barn and retrieve a long leather rein used for controlling large animals. They stood me up.

The corporal was holding the leather now. "You see, we do not think you are telling the truth, about anything. If you *are* a journalist, I am sure you can appreciate the importance of truth." He slapped his palm with the heavy rein. "It is not a proper whip but in wartime one must make do. Do you not agree?"

"No," I said but it was the only protest I could offer. Terror and pain made me mute.

The soldiers began yanking the uniform coat off of me. Buttons flew to the ground. I smelled leather and manure and smoke and human sweat. I thought I could manage to vomit now. . . .

I then heard a familiar whistling sound. The soldiers and I looked at the comrade who was holding the rope that was to be used to bind my hands. An arrow was protruding from his throat; the feathers were just above his collar bone. Blood rushed in two great arcs from his nostrils before he fell dead.

The barn door swung shut with an ominous quiet, just its old hinges protesting a bit. Then there was the clink of its being secured from the outside. We all watched and listened, the five of us. Another arrow came from nowhere, only revealing itself when it lodged in the chest of the second soldier to die. He fell straight back, supine on the floor, his left leg twitching for a moment.

The three remaining soldiers rushed to their P57s but did not know where to aim. I, meantime, was rooted in place, truly as immobile as an ancient tree. The soldiers moved in frantic circles, back to back, watching the narrow openings for their attacker. One young soldier must have seen his adversary for a half second before the arrow split his skull like a midsummer melon.

The corporal and his remaining comrade fired their rifles in the direction of the attack, missing their mark. One bullet careened off something metal and struck the lantern above my head. It swung wildly on its chain and cast the barn in weird nightmarish light. The gunfire also spooked the animals, which began moving excitedly in their stalls. Two knocked loose the boards that confined them and they started loping around the barn.

"Call off your friends!" The other soldier spoke and leveled his P57 at me. All three of us knew simultaneously it was a mistake. The arrow punched through him back to front, no doubt severing his spinal cord and puncturing his heart. He looked at me accusingly, as if I had done this to him personally via some dark art. He fell, not even able to squeeze the trigger of his rifle before his ghost fled from him.

It was the corporal's turn to be terrified. He fired his Pachrov at the barn door, once, twice, thrice; then charged it with a demon's scream. He struck the door with his shoulder and it did give way, but the corporal was off balance and tumbled through the snow. He got to one knee and prepared his weapon to fire . . . then Yadnina's antique rifle efficiently removed his head from his neck. I was fascinated by the length of time his body stayed locked in position before pitching to the side, his life blood rising to the sky like an energetic mountain spring.

I crumbled to my knees and placed my hands over my face. I did not want to see anymore. I stayed this way for some time, until I felt a gentle touch on my shoulder. "Hektr, are you all right?"

"I believe so." My voice was rough. Helena helped me to stand and gather my things.

"We have to go," she said. "There will be others."

She led me out of the barn into the white day. Nina was there with her rifle, which was *taller* than she. The stranger came from around the barn. The battle had taken its toll on him. He dragged his bow behind him and could barely walk. Helena went to his aid and brought him to me. He was horribly thin, his hair long and blowing in the wind, his eyes lifeless and sunken. How he had mustered the strength to wield the bow so expertly was a mystery.

Helena said, "Hektr, this is—"

I stopped her. "I know. It is Ulas Ulasovich, and he is in the Land of the Polar Bear King." I offered him my hand. "Thank you."

Helena probably attributed my nonsense to shock and she may have been correct. We had no time to ponder the workings of the world, any world. We left the dead where they lay and focused our energies on leaving Mink Farm. It had to be difficult for Nina but she understood its necessity. The first task was to get the animals under control and assess their fitness for travel. I tried to be of use but it was mainly Helena and Yadnina who accomplished this; Ulas Ulasovich sat on the front steps barely moving. Nina, the countrygirl, said all five animals were malnourished and poorly shod. The horses, she thought, could make the distance to Iiloskova but the two mules would not get far on their shoes. Ulas overheard her and roused himself from the steps. He said the soldiers should have been carrying replacement shoes and farrier tools. He went into the barn of carnage and came back in a few minutes with what we needed. The stranger held each of the mules and directed me in their reshoeing. Meanwhile, he spoke softly into the mules' ears, to calm them, in a language completely foreign to me, Arabic or Greek or Egyptian, something ancient and lyrical. It seemed to me the stranger could have come down from the moon and was whispering Lunarese to the skittish animals. The process took more than an hour. My job was sloppy but Ulas said it would suffice. I was feeling a lot of things and I was feeling nothing; at that moment, however, I experienced a touch of pride that I had done something to help finally.

While we were working on the mules, Helena and Nina packed what supplies they could find, emptying the house of the little it had left to offer, then systematically robbing the dead soldiers. We figured we could reach Iiloskova in less than two days, if we traveled much of the night, assuming we could keep the animals moving and stay to the road in the dark. By midmorning we were ready and set out, Ulas, Helena and I on horses, Yadnina on a mule; the remaining mule was burdened with most of our supplies.

The going was slow as the road was becoming soft with springtime warmth. I rode in the middle of our caravan. Ahead of me, Helena and her man traveled side by side but they neither spoke nor touched. He was so weary his head fell forward most of the time and bobbed with the inconsistencies of the track. As I watched them, I considered Helena's strange story, which had already taken on a dreamlike quality in my memory. It could not possibly be true—just as Ulas could not possibly be the lunatic, the Prince of Ithaka—yet it seemed to me to be a tale worth telling, worthier perhaps than the Disaster of Lake Aurora; worthier, fuller of meaning, more constructive than destructive.

And what of Yadnina, our own snowmaiden, with hair weaved of sunshine and winter in her blood? She was yet another orphan of the war, and now a refugee from strife. The government had no plan for such children, or at least not a good one. What were her thoughts on this cold but not too cold day? She was a bit behind me; I looked over my shoulder at her. Her blue eyes took in the great expanse of land, the barren snowfields, most likely for the first time. I feared that she saw merely the land's emptiness, when what I hoped she saw was its openness: openness as infinite possibility, as unfettered future.

My thoughts were as mad as Helena's. We both inhabited a world of fantasy—but even in my madness I knew to like hers better, to prefer a love that would not die, literally and figuratively, over everything else.

I took off my mitten and stroked the horse's shaggy mane. It felt real enough. I smelled deeply and took in the horse's animal scent of musk and manure. I listened to its hooves in the softening snow. I did everything but lick its ear. Satisfied, I pulled on my mitten and prematurely watched the unbroken whiteness for a glimpse of Iiloskova, which took on the aura of home, though my brain reminded me it was not.

XXI

Tears, hot with brine, burst from the years of longing.

Odyssey 16

WE ARRIVED AS THE SUN WAS SETTING, in that twilight time between the city's dayfolk disappearing indoors and the nightpeople taking over the streets. Only ghosts were out and they paid us no heed, counting us with their kind perhaps. It had taken more than three days. Two animals perished, the mule carrying the supplies and my horse. The deaths slowed our travel but added to our food supply. The carcasses may have also kept the trio of winter-thin wolves at bay that followed us at a distance until the city's skyline showed plainly on the white horizon. During the journey, Ulas Ulasovich and I were forced to replace two sets of shoes, both by firelight in the snow.

We passed the news bureau and I thought I saw a lamp inside. I considered stopping but only for a second. Division Street was not much farther and the pension there was our goal. Helena and her man were on one horse, Helena preventing him from falling off he had become so weak again. Nina and I were on the other horse, and the few remaining supplies had gone to the mule.

I was exhausted and saw things on the outskirts of my vision, indefinable shapes approaching me suddenly then vanishing. Only half alert, I imagined the shapes to be the spirits of the soldiers who fell at our hands, loitering among the living before reporting for duty in hell. . . .

Hands were helping me down from my mount. I hoped vaguely they were friendly hands but was too tired to care much. I was inside and smelled fried food. Mrs. Strubel, in reality or hallucination, was propping up my head and making me sip tea. Then I slept. I had found a place of peace and I slept. . . .

We recuperated in the pension. Helena and Nina were fit almost immediately and spent most of their time attending to Ulas Ulasovich and me. By the second day I was reasonably recovered. Helena's man was still bedridden but improving. I put on the clothes I had left at the pension, and gladly shed the uniform forever. Mrs. Strubel cut it up for patches. The captain's insignia went into the parlor's coal-burner. I shaved off my beard and trimmed my mustaches. I looked in the mirror and barely recognized my old face.

Yadnina instantly became the darling of the pension, as the Strubels and their guests showered her with attention, which she politely accepted. But most of the time she was quiet and withdrawn, and preferred the company of books to human beings. She behaved as shell-shocked soldiers do. Perhaps I suffered similarly: I still had told no one what I witnessed. It seemed there was too much to say—the events too immense—and I did not feel up to the task yet.

On the third day, Helena came to my room before breakfast. She brought me a cup of coffee.

"You are beginning to write it all down," she said, alluding to the papers on my table.

"Just making some notes—so I do not forget." I was holding a pen but set it next to the ink bottle in order to take the coffee.

"Mr. Polozkov says you are leaving this morning."

"It is time."

Helena nodded. She hesitated. "Do you think the fighting will come here?"

"I do not know. It seems likely."

"Yes, I agree." She smiled, but with a touch of sadness, and said, "'Ulas Ulasovich,' as you call him, has spent his life chasing trouble or being chased by it. I suppose now is no different." Then Helena became more serious. "If the fighting does come here, it will not be a good place for Yadnina."

"For any of you."

"True perhaps. But Mrs. Strubel will have her baby before summer's end. We will stay. Yadnina, however, should go home with you. You believe so too—I have come to know your mind."

I placed my coffee cup on the table. "I do not know how my wife will feel."

"Hektr Pastrovich, you have survived much. You can survive a discussion with your wife."

Helena was right of course, about everything. Tasha had not warmed to the idea of adoption but it was one thing to be cold in the abstract and quite another to deny a poor waif of a girl in person.

We all had a solemn breakfast of fried eggs and coffee, then Nina and I prepared to leave for the train station. We said our goodbyes. I even went upstairs and looked in on Ulas Ulasovich but he was sleeping, so I let him be. Helena borrowed a jacket from Mirska and accompanied Nina and me to the station. It was a short walk and the morning was quite lovely. In the sunlight Helena appeared to have aged, but was beautiful nevertheless. She had taught Yadnina to braid her hair and light bounced golden off the intricate pattern.

With the improved weather, the train was running more reliably. It was already on the southbound track taking on fuel and passengers. I handed Helena a slip of paper with my address and told her to come see us. She smiled and put the paper in her pocket. We knew she never would. She kissed and hugged Yadnina, calling her her "brave girl." I then took Helena in my arms and we kissed each other's cheek.

Nina and I found our seats on the train and waved at Helena a final time. The train was not moving yet, but Helena turned and walked away from us to return to Division Street. I thought good thoughts of her and knew she would be well.

The Prince of Ithaka once called himself "Nobody" but he was mistaken: he should have called himself "Everybody." He was lost and alone and searching for something—but on the verge of finding it too, the next day, or next week . . . or next year. Yes, Everybody would have been a more fitting name.

A conductor, with a tobacco-stained beard and threadbare coat, came by and asked me for my ticket and my daughter's. Neither Yadnina nor I bothered to correct him; and the train began to move.

A Conversation with the Author

by Beth Gilstrap

On a gray March evening (in 2011), I spoke with Ted Morrissey, author of the novel *Men of Winter* (originally published in 2010) and the forthcoming novella and story collection *Weeping with an Ancient God*. We talked about the publishing industry—and the joys and terrors of writing. (Note that *Weeping* was supposed to come out in the summer of 2012, but its publisher went out of business on the verge of its release. Twelve Winters Press is planning to bring out the novella, possibly in an illustrated edition, in 2014.)

What was your impression on the response you received to Men of Winter? *How do you feel about being compared to Tolstoy and Homer?*

Being published by a new, small press, Punkin House, there have been no formal reviews of *Men of Winter* yet, so the reactions have come from actual readers—who seem to like it very much. Among my various jobs, I work part-time at my small-town library, so it's interesting to see the novel's coming and going (so far its going has been pretty regular), and people who realize I'm the author will remark that they liked it. Of course, if they didn't, they probably wouldn't say anything period. A local book club is planning on its being one of their summer readings and on having me come in to read and chat with the members—which should be fun.

The comparisons to Tolstoy and Homer are very flattering of course, but I know they're based more on setting and plot, and not on storytelling ability per se. Ironically, I hadn't read much Tolstoy, much at all, when I wrote the novel, but for the past year I've been reading the Russians a lot, including Tolstoy. Somehow I missed much of Russian literature in my formal education, so I'm trying to catch up. In the summer and fall I read shorter works by Dostoevsky, Turgenev, and Gogol; then this winter I read *Anna Karenina* and have just recently begun *War and Peace*, which is going to take me a very long time.

Homer I know well, especially the *Odyssey* as I've been teaching it every fall for fifteen years now, and I've used several translations, including Robert Fitzgerald's, which is where I took the title from, his translation of Book 11, Odysseus' journey to the underworld.

What inspired you to write Men of Winter?

I actually began writing what would become the novel about thirteen years ago; I finished the book in three years; then it took me ten years (and two literary agents, both of whom gave up in despair about the industry) to find a publisher—my point is I'm not sure I can recall specific inspiration. I'd written a short story as a sequel to Mary Shelley's *Frankenstein* ("A Wintering Place," which eventually found a home at *Eleven Eleven*), and I liked that story a lot. So I decided to write another short piece based on another book I loved, and for whatever reason I started thinking about the *Odyssey*. I've always found Calypso the most sympathetic character in the poem, as her love for Odysseus is totally disregarded by the council of gods and goddesses who decide that the hero should be allowed to go home. I guess it was my thinking about brokenhearted Calypso that started me moving in the direction that wound up with my writing the novel.

In Men of Winter, *you have a journalist/poet narrator; why would you say writers make interesting subjects?*

I like writing in first-person—though I know that mode has been taking a lot of criticism for some time now—and to me it doesn't make sense that someone who isn't a writer of some sort would be able to write well enough to tell a whole novel-length story (I know that's condescending and there are people who write well who aren't writers per se—and I've written first-person stories with non-writers as their narrators). Also, I grew up around the newspaper business and worked as a sports reporter for seven years, so I feel like I have an affinity for newspapering and newspapermen. His being a poet, I suppose, is a nod to Homer.

I tend to like novels and stories whose main characters are writers, but that's because I can relate to them. I'm not sure journalists/writers as main characters are inherently interesting. No matter who or what your main character is, hopefully you can find a way to make his or her situation of interest to the reader.

What were some of the high points and low points of writing either Men of Winter *or* Weeping with an Ancient God?

I actually wrote *Weeping with an Ancient God* before *Men of Winter*, and my understanding, from researching the market, was that I'd have trouble finding a publisher for the novella-length manuscript. My contacts with publishers and agents bore that out: no one had any interest in publishing something shorter than a novel from a no-name author. So I squirreled the manuscript away and set about trying to write something longer, which ended up being *Men of Winter*, even though my original notion was that it'd be another short story. The high points, besides the process of writing them—which I genuinely do enjoy (even though it's hard work at times)—have of course been finding people who like them and who want to publish them. During those ten to fifteen years that I was having trouble finding a publisher for my books, the industry changed because publishing technology changed. On the one hand, it's harder than ever to publish with a name house (unless they're going to make a million dollars off your book, they don't have the time of day for you), but on-demand technology has made it feasible to publish authors in small enough press runs to make it profitable, thus giving rise to many, many small presses.

My lowest points were of course the innumerable rejections I received from publishers, often via an agent. The biggest disappointment came when I'd been contacted by a literary agent because she'd read one of my stories in *Glimmer Train Stories*, and she wanted to know if I had a book-length manuscript. I said yes, I had the novella manuscript (*Weeping*), and she didn't even want to see it; but I'd also just started working on what would become *Men of Winter*, so she said to send it to her when I was finished with it. It took me three years to complete it, and the whole time I had in mind that an agent was waiting to read it. When I finished, I tracked her down (she'd moved to a different agency), and she wanted to read it—but then she declined to represent it. That was very disappointing.

In anticipation of *Weeping with an Ancient God* being published by Punkin House [which was set to happen in the summer of 2012, but the press went out of business before bringing it out], I sent the first chapter out as a stand-alone piece titled "Melvill in the Marquesas," and it was picked up very quickly by *The Final Draft*—and to my surprise I received four other offers of publication (even though I'd withdrawn the manuscript elsewhere immediately), and two rejections that were very complimentary. To be honest, I thought the excerpt in particular was so quirky it might take me quite a while to find a journal to take it. But editors have responded very enthusiastically to it, which has been, frankly, both surprising and vindicating.

What inspired you to write about Herman Melville's encounter with cannibals in the Marquesas Islands?

I'd been a Melville fan for quite a while, even though I hadn't read, at the time, a lot of his work. I always admired that he abandoned the style of writing that would have made him a wealthy man (the sort of writing he did in *Typee* and *Omoo*) and experimented with other forms (especially *Moby-Dick*) that led to the reading public's abandoning him. His last several works were self-published in fact. In particular, though, A&E had a *Great Books Festival* and featured some of the world's greatest works of literature and their authors; it was narrated by Donald Sutherland.

One of the episodes was about Melville and his writing of *Moby-Dick*, and it painted him as a tragic figure, consumed by financial troubles and self-doubt and all kinds of personal and family problems. Yet he didn't do the "easy" thing and write popular stories that would have solved many of his problems, especially his financial ones. From the A&E program, I also learned that it was when he was a young sailor that he first heard the whaling legend that eventually inspired him to write *Moby-Dick*. I started researching Melville's biography, and I read *Typee*, his own fictionalized account of his cannibal adventure —and I soon realized it could make a great story in itself.

But I didn't want it to be a biography of Melville per se; I wanted it to be a genuine work of fiction (dare I say, a genuine work of art). So I did a few things to distance my story from its being a biography, in my way of thinking anyway: I'd discovered that his family name was originally spelled "Melvill" without the "e," so I thought it'd be an interesting twist to use his original name that was not as well known, in fact barely known at all. Also, I was going through something of a Hemingway phase at the time, so I decided to write about Melville in a very spare and modern style, in contrast to his own richly florid and poetic prose, thus firmly transplanting his nineteenth-century story into the twentieth century (now, twenty-first century).

How did you get interested in "revisionist fiction"? What are the beauties and complications of working in this genre?

I'm not sure how I became interested in revisionist fiction exactly, other than I read several examples of it that I really, really enjoyed and admired (coming to mind are J. M. Coetzee's *Foe*, Jean Rhys's *Wide Sargasso Sea*, Valerie Martin's *Mary Reilly*, John Updike's *Gertrude and Claudius*). Having been a life-long bibliophile (bibliomaniac more accurately), the idea of taking characters and settings that I loved and working within their frames and conventions myself was just very appealing, like getting to spend terrific quality time with beloved friends and family.

One of the beauties of doing revisionist fiction, then, is just getting to spend all that intellectual time with an author and his/her characters, etc. I'm not a musician, but I suppose it's a bit like doing a cover of a song that you love—changing it up and making it yours, but because you love and respect the original so much, not because you think the original failed in some way and you want to do a better version. I enjoy playing with the nuances of the original, isolating certain aspects of the tone or imagery, for example, and amplifying it or recoloring it or recasting it somehow; or emphasizing an aspect of characterization that is only hinted at in the original . . . the possibilities are truly endless.

I like to write in a way that makes it unnecessary for my reader to have read the original to make sense of the story—I'm sure, for instance, that there are people who have read *Men of Winter* who've never read the *Iliad* or the *Odyssey* so they don't get any of the allusions, but yet (hopefully) they understand and enjoy it on its own terms. On the other hand, if my reader does have some level of familiarity with the original text, it should enrich their reading experience, and maybe even get them to think about the original work in a way they hadn't before.

What type of research did you do in preparation for this type of writing?

For *Weeping with an Ancient God*, I read a lot of Melville and about Melville. I read with special care his novel *Typee*, which was his own thinly veiled fictional account of his time in the Marquesas Islands. It's important to say, though, that while I used his biography and *Typee* for inspiration, and for period details, I wasn't interested in being faithful to what really happened. There are some episodes that appear in his novel as well, and some things that his biographers discuss, but I felt at liberty to change those episodes and to add wholly original material as my own story needed them. I also did some research on the whaling industry, like the actual process of hunting whales, and on whaling towns like Nantucket and New Bedford— again for inspiration and period details, not in an effort to teach my readers about whaling, and so forth.

Men of Winter was a bit different, in terms of research. Even though it's strongly implied to be set in early-twentieth-century Russia, Siberia in fact, I deliberately avoided pinning it down to a specific time and place. I wanted the narrative to have one foot in the "real" world, and one foot in some other sort of world. I've also tried to accomplish that feel via some other narrative techniques that so far no one has seemed to notice—which either means I did them so well that they're invisible, or that I did them so poorly that they in fact accomplished nothing. I already knew the *Iliad* pretty well and *Odyssey* very well, like the back of my hand, to employ a cliché, so I didn't have to read them especially for this project—they're a part of me like my own family history—but I did research what life in Siberia was like, and I researched European history in the first decades of the twentieth century, especially World War I warfare, and other mechanical technologies.

But I also made a lot of stuff up. I've had a few readers compliment me on my thorough research, which implies to me that they think all of the geographical and period details are genuine, when in fact there are very few details that I included straight from my research. So I do take such comments as a compliment, but not to my thorough research so much as to my ability to write made-up stuff that sounds real. In essence, they're complimenting me at being an accomplished liar. To which I nod demurely and say "Thank you."

Beth Gilstrap earned her MFA from Chatham University, and her work has appeared in *Blue Fifth Review*, the *minnesota review*, *Superstition Review*, and elsewhere. She was also writer-in-residence at Shotpouch Cabin with the Spring Creek Project. Visit bethgilstrap.com.

Afterword

by Adam Nicholson

I first met Ted Morrissey in planning talks for a collaborative writers' workshop series involving the University of Illinois Springfield, the Vachel Lindsay Association, and the Pharmacy, a grassroots art center in Springfield, Illinois; and I first read *Men of Winter* perhaps a month later in preparation for an interview with Ted for the *Lincoln Land Review*, the literary journal of the community college where I worked as an adjunct.*

In a sense, it was assigned reading, so I felt relatively little initial investment in the act of reading the book. At the time, I had only modest expectations for local writers in general. But having come to know Ted through our workshop planning, I knew him to be both passionate and deliberate in his outlook on writing, and to retain a sense of the fun and discovery in it. *Men of Winter*, I thought, would be a fair read.

Fair was a gross underestimation. Within the first page, I was charmed by Hektr Pastrovich's description of Helena. Its contrast of snow-white skin and long, black hair, its figure of "a child traveling alone to meet a guardian aunt . . . in the country" called to mind a mélange of classic fairy tales; and against that fanciful backdrop, the "geometric shape, something like a star" in Helena's intricate braids seemed unequivocally to mark her from the beginning as something magical, or celestial, or divine.

That *seeming* assurance is Morrissey's great strength as author. In fact, Morrissey is persistently equivocal throughout *Men of Winter*, preferring to maintain ambiguity, never fully answering the question of Helena's true nature. Or that of the vagrant "Prince of Ithaka," for that matter. Everything these characters do, from beguiling a pension of boarders to life, mirth, and fecundity, even to dispatching a barn full of trained soldiers with bow and arrow and obscured line of sight, is at least plausible from a real-life perspective, however fantastic in effect. In fact, the very language of Morrissey's descriptions of characters and events serves simultaneously to suggest and to disclaim supernatural essence. "He looked at me accusingly, as if I had done this . . . via some dark art."

This technique of equivocation allows reader response to shape the narrative, but then it does more: it serves as a microcosm of a larger motif of tergiversation and a theme of liminality. Hektr's conflict of commitment between Mezenskov's newspaper and *The Nightly Observer* is a conflict between credibility and sensationalism— between journalistic duty and integrity on the one hand, manifest in Hektr's warfront reporting assignment beyond Iiloskova, and circulation and money, fame and fortune, on the other, manifest in his pursuit of the elusive backstory of the Prince of Ithaka. It is a conflict Hektr never definitively resolves; he not only serves both masters from beginning to end, but he leverages the resources and opportunities provided by one paper to aid his pursuit of a story for the other, softening the demarcation between the two.

Many readers will have noticed that *Men of Winter* in many ways evokes and alludes to Homer's *Odyssey*, especially, in addition to the *Iliad*. Although Morrissey has taken care to ensure that even readers unfamiliar with Homer can understand and enjoy *Men of Winter* as a story in its own right, the novel is much enriched by a familiarity with the Homeric plots and characters. For example, Helena corresponds, at least in part, to Helen of Troy, daughter of Zeus; and the Prince of Ithaka corresponds to Odysseus himself, the Greek king of Ithaca.

For those who recognize the trace of Homer in *Men of Winter*, Hektr's conflict of commitment between two writing assignments invites comparison to Morrissey's own administration of two seemingly disparate literary tasks—the rendering of a revisionist treatment of the *Odyssey* and the creation of an original work— and by extension, perhaps even exploration of his own process and motivations. Does the author view original writing as low-circulation, low-visibility work in contrast to the relative prominence of the classics, and revisions and treatments thereof? Or is it vice versa? Or some hybrid? Or something else entirely? Does he view one task as his quotidian slog, "put[ting] bread on [his] table," and the other as an enticing diversion? Answers are necessarily subjective and speculative, but the questions are engaging and generative.

Readers may also note that, while characters and elements of *Men of Winter* correspond to characters and elements of Homer, the book is not a direct conversion. The Cyclops Polyphemus is embodied at various points, like in the eye of a storm, or in the spunk of a cigar. Morrissey's redubbing the *King* of Ithaca as the *Prince* of Ithaka intimates to his audience that if he is retelling the *Odyssey*, he is telling it slant. Perhaps it is that, like Hektr graying the line between his newspaper assignments, Morrissey is blurring the generic boundary between original and derivative, and creating a transformative twilight zone on the order of a musical mashup. He creates his own genre—or if Polyphemus were to ask, no-genre.

Every reader, of course, takes something different away from a book, and the complex nature of Morrissey's novel likely admits of even more divergent, individualized response than do most books. *Men of Winter* elegantly combines the active literary study evinced in fictional revisionism with the original literary contribution of a novel, while at the same time highlighting the connection between plot and author experience. It is a rich, genre-challenging work that raises stimulating questions, and a valuable addition to a classroom reading list or personal collection.

* The *Lincoln Land Review* interview is available on YouTube, and can be accessed via the author's webpage: tedmorrissey.com/interviews.

Adam Nicholson holds an MA in English from University of Illinois Springfield, where he is an adjunct instructor. He also teaches at Lincoln Land Community College and directs the Pharmacy Literati, the literary arm of the Pharmacy art center in Springfield. Visit the Pharmacy's webpage at thepharmacygallery.com.

Discussion Questions

1) Whenever a story is told in the first-person point of view ("I"), the issue of the narrator's reliability surfaces. Is Hektr a reliable narrator? That is, do you, as a reader, believe he is telling the tale truthfully? One of the things Hektr is *truthful* about is his own sometimes questionable ethics and honesty. Does his acknowledging his own shortcomings when it comes to the truth somehow make him more believable, or does his self-incrimination cast doubt on the tale's accuracy?

2) Reader perception is especially important with *Men of Winter* as the author is ambiguous regarding whether it's a realistic tale or one with fantastic elements. The ambiguity is often associated with Helena. That is to say, is she just an extraordinary woman (crafty, intelligent, widely traveled), or is there something magical or even divine about her? What are other similarly ambiguous aspects of the novel?

3) One of the issues raised in the novel has to do with *family*, and how families are created. What does *Men of Winter* seem to say about the concept of family, perhaps especially in the context of adversity? Yadnina is literally an orphan, but are other characters orphan-like as well?

4) The epigraph to the novel identifies the phrase "Men of Winter" as coming from Homer's *Odyssey*, and in particular Book 11, Odysseus' visitation with the Dead, a necessary step if he is to achieve his goals of reaching home and being reunited with wife and son. There is some disagreement among scholars and translators as to what Homer meant by the phrase. How does the phrase seem to connect to the novel? In other words, who are the Men of Winter in Morrissey's book?

5) Speaking of epigraphs, in this new edition of the novel, the author has added quotes from either the *Iliad* or *Odyssey* at the beginning of each chapter, but they tend to be only obliquely connected with the action of the chapter. Research the context of an epigraph, and discuss how it may be associated with that chapter's action. (The epigraph for Chapter IV, page 33, which derives from the opening lines of the *Odyssey*, may be the easiest to consider.)

6) In the interview, Morrissey says that he "wanted the narrative to have one foot in the 'real' world, and one foot in some other sort of world," and

that he tried to bolster that feeling via some "narrative techniques that so far no one has seemed to notice" (p. 215). What storytelling techniques perhaps contribute to this "real world" versus "some other sort of world" feel of the novel?

7) When Hektr and Helena are fleeing from the soldiers, after the disastrous Battle of Lake Aurora, Hektr suggests that it doesn't matter whether the soldiers are from his country's military or from the enemy's. What does this ambiguity imply about the nature of war? How else is war or violence in general critiqued by *Men of Winter*? Does the novel in any way glorify war or violence?

8) In Adam Nicholson's Afterword, he posits that Morrissey's revisionist approach to Homer may be associated with the status of classics in American culture as compared to popular, best-selling books. What is the status of the classic today? For that matter, what constitutes a *classic*? Moreover, are today's most popular authors creating the classics of tomorrow?

9) The novel concludes with Hektr preparing to return home with Yadnina as his adopted daughter, but it isn't clear how Hektr's wife, Tasha, will react. What do you think will happen when Hektr arrives home? Does the conclusion of the novel anticipate a "happy ending"? Homer's *Odyssey* is largely about the homecomings of the major figures in the *Iliad*, especially Odysseus', of course. Do the homecomings of the *Odyssey* color your sense of Hektr's homecoming in *Men of Winter*?

The author invites you to visit his webpage, tedmorrissey.com/comment, to express your thoughts on these questions, or on any other topic for that matter.

CPSIA information can be obtained
at www.ICGtesting.com
Printed in the USA
FFOW03n0922010715
14754FF